# THE COLD TOUCH OF STEEL

She rummaged around in her flight bag for her hairbrush. She touched something sharp and, surprised, shrieked. Pulling her hand out, she saw a tiny streak of blood on her finger . . .

Reaching in again, she was very cautious. She felt the handle first. Then she fingered the cold metal. And then she felt fear. Real, paralyzing fear.

"Oh, my God," she said out loud, pulling it out.

Her hands trembling, she began to look around. Then she withdrew it from the flight bag. It slipped out of her hands and dropped to the floor, the "clunk" reverberating throughout her silent apartment. She looked down, shaking . . .

It was a butcher's knife.

# CATCH ME IF YOU CAN

## Judi Miller

A DELL BOOK

Published by
Dell Publishing Co., Inc.
1 Dag Hammarskjold Plaza
New York, New York 10017

For my editors, Susan Reu and Maggie Lichota—
thank you for helping me do something different

. . . Across the margin of my mind they came, the wingless birds, the emus and dodos and ostriches and moas, preening their wings in the desert light: a land of slumber, frightening me, where I lay forever dozing in the sands. Would he never come again, protect me from my sin and guilt? I saw them prance staidly in the far corners of the room, at the edges of the walls, through the piled-up picture frames, all grave and unmenacing in the drowned and stifling dusk. Outside the sparrows chirped and fluttered; someone called distantly; I held out my arms.

—William Styron, *Lie Down in Darkness*

# CHAPTER 1

Standing at the top of the hill, Johanna held her beige folding umbrella high. Someone had once quipped that she looked like the British version of the Statue of Liberty. Smiling firmly, she watched the group catch up and mentally began to count heads. Losing a housewife from Michigan at Windsor Castle and holding up the bus while she roamed the streets of the quaint little town, looking for the woman, was not her idea of a good day's work as a tour guide.

The elderly couple, the honeymoon couple, the rather attractive woman alone, the two sisters, and the loud dentist and his quiet wife were all present and accounted for. The wind was gusty on the hill, and she brushed a wisp of wheat-colored hair from her mouth so she could speak.

Taking a deep breath, she launched into her speech about Windsor Castle. It was the standard condensed history lesson, but she liked to think that she had somehow made it her own, and that it was entertaining and amusing. Perhaps when they all got back to their homes in the States, they would pull out their blurry snapshots and think of her a little. And she liked to think that she and her beige umbrella were in one or two photos.

Over the footsteps of passing tourists and shouting above a sturdy wind, her voice was just slightly hoarse and her manner brave and weary. Actually she could have sung *Aida,* but her hoarseness was a little trick she had mastered over the years. When the tour bus dropped everyone at their hotels, it was customary to give a little something to the bus driver and the tour guide. She certainly couldn't live on her salary alone, what with rents what they were in London. Her tips were always high.

There was a shout. She looked at her watch.

As they walked up the hill, they could hear the mesmerizing hup-hup-hup guttural sounds. It seemed as if the red-uniformed guards with their high fuzzy black caps were guarding their queen and her castle from some real and immediate danger. Cameras were lifted and focused, and Johanna waited patiently. And it was a picturesque sight. There were times she wished she could drag *her* camera along.

Especially on a beautiful, untypically British day like this, with the warm spring air and the mounds of white clouds looking like dollops of cream in the china blue sky. And in just hours she would be with Stephen. She knew, just *knew,* he was going to ask her to marry him tonight. They had talked a little and joked about it, and now that he had gotten his raise it was time.

"We are now approaching the tourists' entrance to Windsor Castle. The queen is in residence today, so we cannot see the state Apartments." She stopped, pouted, looked down, and then said, in her most British accent, "She always does this to me." There was a polite twitter of laughter. Johanna liked American tourists. They were jolly and easy to play to. It didn't matter much what she said; it was her timing, really. And that they got a bit of a laugh with all that knowledge.

As if on cue, the troop of guardsmen high stepped by, looking for all the world like toy tin soldiers without drums. Johanna waited indulgently while one after the other the tourists popped out from the group to get a close-up of this oh-so-British sight.

"After this you can do a bit of shopping. Remember, the lamb's wool is just as nice and less expensive than cashmere. Or you can have that famous high cream tea, which is guaranteed to make you plump like the rest of us Britishers." She waited for the laughter to subside, thinking that perhaps she'd missed her calling. She should have gone into the theater. "We will meet at the bus at the bottom of the hill. Just go to the statue of Queen Victoria. You'll see where her hand is pointing—that's where the bus will be waiting. See you then, at four thirty in the bus."

Johanna watched as her little group trooped into the castle. Tours. They poured everything into one ear so fast it was a wonder it didn't spill out the other ear just as quickly.

She rested at the bottom of the hill, taking out a cigarette and letting her body relax as she allowed her thoughts to drift lazily. Tonight she would wear something sexy. Maybe she'd take a cab to Mayfair. No good. It was her mum's birthday next week, and she'd have to scrape up a proper gift.

Tonight she'd take the Underground. And she'd wear the clingy lavender dress with her silver chains. She was meeting Stephen for drinks and dinner in Mayfair, no less. Tonight was a special night. She had been sure all week that this Friday night he would pop the question. Oh, yes. And she knew her answer.

She smoothed the wrinkles out of her navy skirt, then began to wander around, looking at shop windows, thinking she was the happiest girl in all of England. After some of the bloody garbage she'd gone out with, she deserved a chance to be happy.

At twenty-five past four the tourists began to climb into the bus, packages in their arms, mild fatigue and unwelcome crankiness showing from too much sight-seeing. She counted them, waiting patiently as the two sisters ran for the bus as if it would leave without them. After everyone had been dropped off at their hotels, it was just the two of them on the bus, she and the driver. They folded the pound notes and American dollars and counted the pence. It was a good job.

"Drop me off on Harrow Road, will you, ducks?" she said to him.

The sun was shining as she walked to her flat. When she let herself in, she saw that her flat mate, Susan, was out. Susan was a stewardess for TWA. They liked to joke that Susan took them on the plane, and she took them on the bus.

Slipping her suit jacket off, Johanna went into the bathroom to check on the tub. Even over the running water, she heard the noise. Quickly she turned off the tap.

"Susan, is that you?"

There was no answer. The noise was louder this time. Like someone trying to get in.

Clutching the top of her half-opened blouse to her throat, she padded, shoeless, out to the door. Oh, no. She couldn't believe it. Shaking her head, she latched the chain. How stupid of her. You couldn't take chances like that in the city of London. Wasn't it just yesterday she had read in *The Mail* that a woman had been murdered in her flat in broad daylight? What was that damn noise, anyway?

Keeping the latch secured, her heart pounding, she opened the door just a crack. She saw what the scratching sound was. A cat was pawing at the door.

"Hello. Well, how did *you* get in?"

The cat kept scratching, making a sound that magnified in volume as its paws tore noisily at the wooden door.

Dumb cat. Must have gotten in somehow and been mucking about the hall all the while. "Shoo! I've got better things to do."

The cat looked up at her, hissed defiantly, and arched its orange back.

"I'm getting engaged tonight, you stupid feline. Now, *get!*" Johanna laughed and closed the door. She was supposed to meet Stephen at the Red Lion at seven o'clock, and here it was five thirty and she was still doing everything but what she ought.

"When I'm a married lady," she uttered aloud after her bath, "I'll own a car or take a taxi." She sprayed cologne behind her ears and on her wrists and then quickly dabbed some between her breasts.

Susan was working tonight. She and Stephen would have the flat to themselves.

When she walked out the door, she saw that the cat had gone. Outside, it was still light, but the sun had lost its glare. She walked to Paddington Station, which was just around the corner. Taking the Circle Line, she changed at Baker Street to the Jubilee Line and took that to Green Park. A posh neighborhood, Mayfair, that was for sure. And a safe one, too. She could walk to the restaurant. She could walk on air.

On Curzon Street she quickened her pace. The restaurant was on a little side street. She always felt a skip in her heart when she was going to meet Stephen. It had been that way from the beginning. Her excitement was running so high she could feel her toes itch from wanting to walk faster.

As she walked she noticed the street was empty. It was a surprise, then, when she heard the rip, which was followed by a whimper, and *realized those sounds were coming from herself.* The dress, her good dress. *Oh, dear God,* she prayed, not now, not this way. She opened her mouth to scream, but there was no sound as a bubble of blood emerged from her lips. As she felt herself buckling and sinking, she wondered if it was twilight or dawn. Tears poured down her cheeks as she tried to cry out, but as in her worst nightmares, no words came out. There was no one to help her. The last image she saw in her mind was Stephen's face. When she fell facedown onto the hard pavement, the street was so washed in her blood it looked as if it had been painted red.

Just minutes later a group of American tourists turned onto Curzon Street, and a woman spotted her and screamed. They stood frozen in horror as they watched the blood rush forth in little rivulets on the street.

"Call the police!" someone screeched.

"I thought Mayfair was a *safe* district!" another woman cried.

A crowd was beginning to gather. Solemnly they looked and then quickly looked away, talking excitedly. Police began to flood the scene. They yelled for people to move on. A car pulled up and two men got out. One was tall and angular, the other short and round. A woman lying in a puddle of blood in the elegant Mayfair District wasn't an everyday occurrence, for that matter. The only reason Scotland Yard was there and not the Metropolitan Police was because they happened to be driving by.

Detective Sergeant Hollings clucked his tongue to the roof of his mouth. "Look at that. A knife job. Slashed up and no one saw," he said morbidly. Using a handkerchief, which immediately became blood soaked, he picked up her bag and looked through it. "All her money's here. Didn't do it for money, then. Couldn't have been raped. Would have had to have been awfully quick about it, wouldn't he?"

The detective inspector studied the body carefully. The sandy-colored hair was caked with drying blood. The pretty silk lavender dress looked all muddied.

"Just slashed her. Like Jack the Ripper," the sergeant droned on, unable to keep quiet.

The inspector came out of his reverie and looked almost steely eyed at Sergeant Hollings. "Why is it that London is always looking for a new one?" he asked.

"Sir?"

"That's all we need. Another Jack the Ripper. They never caught the first one, you know."

# CHAPTER 2

A pinkish purplish dusk began to streak the village of Hammersmith, a residential area in London. Children had stopped playing in the park. People had gone home to fix dinner. Yet she wandered about, strolling aimlessly, breathing in the exotic perfume of the multicolored flowers. It was the kind of meandering, weaving dance known as walking to kill time.

Ravenscourt Park. She liked the sound of it—like something out of an Edgar Allan Poe story. Somewhere in the inky black that was engulfing the park there was a health food restaurant. Whole food, they called it here. She would eat there soon. Satisfied, she began to walk slower. And that's when she became aware of someone following close behind her. She could hear shoes creaking. They sounded like a man's shoes. It had darkened within the last few minutes. There was no one else around. She walked faster. So did the man. She craned her neck to one side. He was overtaking her.

"Sorry," he said as their eyes met.

He smiled apologetically and walked ahead of her. She smiled back. That was such a very British habit—meeting someone's eyes almost accidentally and then apologizing for invading their privacy.

She glanced at her watch again. Close to eight thirty. She had thought it was earlier. The neighborhood was strangely familiar as she moved through the now-darkened streets surrounding the River Thames. At the end of Ridge Avenue there were two little houses connected to each other. The address was 26A and 26B. She walked up the stone steps to 26A and held her breath for a second. Then she pressed her finger firmly on the doorbell.

The door opened slowly. A short, stout woman with steel gray hair slicked back into a bun opened the door. After inspecting her, the woman opened the door wider.

"I'm Barbara Hargrove," she said. "I understand you've got a flat to let."

The woman replied cautiously, "I'll need a month's rent before you move in."

Barbara nodded her head. The woman let her in.

"I'm Mrs. Lockwood. Lockey, they call me. The flat is downstairs, and you're fortunate it's available. It's a maisonette with a bit of garden in the back. Kitchen upstairs, living room upstairs, two bedrooms and the loo downstairs." Lockey watched as Barbara walked through the flat. She followed her down the flight of steps to the lower level.

After a few moments, she inquired, "Work in London, is that it?"

The woman continued to study this Barbara Hargrove while she poked around the apartment. She was well mannered. Not a brash American. No, nothing of the sort. She seemed like a nice girl. Looked like she could pay the rent, though you could never be sure. Finally she reasoned that if the girl wanted the flat, she could have it.

They came back up the stairs to the living room.

"Awfully large for one woman, don't you think?" the older woman asked chummily.

But Barbara didn't answer. She looked around almost vacantly until her eyes came to rest on the kitchen, then lighted up. She went in. The older woman watched as she stroked the stove, a clean but ancient model, one you might have found in an American apartment in the forties.

"You can replace it if you've a mind, but it works fine."

"No, no . . . I wouldn't *dream* of replacing it," Barbara replied.

The landlady wondered what this young woman's real story was. Everyone had one. Well, she'd find out in time if she took the flat. "Would you like to come upstairs and have a cup of tea while we talk?" she asked.

Barbara turned abruptly. "I want the flat."

The older woman nodded. "Oh, well, then, it's settled, isn't it? Four hundred pounds a month." She studied the woman, waiting for some resistance, but there was none. "Come have some tea, then," she said.

Barbara followed the landlady up the steps, hoping she had put on a good enough act. She had known immediately she wanted that flat. It was so like the other one. But she had thought it would seem odd to appear too eager and not look it over.

The door opened on a splash of yellows and pinks and orangey reds. Everywhere there were flowered prints, overlapping and clashing. The furniture was soft and plump, like its owners. Nottingham lace curtains hung like doilies over the windows. Barbara saw the back of a half-balding man, hunched forward in one of the living room chairs. Before he turned, Mrs. Lockwood shouted, "Christopher, we've got a girl for the flat downstairs!"

The man turned reluctantly away from the television program he was watching. He made a polite attempt to stand, but he was wearing suspenders that had slipped down to his bulging waist and midway he decided to forget it and sank back again into the stuffed armchair.

"Sit down, love. Would you like a slice of fresh lemon cake with your tea?" Mrs. Lockwood asked.

"Yes, thank you. That sounds nice. I don't have a British bank yet, so I can't write out a check. I can only pay you with pounds. For the rent, I mean."

Mr. Lockwood turned and said loudly, "That's fine, miss."

"This here's Barbara Hargrove," his wife said, disappearing into the kitchen, thinking she had made a good choice.

Without turning, still watching the television, the man began, "Terrible thing to happen, wasn't it?"

"I beg your pardon?" Barbara asked politely.

"That girl that was killed in the Mayfair District."

"I didn't hear about it."

Mrs. Lockwood came in carrying a silver tray with a teapot, half of a yellow cake, a small pitcher of milk, and a sugarbowl.

"Happened earlier this evening," he said.

"Milk?" Mrs. Lockwood asked.

"No, thank you."

She handed Barbara a delicate, floral-patterned teacup and saucer.

"Woman slashed to death in the Mayfair District. Like a Jack the Ripper murder," he continued loudly.

There was a shattering crash as the china cup dropped to the floor and broke. Barbara jumped up. She was shaking so hard her hand was flapping uncontrollably.

"I'm so sorry. Oh, dear. I'll replace it," she said, close to tears. "I just felt dizzy, that's all."

Mr. Lockwood turned and actually got up out of his chair.

"Are you all right?" Mrs. Lockwood asked, silently wishing her new tenant hadn't broken that particular cup.

Barbara shook her head frantically. "Yes, yes, I'm fine. Really I am." She reached in her bag and pulled out a clump of pound notes. Pictures of the queen stuck out in every direction from her fingertips. "Let me pay you now . . . for the rent and for the broken china."

The couple exchanged glances.

"Where are you staying?" Mrs. Lockwood asked.

Barbara began to tremble uncontrollably again. "At a hotel. At the Hotel Driscoll."

"The Hotel Driscoll! Why, that's right near where the murder occurred!" Mr. Lockwood shouted.

"How did you get here?" Mrs. Lockwood demanded.

Barbara looked up in the direction of the voices. But all she could see were the floral prints whirling about her. The dizziness was back. She put her hands on the table to steady herself. The room suddenly became oppressive. "I got here by Underground," she managed finally, biting her lip.

"And now you're afraid to go back," Mrs. Lockwood filled in for her. She looked at Barbara, and Barbara nodded obediently.

"You *must* get a taxi." She didn't add that with that wad of money she could afford it.

"Who knows? A murderer like that might strike again, especially in the same area. Or on the same street," her husband said.

Barbara took a wilted tissue out of her bag and blew her nose. They were staring at her. She smiled somewhat timidly. She breathed a sigh of relief. That's all it had been this time. Just a little dizzy spell.

The crowds had thinned out. There weren't many people in the Mayfair area brave enough to be out on the street, knowing what had happened earlier. Nowhere in sight was a woman walking alone. The men from Scotland Yard had driven off in their cars. The woman had been . . . removed. Only one obvious reminder was left. The caked blood on the sidewalk. A day's rain might wash some of it away. Maybe.

A man stood staring down at the sidewalk, studying the blood. His shoulders still shook, but no sounds came from his hoarse, raw throat. In his pocket was a tiny mauve-colored velvet box. Inside it was a diamond engagement ring. Her mum had helped him pick it out. His name was Stephen Knight.

He had waited at the restaurant patiently. Because Johanna was so capable and so organized, he figured if she was late she had a reason. The waiter had offered him a menu so many times it was getting embarrassing. Finally he decided to leave and go to a telephone box. No answer at her flat. Of course not. Back to the restaurant. A beer then, while he was waiting. Looking at the diamond sparkler. Another call. Three more calls. Two more beers.

And then finally he called her mum. It had all been so unreal. A neighbor answered and said she couldn't speak . . . Oh, yes, he was the fiancé . . . Oh, dear, then he hadn't heard, poor lad. Heard . . . what? And then the phone was left dangling in his hands, and people who passed the big red booth heard a long, loud scream and someone ran to get a policeman. They thought he had gone mad. Well, he had, a little.

And now, staring at the sidewalk at what was left of Johanna, he made a vow. One day they'd find the man who had done this. The crazed, evil son of a bitch. Yes, they'd take care of him so they could put him on trial. And then when they had him, safe and secure, he, Stephen Knight, would sneak up somehow, in disguise, past all the guards, and with a knife, he'd slit his back and watch his face while his insides poured out. Just like Johanna's had. All over the sidewalk he was standing on.

But he'd let *them* find him first. If they had been doing their job, this never would have happened. Oh, yes, he'd wait. Then they would have two murders on their hands.

But they would catch only one murderer.

# CHAPTER 3

The desk clerk looked up into the sparkling dark, heavily made-up eyes of the woman who had said, "Hey, you." He noticed the dark shiny hair pinned behind one ear with a clip and the long, dangling rhinestone earring. She was, for this midtown hotel on Lexington Avenue on New York's fashionable East Side, what they might have called "jazzy" years ago. He couldn't help but meet her inviting sassy smile with an appreciative grin of his own. She was an attractive woman.

"Any place good around here to have dinner and a drink?" she asked.

She was wearing a white, low-cut jumpsuit. He was trying very hard to look her directly in the eyes, but he was having a hard time not looking at her very obvious, very meant-to-be-looked-at cleavage.

He cleared his throat. "What did you have in mind?"

As the words came skipping out of his mouth he knew it had been an indelicate choice. He saw the tiny smirk of a smile that began to slip across her mouth. Oh, she would come back with a man, he was sure. Then he wondered for a moment if she could be a . . . No, not at that hotel. It would be economically unfeasible for her, although she could be a high-class one. No, it was unthinkable.

"There's a tavern across the street specializing in steaks and chops, and then there are several burger places; some have dart boards. And then there's a fine little Italian—"

"The tavern sounds fine," she said. Winking, she thanked him and turned to leave.

The desk clerk found himself feeling relieved as he watched her walk out through the revolving doors.

Squinting in the dusk, she spotted the tavern across the street. Aware that men were turning to follow her with their eyes, she sauntered across Lexington Avenue and into the dimly lighted restaurant. She caught the bartender's eye immediately. First stop, a drink. Sitting on a bar stool, noticing that she was the only single woman at the bar, she ordered a Bloody Mary.

It was Saturday night, but there was a definite slump in the traffic. A couple, two men, and another single man were seated across the circular bar beneath red-fringed imitation Tiffany lamps. The single man, who had blue eyes and sandy hair and looked as if he were in his midforties, was looking directly at her. She lowered her eyes demurely and then looked up quickly into her merry eyes.

In less than two minutes he was sitting next to her. "I should have sent a drink over," he began.

She looked at him appraisingly and then laughed. "I can only drink one at a time."

"Hi, I'm Mike Holler. I'm a scream," he said, sticking out his hand, friendly as a puppy, "and a liquor salesman. Glad to meet you."

She shook his hand, at once flattered and amused.

"And you're . . . ?"

"I'm Enid. Enid Thornton. I'm a model."

"I'm impressed. You live in New York?"

She took a sip of her drink. Then she said, "I'm staying at the hotel across the street."

"What's the name of it?"

She laughed, sliding her tongue over her teeth, again seeming to size him up. Then she opened her bag and took out a big black plastic square with a key dangling from it. She studied the raised white lettering. "Hotel Lincoln," she recited, holding the key up and waving it. Then she put it back in her white bag and snapped it shut.

"From out of town, then."

She looked into his face, smiled, and said nothing.

"Hey," he said in that fresh, engaging manner he had, "I really wish you'd have dinner with me here. I just hate to eat alone, and my expense account is enormous."

She looked at him, again seeming to taunt him. "You make an offer a lady can't refuse."

His eyes lowered to her neckline.

She felt the usual tingle she experienced when she was meeting a new man, especially one as attractive as this one. It was a challenge. "I'll just go to the ladies' room and powder my nose," she said, tossing her head and giggling.

There was a slight smirk on his face. She lived across the street in a hotel. How convenient.

"Ta-ta," she said, then disappeared down the darkened hallway where the bathrooms were.

He waved a little good-bye, smiling contentedly.

In contrast to the almost bordellolike atmosphere of the restaurant, the bathroom was brightly lighted and cheery. A black matron sat in a boudoir chair.

Enid sat down at the long pink counter and began to study her face. She looked a little droopy. In her bag, somewhere, was a tiny tube of eyeshadow, a silvery gray one. Digging around, she couldn't find it. Finally, exasperated, she just dumped the contents of her bag out onto the counter.

Lipstick, comb, compact . . . There it was, her eyeshadow. Mary Quant. She just needed to accent her eyes, especially under the dim, seductive lighting.

She took her fingertip and oozed a little shadow from the tube onto it. Then she rubbed her eyelids until they were shiny. She put the tube back into her bag. That's when she saw them. She bent to look closer. At first she thought they were two little shiny bugs crawling across the counter. She picked one up and examined it.

Gold and pink stripes twisted at the end with brown and white bonbon ties. Chocolate éclair candies. Royale. The queen's favorite. Well, la-di-da. She should eat them. And then you-know-who wouldn't find them. Speaking of you-know-who, she combed her hair back behind one ear so that her rhinestone earring showed more. Then she let her hair hang in front on the other side, combing it faster and faster.

And then she couldn't comb anymore. She had to grab onto the counter, gripping it with her fingers. She leaned her head back and then rocked forward, moaning and crying.

The black matron leaped up from her chair. "You okay, miss? Can I get you anything?" The matron ran her hand over the array of antacids, aspirin, tissues, hand lotion, and perfume.

She gazed up at the black woman, a sweet-faced lady who looked almost saintly at the moment. Then she batted her eyelashes as if she were blinking contact lenses into focus. Gripping the counter, she felt her whole body trembling. Then she was quiet. Mechanically she began putting the spilled items back into her bag.

"You *sure* you're okay now?" the matron asked, concerned.

"Yes, I'm okay, really. Thank you. You're very kind."

She got up, gained her balance after a moment, and grabbed her bag. Then she put her hand on the door and pushed it very hard. The attendant breathed a thankful sigh of relief as she left. Never in her years of working here had she ever had any real trouble.

The matron turned to straighten the counter. Why, there were two little pieces of candy lying there. Had that woman left them there? She wasn't quite sure. Hadn't she put everything into her bag? Scooping them up, the matron tossed them into the pocket of her apron.

Enid rushed through the restaurant, eager to get out. Mike Holler stood up. He had selected a table for them in the front, near the window. There was a fresh drink at her place waiting for her. At first he thought she had to rush across the street to her hotel for something she had forgotten.

He almost knocked over a chair trying to stop her. "Enid?"

She turned and looked at him.

"I have a table for us."

She just stared at him.

"C'mon." He grabbed her arm and began to pull her over to the table he had selected.

She shook her head, refusing to move.

"Oh, hey, now, you said you'd have dinner with me. You promised."

Her lower lip trembled, and she shook her head slowly as if she were seeing something horrible. He took a step back.

"Are you sick?"

She didn't answer. He opened his mouth to plead with her. And then she spoke.

"Who are you?" she said very slowly in an icy tone of voice.

He started to laugh. But mainly because he was nervous. And a little scared. He felt as if he had just propositioned a nun, for Christ's sake. "Mike," he said in a higher-pitched voice than usual. "We just met."

She turned abruptly and walked out of the restaurant.

"What the hell is going on?" Mike wondered as he went back to his table and his half-finished Scotch and soda. "Broads," he said to the waiter. "You know? I'll never understand them."

She dashed across the street, ducking her head, clutching her hand at her neck. There was a screech, a horn honked, and a loud cabbie's irate voice yelled, "Why don't ya look where you're goin', lady?"

She rushed through the revolving door, which spun around, depositing her a second later in the bright lobby with its glittering chandelier.

The desk clerk glanced up, and when he saw the woman in white he knew it was her. Watching her wobble across the carpeting, he thought that she'd had one too many. Then he watched her weave her way to the elevator. If he had been making a five-dollar bet, though, he would have lost it. He could have sworn that Room 712 would have been a double occupancy that Saturday night.

Mike Holler sat at the table, alone, his face tinged pink with fury. He wasn't hungry. After a few more drinks, he thought he had it figured out. She had the hots for him. Anyone could see that. The clue was the key! The way she dangled—hell, waved —the key in front of his face. How could he forget the room number. Room 712. She was playing a game with him, and he was too dumb to catch on. He was supposed to go across the street and knock on her door. He'd say it was hotel management or something like that. Could be that's what she expected him to do.

Practically knocking the table over as he got up, he slid the chair out and signaled the waiter for the check. Oh, yes, this would work out just fine. And he wasn't beyond using a little friendly persuasion with women. Contrary to all this liberated women's stuff, he knew they liked force. Every woman secretly wanted to be taken, to be raped. And this woman definitely wanted him. He had known it from the beginning. But then, very few women could resist Mike Holler. And this little tease was going to love every minute of it.

At exactly eleven minutes to eleven that twenty-second of May, Irwin Dinkle came cruising up Park Avenue. The windows were open in the cab, and his arm was sticking out in the breeze, under his short-sleeved shirt.

He had just dropped a fare off at Seventy-ninth and Park. Sure was a nothing area this time of night. The next corner he'd turn around and go down Park Avenue toward midtown. Shows were letting out; people went for after-theater suppers. He wondered, his mind rambling, whatever became of the big nightclubs. Part of another era, he guessed. And then, squinting, he saw something.

It was maybe two blocks up, but it stood out because the person was wearing white, which looked almost fluorescent against the night and the dark buildings. The figure looked like a ghost. But the arm was up and he had to stop. Besides, it was a rich neighborhood, this upper Park Avenue, and the tips were bound to be high. He hoped the person was going downtown. That would fit his plans perfectly.

He cruised slowly, his light on, not really thinking of anything important when he saw the arm go down, and then the whole white cylinder tube of a body crumpled and sank from his view. He stepped on the gas. He *had* seen someone dressed in white standing between two parked cars hailing a taxi, hadn't he?

He stopped the cab and got out on the traffic side, walking

around to the side where the figure had been standing. He looked down and in the light coming from the street lamp saw a puddle. It was red. The blood that was rushing out of the figure in white. Blood! His mind was stalled. She was a woman, and she wore some kind of classy white outfit that was now white in only a few spots. Blood! But how? When? Where?

Her face was turned to the side as if she were asleep, but he saw that one eye was wide open. Her back was slit in two, from her neck to the base of her spine, and the blood gushed out of this oblong gash. One hand flew to his forehead and the other clapped across his mouth. This woman had just been killed.

He ran up the street. Maybe the man had fled up Park Avenue. Or maybe he had cut up Ninety-sixth Street. He shook his head, out of breath, exhausted, although he had hardly run half a block. He turned toward the dead woman as if he expected her to get up and walk away. She was still lying there. Then, with a jerk of his body, he ran as fast as he could in the other direction. But he could see from the light of the moon that the streets were empty. It was still, unnaturally quiet.

He was completely out of breath now. His legs moved under him as if he were running on a treadmill. He stopped. His breath was coming in short, panicky gasps and he felt strangely dizzy.

A woman murdered on Park Avenue. Park Avenue? He snickered then, knowingly. Nowhere was safe. He should know that. He dashed back again to check on the dead woman. He could have stopped it, he thought guiltily. If only he had seen something. Where had the man with the knife come from? He stepped back and surveyed the area. Of course. All the killer had to do was jump out from behind one of the parked cars, then sneak away.

He looked down at her. Hooked on to one of the fingers of her right hand was a white bag, a blood-soaked clutch, with a gold chain. The bag was closed.

He should check her purse, find out who she was. Maybe there was a clue there. If there were a lot of money, did he have the willpower not to take it? He plucked the purse up and, shaking, snapped open the clasp. There was a wallet. Inside, in a plastic holder, was an I.D. card. The woman's name was printed in block letters. Enid Thornton. In the wallet was eighty-three dollars. She hadn't been robbed. Quickly he put it all back. "Keep your money, lady," he whispered. He hooked the gold chain around the pointed finger just as he had found it. He would call the cops now, that's what he should do.

He stood there, his arms heavy at his sides, his head bowed, and stared at the widening puddle of blood seeping from the woman. He shook his head in slow realization. Then he wiped his runny nose with his arm. Turning, he began to run again, almost smacking into the bumper of his cab.

How stupid could he be? If he called the cops, he would be questioned, followed. They'd never leave him alone. God. They might even consider him as a suspect. Sure they would. Frantically he found the door handle to the cab and fell into the front seat. A car was coming by. He could see it in his rearview mirror. How many had driven by but not stopped? Who stopped in New York? He turned the key to the ignition and peeled out of his spot, driving fast up Park Avenue, away from the dead woman. He saw someone standing with an arm raised, but he kept going. The hell with a fare right now. He needed a safe little side street—quick. One where he could open the cab door a little and throw up in the gutter.

One thing Mike Holler was better at than most people was holding his liquor. And he had stopped counting a long time ago. Sitting at the half-empty circular bar, he flicked the ashes from yet another cigarette and started to hum.

A man on the far end of the bar leaned in toward him, toppling a little, and said, with some difficulty, "Somebody's happy tonight."

Mike grabbed a handful of peanuts and swirled his Scotch around in his glass stoically. "Nope," he replied, smiling amicably. The rest was none of anyone's business. He'd thought, for sure, that he was going to score. Oh, yeah, that was a rejection, all right. And he didn't like it. Not at all.

He was looking straight at the bartender, a huge, beefy man who rarely showed any emotion on his expressionless face, when he saw the man's mouth drop open. The other man at the bar swiveled around next. Mike was the last to turn. He gasped.

The woman at the door was wearing a white, low-cut jump-suit. She was smiling. Her hair was dark and lustrous, pinned behind one ear with a hair clip. A sparkling rhinestone earring dangled from a pink exposed earlobe.

"Hiya, Mike," she said seductively.

"Enid?" he said dumbly.

She nodded reassuringly.

"But I knocked and knocked on your door, and you never answered. I could have sworn you were there. Finally they asked me to leave."

"Poor baby," she said, her lovely red lips in a pout.

She walked slowly, deliberately, to the bar while all three men followed her with their eyes. It could have been the dim lighting, the lateness of the hour, the lack of females, or the moody blues droning from the tape deck behind the bar. But watching her move, mesmerized by it, they might as well have been watching a sex goddess on the screen. She was to them, at that moment, a dream. A vision.

Sliding slowly onto a bar stool next to Mike, she crooned, "Shall we have dinner now?"

The bartender, his elbows on his chin, bending over the bar, said, "They stopped serving dinner a little past ten, miss. It's around midnight, now."

Enid eyed him up and down angrily. Then she glanced down at the delicate gold watch on her wrist. She was shocked to see he was right.

Mike ordered another drink and said, "And one for the lady. What was it you were drinking, sweetheart?"

Enid smiled. She liked that. Sweetheart. Princess was better. "A Bloody Mary," she replied.

"Now, where are we going to have dinner?" he said softly. He grabbed her hand. "I'm so glad you came back. You're a little tease, aren't you?"

She stared at him coyly, choosing to answer only the first question. "Oh, I don't know. Anywhere you say." There was just a tinge of a bogus southern accent in her voice.

"I know," Mike said expansively, noticing that his speech was beginning to slur because he was getting tired, "we'll have dinner at the best place of all."

"Where?" she answered, laughing, moving closer as if to share a secret.

"Your place," he shouted jauntily. He knew that he should be angry at this woman, but he was caught, trapped in a spell he couldn't understand.

"Are you really hungry, Little Miss Model from Somewhere?" he asked, winking at her.

She met his gaze boldly and subtly thrust her chest out. "Maybe not." She laughed. "Have something better in mind?"

"Oh, you bet, I do, sugar plum."

Enid threw back her head and a husky, throaty laugh spilled out of her mouth. Mike liked that as much as her delicious giggle.

"Are you going to behave?" he asked, offering her his arm.

"Sure," she replied, giving him hers.

The two of them strolled out of the restaurant as if they were taking a turn around a winding southern veranda. They walked slowly across the street, not having to dodge traffic because it was well past midnight. Chatting and laughing, they came through the revolving doors and into the lobby.

The desk clerk looked at them and snickered behind his hand. There she was with a man, and she had her key with her. Well, he could call them, couldn't he?

Arm in arm, the couple, laughing gaily, walked to the elevators. Their bodies touched slightly as they walked. Enid pressed the elevator button. It opened immediately. Mike stepped in.

She pushed him away. "Naughty, naughty," she teased.

He came closer, thinking it was a joke.

"You *can't* come up. I'm tired."

"Huh?" And then he looked into her cold brown eyes, and he knew she meant it. "Now, wait a second, Enid," he protested. "Wait just a little second, here." He almost lost his footing. "Look, you *know* I'm coming up. You want me to." He had his arm on the wall near the elevator, blocking her from leaving.

"Oh, no, I don't." She laughed haughtily. "What kind of girl do you think I am?"

He squinted, looking at her in disbelief. "Now, lookeee here . . ." he began to shout.

But she cut him off. "Next time," she whispered invitingly.

He was just about ready to push her into the elevator and then force his way into her room when a man walked up and said, "Any trouble here, miss?"

She nodded helplessly.

Mike looked at the scene to come. Big, strong stranger protects damsel in distress. Suddenly he felt disgusted. She was a tease. And she was a pro. He had fallen for it . . . twice.

Raising his hand as a parting gesture and indicating the winner, he said, "Enid, you're a real remarkable lady, and I hope I never run into anyone like you again."

He turned and walked away, heading across the street for the bar and one last nightcap before it closed.

Twice she had done it to him. He must be a glutton for punishment. There was something wrong with that lady. Very wrong. He didn't know who the hell she was. Shit, he doubted if she did either.

# CHAPTER 4

It was the doorman who spotted her first as she stepped out of the cab midmorning. He tipped his cap and held out his hand for her valise. "Morning, Miss Hargrove. How are you this beautiful Sunday morning?"

The bright red of the doorman's uniform and the gold braiding of his cap shone snappily in the blinding sunshine. She looked at the flowers budding in the strip of grass running down the middle of the avenue, and then she thought of winter, when there were little lights on the shrubs at Christmastime. Upper Park Avenue had been a nice place to live. She would miss it.

Upstairs she turned the key to an empty apartment. Blues and whites basked in the sunlight that flooded in through the windows. Everything looked clean and bright and open, so different from the flat in Hammersmith, which was dark and airless. But, somehow, she knew she would be able to carry out her work there.

Barbara set her valise down in the large living room. She should take time for a little nap to recover from the jet lag, but for some reason, she just wasn't at all tired. It could wait. She could see her answering machine sitting on the big desk in the living room. The tiny red light was flashing on and off. It always reminded her of a little heart beep.

She had three messages. Unwinding to zero, she pushed the start button and watched it crawl across to one. The message was from Eva. Dear, sweet Eva, a childhood friend who had become like a sister to her. She would have to call her because Eva worried about her constantly. Eva didn't think that she knew how to deal with her grief properly. Barbara put the palm of her hand to her forehead. One of those headaches was coming on again. Well, what did you expect after flying in a cramped plane all night?

She depressed the start button, and it slid from one to two. As the message played back, she became more and more bewildered. It was a Dr. Walters returning her call. There was only one problem. Who was he?

Number three. Her lips parted in surprise as she heard the soft-spoken, shy voice. "Hi. This is Jonathan. Jonathan Segal. I —um just called to say hello, and I wondered how you were doing." He left his number.

A slow smile crept across her mouth. Jonathan had called her. All she had to do was return his call. Hesitantly she picked up her turquoise phone. Then she put it down.

A cold drink. That was what she needed. Then she would call him. She opened the refrigerator door, and it lighted up the whole darkened kitchen area. There wasn't much food. She'd have to go shopping soon, but it wouldn't do to buy too much. Ginger ale. That was what she wanted. She reached for the big bottle on the top shelf with one hand and with the other opened the freezer compartment for some ice cubes. One slid across the wet sink counter and fell on the floor. Stooping to pick it up, she felt a dizzy spell coming on. Trying to stand up was like trying to ice skate on the wet floor. Frightened, she grabbed her drink and walked out of the kitchen and into the living room. But she didn't make it. Later she wondered if her heel had caught in the rug first, before she passed out, or the other way around.

When she opened her eyes—she never could figure out how much later—tiny stars danced in front of them, and she had a throbbing, blinding headache. A little tear trickled out of her eye, and she let it slide down her cheek, tasting the saltiness of it. She was flat on her back on the floor, every muscle and bone ached, and for a few seconds, she didn't know where the floor was.

How dangerous. Why, she could have banged her head on the edge of a sharp table, or the glass, which had rolled across the floor, could have shattered. She could have cut herself. But all that was nothing compared with the real terror she felt. She had lost control over her mind and body. She couldn't trust herself.

What had she been thinking about before she'd blacked out? She couldn't remember. Boosting herself with her hand on the floor, she finally got up, stumbling slightly. She looked at her watch. A few minutes had gone by. She had only fainted, that's all.

She stared at the phone and then walked heavily, unsteadily toward it, picked up the receiver, and dialed. Thank heaven for little favors. There was an answer. "Hi, it's Barbara," she said cheerfully.

"Oh, you're back."

"It happened again," she replied quickly, her tone changing to one of defeat.

"Again? Didn't you call that doctor?" her friend asked, concerned.

"What doctor?"

"The one I told you to call. Dr. Walters."

So . . . the message wasn't a mistake. "Eva? Don't get angry, huh?" She paused, closing her eyes. "I just, well, I forgot what kind of doctor he is."

"He's a psychiatrist, Barbara."

Barbara was silent.

"And he can help you. Really he can. You must admit, you haven't been yourself. Especially since it happened."

Barbara thanked her. Then she said good-bye and hung up.

The white, gauzy curtains on the window facing out to Park Avenue were billowing out, looking clean and somehow ghostlike. So that psychiatrist was really calling her. That meant she had called him, but she didn't remember. Maybe she didn't want to. She knew she didn't really want to go. But it was strange. Lately she couldn't remember much of anything. She couldn't even remember coming back from London.

Usually Irwin Dinkle went out for the papers in the morning so that he could look at the Help Wanted ads. This morning he had gone out earlier than usual. He wasn't looking for a job, though, in the Sunday papers. He was anxious to find out something, anything, about the woman in white who had been murdered on Park Avenue the night before. The murder he could tell no one about.

His eyes had been caught by the headline in the *New York Post:* BEAUTIFUL BRUNETTE MURDERED IN BATHTUB. Well, that wasn't it. She was swimming in a pool of blood on Park Avenue. Grimacing, he took the piece of doughnut he was dunking in his coffee and placed it on the saucer.

Then, thumbing through the paper, he found it on page five. Just a small story in the lower-right-hand corner, headlined PARK AVENUE SLASHER. Hungrily, he devoured every word. When he was finished, he slapped the paper together and paced the apartment.

The newspaper had said the woman was . . . unknown. No identification had been found, and yet he had opened her bag and he knew who she was. In the whole city of New York only he knew who the woman in white was who had been murdered on Park Avenue the night before. How do you like that? Why . . . she must have been mugged after she was murdered! And on one of the most elegant avenues in the world.

Shaking his head furiously, he reached into the closet and pulled out the white pages. As he flipped through the phone book he asked himself, Why the hell was he doing this? and he honestly had no answer. Just a compulsive need to know more about her. Thornton, Edward; Thornton, Elaine; Thornton, Elmer; Thornton, Ewell. He looked once more. No Enid Thornton. Tossing the phone book back in the closet, he figured maybe she was unlisted. Maybe she was married. Poor guy, her husband.

He sat down on the couch and punched one of the cushions. Everything in his upbringing, his background, his sense of decency told him he should go to the cops and tell them the name of the woman who'd been slashed on Park Avenue. But he fought hard with his sense of what was right. Because it was too beautiful of a setup. He could hear it now. "And why did you wait so long . . . ?" The longer he waited, the worse it would get for him, and it would have been bad enough if he had reported it last night.

The woman is dead, he told himself. If he gave them her name, would that bring her back to life?

One detective sat, her legs up on the desk, her hands folded over her chest. The other was sitting backward on a chair. They were both concentrating. They looked up at the high ceilings and almost through the clotted institutional green paint. The Nineteenth Precinct, stretching from Fifty-ninth to Ninety-sixth streets, from the East River to Fifth Avenue, covering some of the wealthiest sections of Manhattan, had one of the most forlorn, decrepit precinct houses in New York City. It was almost one hundred years old. Visiting police officers were reluctant to use the bathrooms.

"I *want* that case," Detective Carolyn Kealing said, swinging her long legs off the top of the desk.

"Yeah, so do I," replied her partner, Detective Tammy Zuckerman, in a pronounced Brooklyn accent.

"So, we go for it," Carolyn announced, standing up.

"Yeah." Tammy winked at her.

They walked slowly, casually, one on one side of the desk, the other approaching from the other side of Detective Hank Patuto's desk.

"Hennnreee," Carolyn sang, her blue-green eyes twinkling.

He looked up sharply. Both women were scrutinizing him.

"You know, we were just talking about you, and we think you look a little peaked, working Sundays and all," Tammy said.

"Maybe you need a little vacation," Carolyn added. "That trip to the Caribbean you want to go on."

"Or maybe Bermuda. I hear it's nice this time of year," Tammy chimed in.

He looked at them from eyes rimmed with lines of fatigue.

His shoulders sagging, he nodded as if he had been caught and was confessing. "I am tired."

Tammy almost snickered out loud. His sexual and romantic exploits were legendary in the department.

"But I can't afford a vacation, you know."

They both clucked sympathetically. Tammy put a comforting hand on his shoulder, and Carolyn took a compact out of her bag. She held the small mirror up to his face.

"You just don't look good, Hank," Carolyn said.

He looked in the mirror, stuck his tongue out, and studied it.

"Why don't you let us take some of that paperwork off your hands?" Tammy crooned in her best motherly tones.

He was visibly moved. For a moment. Then he jerked his head up. "Okay, girls, what's the catch? Why are you being so nice to me?"

Tammy and Carolyn shook their heads as if they were sorry for the world that had corrupted his faith in the goodness of human nature.

"Henry . . . Hank, we want to help," Tammy said soothingly.

"Well, I could use a little help. It wouldn't hurt. You have spare time, is that it?"

They shrugged in unison, taking their cue from each other.

Carolyn was quickly ruffling through the papers on his desk. "And you know what, Henry? We even have time to take some footwork off your hands."

Tammy had the opening she was looking for. "Like this woman who was slashed and found on upper Park Avenue last night. No I.D., no nothing, pain in the neck, no glory. We'll take that off your hands."

Hank shrugged. "Gee, thanks," he said feebly. "I don't need that case. You're right." As they walked away he was sitting there holding his forehead with one hand and feeling his glands with the other. His tongue was still sticking out.

Carolyn and Tammy walked to the door, down the steps, and came into the almost nonexistent lobby on the first floor of the Nineteenth Precinct. They waved to the patrolman standing in front of the flag behind the small precinct desk, stopping in front of the I Love New York sticker on the front door. Then they ran down the steps, cackling openly.

"Like taking candy from a baby," Carolyn said.

"What woman goes out into the street without a bag?" Tammy asked.

"Where do you want to go for lunch?"

"Not around here."

"What woman goes out without a bag? Someone who's running away from somebody," Carolyn answered as they got into their car, which was parked in the small precinct driveway.

Tammy backed the unmarked Chevrolet into the street and drove toward Third Avenue. They were pensive as Tammy headed across Sixty-seventh Street. "Chinatown?" she asked.

"Sounds good. You know, she could have dropped it."

"Nothing was found nearby. But she was pretty dressed up. White pants outfit. Evening wear. Would you have carried a bag?"

"Sure," Carolyn said. "I wouldn't put my lipstick in my pocket."

"Maybe the bag was taken," Tammy said suddenly.

"You mean *that* was the motive? Someone stabbed her for money? Maybe she resisted?"

"No," Tammy replied tentatively. "Actually I was thinking it was the other way around."

"I don't follow."

"Well, she was murdered. For that reason it was a homicide."

"Yeah."

"So," Tammy continued, "that was it. There she lay on Park Avenue, slashed. Blood all over the white outfit."

Carolyn nodded. "I think I see what you're getting at. Somebody found her. Didn't report it. Took the bag. Got the money. It was somebody's lucky night."

"Right," Tammy agreed.

"You know," Carolyn said, running her fingertips through her sleek strawberry blond hair, "we're downtown. Why not stop in at the Transit Authority Building?"

"I beg your pardon?"

"The bag. Just maybe if she were mugged, the mugger ran

away. He could have taken the money and left the I.D. in the bag on the subway or the bus. Happens all the time."

"Well, it's a long shot," Tammy said, "but we could try. After all, we're right here. Of course, we don't know what the bag—if there is a bag—even looks like."

"Let's just say it was white or gold or pretty or dressy," Carolyn replied.

Tammy maneuvered the car into a parking place, and they both got out, walking toward their favorite Chinese restaurant. Carolyn began to giggle suddenly, and soon she was laughing helplessly.

"What? What's wrong?" Tammy asked her partner.

"Look what we did. We took on an extra case. We're following a harebrained idea that the woman was mugged after she was murdered . . . not murdered because she was mugged and might have resisted. Now we're going from here to the Transit Authority to look for a bag we can't even identify. Why?"

"I know, Tammy. I was just asking myself the same thing. I guess we're workaholics."

"And it's an interesting case. We don't know who was murdered . . . let alone who murdered her," Tammy said.

"Which accounts for half the homicides in New York. But this was Park Avenue. Isn't that what gets you?"

"Yeah," Tammy admitted, "that's it. Because now it's not safe for a woman to stroll down Park Avenue. And that's scary."

"Yeah," Carolyn agreed. "If Park Avenue isn't safe, *what is?*"

# CHAPTER 5

The mother lived on King's Cross Road, not too far from St. James's Church. She was a widow. That was all Detective Inspector Cavendish knew of her as he stood on her doorstep on a drizzly Monday morning, ringing the bell. He was rather surprised to see a young man open the door instead of her.

"I'm Detective Inspector Cavendish from Scotland Yard. I have an appointment to talk to Mrs. Haydn about her daughter Johanna."

The man eyed him up and down with distaste and let him in, ignoring the hand Cavendish offered. He walked ahead and Cavendish followed him down the darkened hallway. At the end of it a door was ajar, and they went into the flat.

Finally the young man spoke. "Mrs. Haydn is taking a nap," he said with finality. "I can answer all your questions. I'm Stephen Knight, Johanna's fiancé."

The detective inspector nodded, his face impassive. But he did have an appointment with the victim's mother, and it wasn't yet eleven thirty in the morning. How could she be napping?

A slow smile spread across Stephen's haggard, unshaven face. The eyes had gray rings under them, and for a moment, they sparkled with a fervor Cavendish had only seen in the eyes of revolutionaries or religious fanatics. Stephen Knight hesitated as if he were waiting for applause. His eyes held the inspector's until even Cavendish had to look away. Something was wrong here. He had been with the Yard long enough to trust his instincts, which had been finely tuned and carefully developed over the years.

He cleared his throat. "Yes. Well, then, I do have some questions to ask *you*, Mr. Knight."

"Fire away."

"Did Miss Haydn have any enemies that you know of? Men that might have carried a grudge? Men that she may have slighted in some way?"

The man stiffened his back and suddenly looked as if he were growing taller. "See here, we were about to be engaged."

Cavendish carefully softened his voice. "But, what about . . . old boyfriends?" he asked sympathetically.

Stephen Knight shrugged.

Cavendish had a way of studying a person and, at the same time, looking as if he had nothing on his mind but the weather.

"Her roommate . . . ask her!" Stephen Knight said finally in an explosion of anger.

"Splendid idea," Cavendish replied. "Where were you, Mr. Knight, when the murder took place? Where were you at around seven o'clock?"

Stephen looked at the man incredulously. "Where was I? I was sitting in a restaurant called the Red Lion on Half Moon Street, right in the Mayfair District, waiting for Johanna. I had in my pocket a tiny velvet box containing an engagement ring. She never even knew I wanted to marry her!"

Cavendish nodded his head sympathetically. "And you were there all evening?"

"Why, no," Stephen went on indignantly. "I left to call her flat."

"When?"

"I don't remember exactly. I suppose I waited a half hour first, then called. I called a few more times after that, and then I thought of calling her mum. And then I found out." His voice rose in anger.

"I see," said Cavendish.

There was a creak in the floorboards and both men turned.

"Can I get you a cup of tea?" the woman, Johanna's mother, offered as she moved slowly, like a woman of eighty, into the parlor. Cavendish waited until she had found herself a seat on the sofa and plumped up the cushions.

"I thought I heard voices," she said.

Cavendish stood up and introduced himself. He was quite sure Stephen Knight had told her the appointment had been canceled, for some reason. But he said nothing. He looked around the flat very subtly. It was large but made smaller by all the clutter. It looked like it hadn't been tidied up in days. Everywhere were ashtrays full of cigarette butts, stacks of old newspapers, dirty tea cups and dishes lying about on the floor. He turned his gaze back to Stephen Knight, who was, unknowingly, holding an inch of solid ash on his cigarette.

"I'm sorry to bother you so soon after . . ." Cavendish began delicately. He had said it so many times to so many people. "But did she complain of crank callers or that sort of thing?"

"No," her mother answered simply.

Cavendish noticed the resemblance immediately, though he had only seen the girl in the morgue. There was the same blunt angle of the haircut against the high cheekbones. "Was she unhappy about something?"

Mrs. Haydn clapped her hand on her thigh and let out a little squeal. "Johanna? Come on. She was the happiest girl alive. Always joking, always helping people. It was a joy to be around her. She loved her job and she was a good girl." There was a pause, and then the woman began to sob uncontrollably. "Why does God take the good? Does He have some kind of master plan we don't know about?"

Detective Inspector Cavendish closed his eyes. It was inevitable. The tears, the entreaties. Once it all but broke his heart, but now, while he was not hardened to it, he was accustomed to it. It made him want to solve the case even more quickly. And this was a mean one.

He waited a respectable number of seconds, and then he directed a question to the man. "By the way, what do you do, Mr. Knight?"

"I'm in computers."

"And with what firm?"

"Thomas Cook."

"Oh," Cavendish said, and the map of London he kept in his mind rolled out a Thomas Cook office right near the sight of the murder. He stared at the obviously angry young man and took in the weeping mother. It was a useless interview as far as he was concerned. He would get back to it later.

Then the woman said something, sniffling as she talked. "I know who killed her."

Cavendish looked at her sharply.

"Oh, yes. It was one of those American tourists that she liked so well. I don't know why he did it, mind you, but it makes sense, doesn't it? Who else would have done such a hideous . . ." She began to weep more loudly.

Detective Inspector Cavendish stood then, his tall, lanky body seeming to unroll from the low chair. A tourist. That would be a headache to investigate. His eyes narrowed as he saw Stephen Knight smirking at him.

No one offered to show him the way out, so he found it himself. As he stood on the stoop looking into the dreary rain, he decided that Stephen Knight's behavior was decidedly unnatural for a young man whose fiancée had just been murdered. He exhibited no signs of grief.

Cavendish had seen a lot in his long career. Murderers were interesting people. Especially those who committed crimes of passion, or those with some deep-rooted pathological problem. Yes, it was quite possible that Stephen Knight had left to make that phone call to his fiancée. Then he shoved the knife into her back and returned to the restaurant to wait and play the charade.

Barbara changed her blouse once more and cursed herself for being such a coward. He had told her to come today, and now she was so nervous she was going to spend money on a cab when she could have taken a bus.

She had never met a psychiatrist before.

The doorman hailed a taxi going by, and though it was a cool day, she felt sticky somehow. Slumping into the backseat of the cab, she told herself one more time that it would be just one visit, and that when she made the final move to Hammersmith, she would be very careful of her money. No matter how much she had, it would one day run out.

When they pulled up to the high-rise apartment on Seventy-first Street near Central Park West, it was so high she couldn't see the end of it through the cab window. Behind the big glass windows at the front of the building, she could see the glitter of the chandelier. It reminded her of a Sheraton Hotel.

Shaking slightly and feeling totally terrified, she made her way to the desk in the lobby. Announcing her name, she watched the desk clerk as he read slowly over a list.

"Okay . . . Hargrove. You can go up."

She felt as if she wanted to bolt and run. And then at the elevator, she felt a wave of dizziness pass over her. Someone behind her stepped forward and looked at her strangely. The doors opened, and she got on. At the seventeenth floor, she stepped out of the elevator and looked around frantically for the apartment, knowing it was too late to turn back.

She rang the bell and then found that the door was open. It opened into a tiny waiting room. There were two chairs. She sat down in one. The walls were stark white. On it were two water-color prints, which she knew immediately she didn't like. They seemed cold and impersonal to her. In a vase were exquisite little budding roses. Artificial flowers.

She heard someone coming and looked up. A woman walked out, her eyes downcast, her face grim. Small beads of perspiration began to pop out on Barbara's forehead. Her blazer, she had to take it off. Why didn't they have air in these offices? Her fingernails snagging on the dark linen, she all but ripped off her blazer. And then she realized someone was watching her. She looked up into deep blue eyes, black wavy hair, and a very serious face. Embarrassed, she looked away.

"Hi! I'm Dr. Walters!" He stuck out his hand.

She stood up and let him pump her hand. Then they walked down the hall to the inner office. It was small, too, and effi-ciently compact. Besides a small forest of plants, the office had a beige fabric couch and two chairs, one matching the couch, the other a black leather recliner. There was a desk, and the wall was lined with bookshelves.

She sat in the black recliner and leaned back. He stood over her, slightly amused.

"You're supposed to sit over there," he said, pointing to the chair opposite the black recliner, across the room.

Embarrassed, she uttered a little "Whoops" and, almost falling out of the chair, scooted across the room to the little chair opposite the recliner. As she sat she found herself sinking down into its cushiony seat. She felt his eyes bore through her like he had X-ray vision. It made her want to squirm. The dizziness she had felt before washed over her like a wave, and she desperately tried to cover it up.

She couldn't meet his eyes directly. He began to smile at her encouragingly, but she couldn't say anything. She was relieved when his mouth opened and he began to speak.

"So what's happening in your life?"

Barbara almost gasped. Did she have to tell him that? She thought Eva had said something. She was the one who recommended her.

In a thin, reedy voice she barely recognized as her own, still trying to avoid those eyes, she spoke. "I've had some fainting spells and I get these headaches"—he just kept staring at her— "and there's some dizziness," she said nervously.

She swallowed and looked at the picture above the couch. It was an oil painting. It looked like one of those paint-by-number jobs.

"My father died two weeks ago. That's why I'm here."

"Oh, I'm sorry to hear that," he said sympathetically.

She nodded. Suddenly in his presence she felt grief stricken, but in reality, she had known her father was going to die. His doctor had wanted him to stop drinking years ago.

"And your mother?"

"Dead," she answered crisply.

He looked at her long and hard, but for the first time, she felt this rather abrupt, impersonal man might have some warmth and compassion.

He said, almost pitifully, "So, you're feeling all alone."

"Yes," she replied, matching his tone. But she had always felt alone, she supposed.

"And what about men? Are you seeing a man?"

She was going to say no, but then she thought of Jonathan. He was a man and she would call him back. They had been friendly and would probably get together. "Well, yes," she said.

"And the sex is good for you?" he asked.

She fidgeted with the top button of her blouse, lowering her eyes demurely. "Oh, there's no sex or anything like that."

"I see."

Then there was a long pause. He was still looking at her, waiting. But she didn't know what to say or do.

Finally he broke the silence by asking, "Is there anything you want to tell me or ask me?"

She was so tongue-tied she couldn't speak. Then she felt a stab of pain. Oh, no. Not here. The headache again and the swirls of dizziness. Oh, God, she was so embarrassed. She bent over to hide it by reaching for a tissue. He kept a box of mustard-colored tissues on the floor. A cube. A cute cube. She knew she had to sit up again. Somehow.

Then he was smiling at her.

She tried to smile back, confused.

"I don't think you need to come for more than a few visits. But I do want to recommend a complete medical checkup. Those fainting spells and headaches may not be psychological." He paused to smile merrily, letting her know he was human enough to knock his own profession. "Not everything is psychological."

She returned his smile.

"But I think your grief for your father is very real. Grief does strange things to people. Especially since his death was so recent. We can talk about that at your next visit."

She nodded.

"And also about your mother."

She shuddered.

"Well, I see our time is up."

She reached into her bag. "What do I owe you?"

He smiled. "Oh, I can bill you at the end of each month."

"No, let me pay you now," she insisted. She might be in

London and miss his bill. While she was writing him a check, she thought how the time had flown. She could hardly believe fifty minutes had gone by.

Dr. Walters relaxed in his chair. She had opened up. He thought he could help her. Short-term therapy was his specialty. It was the sign of an old-fashioned psychiatrist not to let his patients go and grow. But before she left him, he'd see to it that she was a little more aggressive sexually.

She shook hands with him rather awkwardly, and they made another appointment. When he asked for her address for his files, she reached in her purse, handed him a business card, smiled, and left.

Dr. Walters headed for his answering machine, as he usually did between appointments, to return his more urgent calls. As he was dialing he looked at the card. Then he hung up the phone and checked his appointment book. Funny, he had thought her name was Barbara Hargrove. That's what he had written in the book. That was the name on the check. But the little white business card had a different name on it. Then he laughed knowingly. Well, that was typical of patients, especially the new ones. Sometimes they unwittingly left gloves or briefcases or magazines in his office. She had obviously been so excited by what they had been talking about that she left the business card of someone who had given her one. He threw it in the wastebasket.

Just five hours after she had left New York on Tuesday night, TWA's Flight 843 began the descent into London's Heathrow Airport, landing at 6:10 Wednesday morning, London time. The harried stewardesses, trying to be polite to the cranky passengers, were clearing away the last of the coffee, tea, and pastry snack. Seat belts were fastened. Cards to fill out for entry into the United Kingdom were being hastily scribbled out, and passengers were grumbling about the inhumaneness of stuffing so many people into such a cramped space and charging so much money for it. Everyone wanted only one thing: to curl up on a soft bed and go to sleep. But instead they were going to have to face the grueling procedure of waiting and standing and showing their passports to enter London.

She sat in the last row of the far right aisle, yawning. Her black slacks were only slightly wrinkled, and her white blouse and red vest had withstood the long trip. She was tired and irritable, like the rest, but genuinely happy to be home again.

"Stay awake," she kept urging herself. "You can sleep all day."

And then the crowds thinned out and dispersed, and finally she was collecting her luggage and getting a red airbus into London. Eventually she caught the Underground.

When she got off at Hammersmith Station, she wheeled her luggage down the street, thinking of the nice sleep she would have. The weather in London was lovely, too. The sun was big and visible and shining all over. Bit of a surprise for London at the end of May.

She rang the doorbell and then waited.

"Why, miss?" the voice said. "I didn't expect you so soon, but it's ready now." She opened the door to the flat. It was bare. "Look," Mrs. Lockwood said, "there's a loft bed built into the living room. An earlier tenant left it, so it's yours. I'll get some bedding, and you can curl up there until you get a few things. Been flying all night, have you? I don't understand why they torture people that way."

She nodded sleepily.

"Well, I'll leave everything outside your door," the woman said. She seemed reluctant to leave. "The keys are on the kitchen table." Finally she backed out and the door slammed shut. She went back upstairs. Very private, this Miss Hargrove. In months, she'd know all about her, and Miss Hargrove wouldn't even know it. Oh, she had ways. And that was her hobby, you might say. People.

The very private Miss Hargrove took everything downstairs and began to unpack. She always felt so much more organized when things were taken care of and put away in the right place.

Her dresses and skirts and shoes could go in the larger bedroom. The other bedroom wasn't her concern right then. She hung her clothes in the closet. Her carry-on luggage was plopped down in the corner on the floor. It was just a TWA shiny beige flight bag, but it came in so handy.

There was no dresser or night table yet, but when there was

she'd have to get some table lamps. It was dreadfully dark in the bedroom. The hall was dark, too. She darted into the bathroom, putting some hand lotion, face cream, and her toothbrush and toothpaste on the shelves. There'd be less to take back next time.

Then she rummaged around in her flight bag for her hairbrush. It was down there somewhere, she knew. She touched something very sharp and, surprised, shrieked. Pulling her hand out, she saw a tiny streak of blood on her finger. She sucked on it. A glass bottle must have broken. "Damn," she whispered. "I should have packed more carefully."

Reaching in again, she was very cautious. She felt the handle first. Then she fingered the cold metal. And then she felt fear. Real, paralyzing fear.

"Oh, my God!" she said out loud, pulling it out.

Her hands trembling, she began to look around. Then she withdrew it from her flight bag. It slipped out of her hands and dropped to the floor, the "clunk" reverberating throughout the silent two-story apartment. She looked down, shaking.

It was a butcher's knife.

# CHAPTER 6

They had contacted the last of the names taken from I.D.'s in bags found on the Transit Authority's lost-and-found shelves. They were well aware that there were plenty of bags that didn't have I.D.'s. Just as they knew they could be looking in the wrong place entirely. The bag they weren't even sure the victim had been carrying might not have ended up there at all.

Sitting with her shirt rolled up to her elbows and chewing on a pencil, Carolyn finished her calls. Spread out before her was a list of names. She looked up at Tammy, who sat at the desk next to hers, and announced, "They're all alive." Then she shouted, "Hey, Hank! What's with that case—the woman slashed on Park Avenue? You got anything?"

"Nah, talking to people in the neighborhood. You got anything?"

"Nah," Carolyn returned.

"Listen, thanks for your help," he said.

"Don't mention it," Carolyn replied.

The phone rang on Tammy's desk. "Detective Zuckerman, Nineteenth Precinct." She signaled to Carolyn frantically as her eyes grew wider. "Yeah . . . Yeah . . . Yeah . . . Can you give me the name off the card, and we'll pick it up later? . . .

Yeah . . . Yeah." By the time she hung up, Carolyn was at her desk. "You're not going to believe this," Tammy said, her voice low, leaning in across the desk. "That was Jay Street in Brooklyn. They found an interesting bag—with blood stains on it. And, get this, it was white . . ."

"And . . . ?"

"And it had an I.D. in the wallet. Name is Enid Thornton."

"Did the wallet have any money in it?"

"Empty. Picked clean," said Tammy.

The two women fell silent as they saw Hank Patuto walking up to their desk. "You know," he said, "now that you mention that Park Avenue murder . . ."

They looked up at him, expectantly, waiting.

"Don't you think it's possible that she might have been carrying some sort of handbag, and that it might have been taken?"

They nodded solemnly.

"But—and here's the kicker—she may have been stabbed and left there and then someone came along and snatched the bag. Huh?" He looked at both women eagerly.

"It's a possibility," Carolyn replied cautiously.

"So maybe you girls can call around. Lost-and-found places, you know. The Transit Authority has one. Where is it? Brooklyn somewhere?"

"I think," said Tammy. "Jay Street."

As he walked away the two women held in their laughter. " 'You girls'?" Tammy repeated, half gasping. Then she said quietly, "Call information first, then run a computer check. I'll bet this is the one. Then we can go from here."

"So the lady lying on a slab in the morgue with a tag on her can get a decent burial," Carolyn commented, pity in her voice.

"Yeah," Tammy said, wincing.

And almost directly above them on the next floor was a detective who was wishing someone would relieve him of his paperwork. Right at the moment two very nervous, concerned people were standing in front of the desk of third-grade Detective Gary Goldstein. The man was twisting his hat around in his hands, and the woman was nervously flicking imaginary pieces of lint off her suit jacket. They had never before been inside the Nineteenth Precinct—or any precinct house in Manhattan, for that matter.

The detective motioned them to two chairs beside his desk. They sat down and he studied them. Expensive-looking was his first impression.

"We're here to report a missing person," the woman said, "my sister."

The detective sat poised at his manual typewriter, a relic like everything else in that precinct. "How long has she been missing?"

"I called her Sunday morning, and there was no answer. I left a message with her machine. I've been trying ever since. That's not like her."

The detective stopped typing, sighed deeply, and scratched his head. "You mean you folks want to report a missing person who's been missing two days?"

"Well, it may be longer," the woman said defensively. "We don't know. I haven't talked to her for a while. But we checked her apartment and talked to the doorman. No one's seen her since Saturday. I just know something's wrong."

He nodded. They're playing my song, Detective Goldstein thought. Sunday, missing. Tuesday, bother us. On Wednesday, she shows up. He cocked his head. "Where do you live?"

"Scarsdale," came the quick reply.

Goldstein nodded his head as if to say, "It figures." "Listen," he said, "you folks probably don't know that a person isn't considered really missing until five days have gone by. We can't trace this woman until Thursday, at least." Then the tone in his voice changed to sympathetic and cajoling. "She's liable to turn up, huh?"

The woman shook her head, her lips pressed together firmly. "Maybe not."

"She married?" he asked.

"Divorced," the man said.

"Date any other men?"

The woman stiffened and said huffily, "Yes, but they are all respectable gentlemen."

"And your sister? Where does she live?"

"Around the corner," the woman said, "on Sixty-eighth and Park. That's why we're here."

The man leaned in and looked at the detective earnestly. "Look, we really think something happened to her. You should check into this immediately!"

Goldstein shrugged. "She has to be missing five days before she's a missing person."

"Whose law is that?" the woman challenged, outraged. "That's nonsense. I'm a taxpayer. What if she's in trouble? She has to wait five days to be saved?"

The detective shrugged again. "I don't write the laws, lady; I just enforce them. I'll need her name."

"Polly Manklin," the man said.

"When did you last see her?"

"Last Wednesday we all went into the city for dinner," the woman said. "Can't you start counting from there?"

"I'll need a description," Goldstein went on, ignoring her remark.

The woman opened her bag and pulled out a snapshot. "This is the most recent photograph we have of her."

Goldstein took it. Attractive woman. No spring chicken. But a looker. Dollars to doughnuts she was shacked up somewhere with some young stud. He could psyche out the rest of the scenario. The older sister was like a mother hen, and the younger sister decided to make hay and the hell with reporting in.

This scene was enacted above a layer of peeling cement that separated them from Detectives Tammy Zuckerman and Carolyn Kealing. They had often joked, sitting at their cigarette-burnt desks, that if the walls could talk, all they would have to do was take notes and write a book. About a hundred years of crime in New York's glamorous East Side.

The first possibility that left their list was that Enid Thornton was in the phone book. Second, that she had an unlisted number. Now they had to find out if she was married, divorced, had a stage name or what.

One hour later Carolyn fell into one of her minidepressions. Tammy liked to tell her it was because she didn't talk out her feelings. Carolyn disagreed with the volatile, motherly detective. She wasn't cool, and she wasn't really hiding much. It was just that she got disappointed and tired sometimes. Police work did that to you. And, unlike Tammy, being a single woman and a detective was no easy feat.

Carolyn put down the phone and swiveled around in her chair. "Tammy? Nothing. Really. It just doesn't check out. No credit cards. No bank. No professional affiliation. No husband with wife named Enid."

"Well, you've only been at it a little over an hour. So, what do you expect? Miracles?"

Carolyn shook her head. "No, I don't. But I have a hunch there is no Enid Thornton. She doesn't exist."

A group of somber, unsmiling Japanese tourists sat in the lobby of the Hotel Lincoln. Their tour guide stood in front of the desk, pleading with the clerk.

"You said the rooms would be ready at noon. Here it is almost one, and they're still waiting to get in. Do you know how many hours these people have been up?"

The desk clerk nodded. They had played out this scene together many times. The rooms were never ready on time, but it looked good for both of them to go through this charade. "We're trying our best," he said crisply.

The tour guide went back to the crumpled group and translated what the desk clerk had said into Japanese. There was a polite but unanimous groan.

The assistant manager then went up to the eighth floor. He spotted four maids and told them to leave their work and go to the seventh floor. There was a group of tourists waiting to get in.

Olga Grunwald pulled her big white tub of a basket out of the door and unhooked her vacuum cleaner. None of this was really important anymore. She just went through the motions. In a week, she was getting married and quitting this job. He didn't want her to work as a maid in a hotel anymore.

On the seventh floor the elevators opened almost together and disgorged the maids, who wheeled their baskets in different directions. Olga had been given the key to Room 712. Humming, she went in the door and began.

She nimbly stripped a bed and remade it with fresh sheets. Tonight was the night she would go to the dressmaker to get her wedding dress fitted. It was white with a high lace neck and looked like the dress her grandmother wore in the old, faded wedding picture. She thought it was the most beautiful dress in the world. And she had spent more than she should have on it.

As she was going to make up the other bed, she tripped over an open bottom drawer and, letting out a loud "Ouch," pulled her ankle away. It was just a scrape, but it stung. She looked at the drawer, and that's when she saw the big white square in the back. Someone had left something.

Reaching inside, she lifted out a white leather bag with gold snaps. It was lovely and obviously expensive. She stroked the buttery soft leather with her finger. Then she opened it up. More leather. A tiny brown case. She flipped it open and saw the credit cards tucked inside. Lifting out a Visa card, she ran her finger across the raised letters. Polly Manklin. She turned it over and looked at the signature. Slanty, with long, sweeping curves. In a tiny gold cloth change purse were six ten-dollar bills.

Olga looked around as if someone had seen her. She should turn it in. But it was such a beautiful bag. She could carry it to the reception after the wedding. And the money . . . sixty dollars. That was just about how much she had gone over her wedding gown budget.

She bit her lip. Never had she done anything like this. But then she remembered the sharp way the assistant manager had insulted her the other day. Accused her of being slower than a turtle. And in front of everyone. It was humiliating. He just needed someone to single out and holler at. Make an example of. She was the fastest maid they had, and everyone knew it.

It was, after all, the perfect crime. She was an eighth-floor maid, and there would be no record of the fact that she had cleaned this room. Besides, she would be gone next week. And anyone could have taken it. Even the new people who occupied Room 712. Carefully she unbuttoned the top of her uniform and laid the bag flat across her midriff section. Then she buttoned her uniform and hiked up her apron to cover the slight bulge. Replacing the towels, glasses, and soap in the bathroom, humming nonchalantly, she finished up and locked the door on Room 712.

Johanna's flat mate, Susan, sat crying softly. "I think she knew that Stephen would ask her to marry him that night," she said. "I told him that. I don't know if it made him feel better or worse, poor bloke." She looked all around the room. "I can't believe it. Just can't believe it." She indicated with a glance a pile of luggage and boxes, what was left of her former flat mate. "I'll have to get someone new, you know. Can't afford this myself. Should move out. Maybe the murderer will come back . . ."

Cavendish looked at her. "Do you think that might happen?"

Susan trembled. "I don't know. You asked me about her old boyfriends. She met Stephen when she moved in here. But she always referred to the old ones as bloody garbage. Still, that doesn't mean they'd come after me, does it?"

The detective inspector said the nicest thing he could think of saying, but he couldn't be sure he was really helping the woman. "Well, she was murdered in the street, you know." If she were his daughter, he would have her moved out of the place.

It was clouded over when he left and it looked a little threatening, but it hadn't started to rain yet. Sergeant Hollings was trailing Stephen Knight in front of his apartment on Sumner Street. He should check in to see if Hollings had anything to report. Driving through the streets, he noticed how crowded, alive, and bustling London was. Everywhere people were shopping, strolling, enjoying the May weather. And as he drove he knew that somewhere in the city of London was a man who had killed a lovely young woman who loved her life. He could pass him in his car and not even know who it was. He glanced down at his watch. Not yet nine o'clock. Drizzling miserably now. He could go for something light, maybe a bun and coffee. On second thought, he decided to stop at his office first.

Passing through the archway, he thought of the Yard as an army of about twenty thousand men encamped in about seven hundred square miles. It was when he arrived in his office that he did something he rarely did. Maybe it was the slow, unrewarding case, but he lost his temper.

Sergeant Hollings was standing in the doorway, waiting for him.

"You're supposed to be tailing Stephen Knight!" he blasted, momentarily shocking the sergeant. "And you're supposed to be doing it until you're relieved!"

Hollings braced himself under the verbal attack. "I know, sir . . ."

"Well, what did you get? Where did he go? *Do you have anything?*"

"Nothing. He doesn't come and he doesn't go."

Cavendish was barely listening. There were voices all around him. Men were crowding into his office. A voice he couldn't see spoke first.

"There's been another murder. Same as the first."

Cavendish looked around the room.

"That's right," Hollings said quickly. "Identical M.O. Woman got slashed in the back by a knife. Call came in around ten minutes ago. I rushed over here."

"Where?" Cavendish demanded.

"Underground," came a voice.

"Underground?" Cavendish repeated incredulously.

"That's right, sir," Hollings said. "Just a few minutes after the rush hour had cleared out."

Cavendish stroked his chin with his thumb and forefinger. "Clever job," he said to himself.

"This time we have a witness," Hollings continued. "Saw someone running away after the murder."

"Well, did you talk to the witness?"

"Actually, sir, the witness spoke to a policeman on the scene. He gave a description, and then he got swallowed up in the crowd. We don't have a detailed description, but there's something."

"Well, what did the man look like?" Cavendish asked quickly.

"Actually, it wasn't a man that got away. You see, sir, it was a *woman.*"

# CHAPTER 7

She was awake even before the loud pounding on the door began. She could have ignored it and she might have sunk back into sleep again except that it was the urgent voice of Lockey, the landlady. Maybe there was some emergency. Scampering down the steps of the loft bed, holding her head with her hand because she could feel one of those headaches coming on, she reached the door and opened it. Mrs. Lockwood's plump hand was raised in a half knock.

"I thought you might be sleeping in this morning, you know? So I've brought you a nice little bit of breakfast and a cozy chat."

Barbara looked at the woman with her determined gray eyes, holding the tray in her hands. There was no way out of it.

"I baked some scones," the woman said with the softness of a drill sergeant.

Barbara smiled in spite of herself, rubbed the sleep out of her eyes, and noticed that her headache was fading slightly. She was barefoot and wearing navy silk pajamas with white piping.

Mrs. Lockwood brushed aside her and began bustling about. On the tray were a small teakettle, the scones, a small tub of butter, and some jams. It really was very thoughtful.

In a minute the table was set, and the tea was on. "There you are, love. I like to get to know my tenants. It's so much chummier, don't you think?"

Barbara nodded and her head started to throb again. She massaged her temples with her fingertips.

"You okay, ducks?"

"Oh, I'm fine. Just one of my headaches."

"Aspirin, then?"

"Oh, that doesn't work with me."

"Well then, eat something and you'll feel better," she instructed, smiling, showing crooked teeth.

Barbara looked up, alarmed. "Oh, no! I lost my watch. My gold watch."

"Is it downstairs? Maybe you left it downstairs."

"Downstairs?" Barbara asked dully, looking over at the winding stairway. "No, I didn't go down there, did I?"

Mrs. Lockwood saw an opening. A chance to learn more about Barbara. It was much like the soap operas. Everyone lived one. If one just listened, there were a thousand stories. And it was much more interesting than reading a book or watching the telly.

"Is it a good watch?" she asked.

"My father gave it to me," Barbara answered without emotion.

"How nice. And how does he feel about your living here?"

"He's dead."

"Sorry. I thought your boyfriend might have given it to you."

Barbara blushed. Mrs. Lockwood registered it. She beckoned the barefoot girl, who was standing absently and biting a clump of her hair, to sit down.

"This is really so nice of you, Mrs. Lockwood," Barbara said courteously, sitting down.

"Not at all. Now, none of that. Call me Lockey. And think of me as your second mother. How is your mother, dear?"

"She's dead."

"Oh, dear," Lockey said. "Sorry."

Suddenly Barbara began to choke on her scone. Lockey jumped up to get her a glass of water. While she was running the cold water, she looked down. In an open drawer that held the silverware tray was a sharp, shiny knife. Nothing else. No spoons, forks, teaspoons. Just a big, fat butcher's knife.

Lockey came to Barbara's rescue with the glass of water long after Barbara had stopped coughing and sputtering. Lockey wondered about that knife. What a mean, nasty thing to do. It was left there, no doubt, by the former tenants. A couple she had asked to leave because they couldn't meet the rent. Odd sort. They hadn't gotten along anyway. Probably left it out of spite.

Barbara looked at her and then at the food and tea things on the table. She suddenly wished the woman would leave. She had things to do, to straighten up, to buy. She hadn't even begun her work yet. She hadn't written one single word.

"I'm a writer, you know," she said to the woman at last.

There it was. Part of the story. Like a perfect piece of a jigsaw puzzle. "Do you write books, then, love?"

Barbara was beginning to regret her disclosure. Now she'd never get her to leave. Lockey had crossed her ankles and popped one more half scone into her crumb-dotted mouth.

"Yes, I'm writing one about . . ." Barbara stopped. It was really none of her business.

Lockey licked her lip. And waited. She broke the silence with, "Oh, I get it. And you want to get to work and busybody old Lockey is preventing you."

Barbara put up her hand as if to stop her. But she was thankful the woman had caught on.

Lockey stood up and began cleaning and clearing off her things from the table. "Well, the Mister is always saying I should mind my own business. 'Lockey,' he says, 'Don't be such an old biddy.' "

Lockey looked at Barbara from the corner of her eye. Not much this time. But she'd stop back again, watch out the window. Nothing escaped her. Actually there was nothing else to do all day. The true story was that the Mister had told her to watch her step. One day her nosey ways would get her in a big lot of trouble. Lockey smiled to herself. The trouble was there was nothing terribly exciting about her new tenant.

* * *

The day had mellowed to a dusky pink, and there was a streak of red floating across the sky. Detective Inspector Cavendish wanted to remember what that looked like. What he wanted to forget was his more-or-less-terminal headache. It had started this morning after the news of this latest murder. Right after that, he had bent down to pick up a pencil and bumped his half-balding head on the desk as he came up. Getting up suddenly, his head feeling raw and fiercely painful, he hit his knee so hard against the corner of the desk that he would have screamed out had his head not hurt so much. Since then, he had been uncharacteristically cantankerous and tight-lipped. And four aspirin hadn't touched his headache.

Maybe after this one case, he thought, he would retire. He was getting too old and cynical for this sort of thing. Women murderers running around the Underground. Talk of another Jack the Ripper. His damn clumsiness today. This case could be his swan song. On the other hand, according to his wife, he always talked like this on a gloomy day. He would never retire. He was too much a fixture at the Yard. What would he do? Putter around the garden?

This last murder was a "first" for London, so to speak. London's "tubes"—or Underground—were a model of efficiency and cleanliness. New York tourists envied the civilization of it all. There were even little vending machines, that worked, that had Cadbury chocolate bars. Now one vending machine had to be scrubbed until the blood stains came off. But nowhere could they find decipherable fingerprints.

So now the London Underground had a bad reputation because of the bizarre murder that had taken place this morning. He wondered if rush hour would be crowded or if passengers would find some other way of getting home. Cavendish felt almost humbled by the clever and cunning mind of the person who had pulled off such a daring feat. The fact was that the murderer rode the Underground to Warren Road. At which time the murderer sneaked off, unsuspected, waited a bit until the throes of people flushed out of sight, and picked one lone, bloody unfortunate straggler to kill. One innocent who didn't keep up with the crowd. And the killer picked a perfect moment—a minute or two after the rush hour. Maybe the woman was dawdling because she was thinking pleasant thoughts. He hoped so.

No, his job wasn't all Agatha Christie and glory. He should have been a bricklayer. Almost had thought of it at one time. Good job, that. Payday. Couple of ales with the mates. Steady work. No surprises.

Like what they had found out at the end of the day. Yes, there had been a witness who had seen a woman running away. But several people had called in. They claimed to be in the Underground after the murder or up on the sidewalk, and some had said they had seen a man running away. Each witness gave a different description of the fleeing figure.

Stephen Knight approached the house slowly. He came as soon as he had heard. He was needed here.

The man shuffled slowly down the street to his house. Even though it was dark out, Stephen knew who it was. Down the street he came, empty eyed, wearing a checkered hat and a grim expression.

Stephen stepped out of the shadows. "She was yours, wasn't she?" he asked bluntly.

The haggard-looking man stepped back. Then he said, "Go away. I don't want to talk to any more reporters."

Stephen put his arm around him. "I'm not a reporter . . . I'm your friend. Maybe we can work together."

# CHAPTER 8

Dear Trivia Bits:
There was a little girl on a soap called *Tomorrow Is Another Day*. The soap was killed. But the little girl was killed way before. Why? I thought she was so good. "Cookie" was my favorite child star. I was her biggest fan. Whatever happened to her? Did she grow up and leave the business? Please tell me why this Cookie crumbled.
"I miss Cookie."

Dear "Miss":
To the best of our knowledge, Cookie simply grew up. She outgrew the part. Her mother, who always acted as her agent, wrote Cookie's farewell letter. She left the business at age twelve, and it is suspected that she may have left the country to live elsewhere.
Trivia Bits
*Soap Opera Guide*

Barbara lovingly fingered the clipping. Eva had cut it out to show her. She had seen it first. Barbara had had it laminated at a print shop, but it wasn't inspiring her. Nothing came from her ballpoint pen.

She was sitting in one of the rooms downstairs, looking out on the green and gold garden. She looked down at the empty page and then got up and paced around. Where should she start her book? Writing was harder than she thought.

Nothing on the paper yet.

She could begin with her father. Dear old Dad. He had left her his insurance money. So she need never work or worry again. But it wasn't only his money that had left her so well off. He had left her *her* money. Because long, long ago he had hired a lawyer to protect the money she had earned when she was a child. Seems dear old Mum was dipping into the till. So the money had to go into a trust fund, payable in full at the time of his death. She would get the money when he could no longer take care of her. Not that he'd done such a wonderful job of doing that before.

So she would never have to take a secretarial job again. Oh, God, how she hated those. The monotony, the boredom, the humiliation of working for arrogant men and women when she knew that years ago she had been somebody. A star. But now she was rich. Everybody thought she was somebody again. She could do anything she wanted. Like take this flat in Hammersmith. Some life she had led. Some parents she had had.

Nothing on paper yet.

She remembered how her father's girlfriend had wept at his funeral. Molly. Strange they had never been friends. No, there was no jealousy or competition. She hadn't known her father was that close to a woman. She and Dad had lived like strangers in the Park Avenue apartment for nearly fifteen years. Molly had cried louder than Barbara at the funeral.

She had to hand it to dear old Dad. She had gone to a wake held at a bar. It was supposed to be a memorial service. Even at the funeral home, there had been uproarious laughter. She had wondered if her father could hear them. But though she felt like shouting, "Shut up, it's disrespectful," she didn't. She couldn't. The reality of it was that her father had always belonged more to his drinking cronies than to her.

And the way it had happened. He had fallen off a bar stool in the back of one of his favorite haunts, and they didn't discover him until the next morning when the man came in to mop up the place.

There was old distinguished Ryder Hargrove, paying his final dues, lying sprawled under two stools with a shit-kicking smile on his face. The smile was what deceived the maintenance man. He tried to wake him first by nudging him with the tip of his shoe. Then he tried to shake him awake. He thought the guy was just sleeping it off. On the floor in a perfectly fitting nice suit.

She thought of her father's silly smile. Even stone-cold dead, there was that smile. She had asked the coroner to wipe it off his face, but he couldn't.

And still nothing on the blank yellow-lined paper in front of her.

At the wake Barbara had whispered to Eva that she had to get out of there. She couldn't breathe. "Now comes the maudlin part," she told her friend. "They'll all go out and get drunk, and tomorrow it will probably rain and I'll have a funeral's worth of soppy zombies coming to pay their last respects." Their poor wives. Maybe that's why Dad never married his Molly. He couldn't do that to her. As it turned out, it hadn't rained at her father's funeral. It was a cheery, hopeful sunshiny day. But nobody was sober.

No, she couldn't write about that. No one would want to read it.

The problem was starting. Maybe she should begin with the title. She had wanted to call it *Tomorrow Is Another Day*. But no one would remember the soap anymore. She could call it *Cookie*. Finally the words came to her:

Cookie. They had gotten away with it until she was twelve. And then they had killed her because she had started to mature. They said Cookie had to go. Then she found out later that they had lied. They had actually replaced her after all with another girl. Only this little girl demanded to be called Corrinne. And then in years to come, Cookie was forgotten. Corrinne, played by the same girl, stayed on and on. Biting her lip, she remembered what one of the cameramen had said when they got the news: "Well, that's the way the cookie crumbles, kid." She had never liked him and neither had Mum. Mum who had fought so hard not to have Cookie killed.

The Information Room at New Scotland Yard acted as a clearing center. Matters that required police attention were received and distributed. More than three thousand police vehicles, boats, and motorcycles all equipped with radio sets were in two-way communication with the Information Room.

The room was staffed by experienced police officers who received the telephone calls, accurately recorded the information, and initiated action.

The night the woman was murdered in cold blood in the Underground the wires were jammed. Everybody had inside information about the bizarre murder. One woman called and said it was her upstairs lodger. Another man called to warn them there would be another killing soon on the Underground near Knightsbridge. He was dubbed the "Soothsayer."

The traffic control room at the Yard had a large-scale map linked to a computer system. A system of television cameras watched danger points and traffic holdups in various parts of London. But the busiest division by far that rainy May Wednesday night was the Criminal Investigation Department. Called the C Department, it was headed up by the assistant commissioner of crime.

He had assigned the two murders to Detective Inspector Douglas Cavendish, who had in turn appointed Sergeant Hollings as a deputy. Though they would have many men from the Yard on the case, there were other less notorious crimes in London to take care of. The public believed that that was all Scotland Yard was doing. Looking for the murderer of two women who had been slashed down the back with a knife.

Cavendish and Hollings were sitting in the Detective Inspector's office. Outside, the dreary rain continued, falling steadily now. Cavendish was twirling his mustache. Another young woman. Old enough to be his daughter and yet young enough to be almost one third his age. Cavendish flicked a toothpick in and out of his mouth.

Hollings had the latest reports. "She was three months pregnant," he said, somewhat sadly.

Cavendish spit his toothpick out. He didn't like to hear news like that.

"The husband, Brian Harrington, refuses to talk to reporters or police or anyone."

"We'll get him as soon as he comes out of his grief . . . poor lad." Cavendish crinkled his forehead as he thought of Stephen Knight and how much trouble he had given them. He got up, walked around his desk, and sat on one corner. "Any similarities on the M.O., other than the slashing?"

"Jane Harrington was a short blue-eyed redhead, and Johanna was taller, wheat-colored hair cut medium length."

"The clothes?"

"No similarity there, either. Jane was wearing a navy suit. She was on her way to her job. Johanna, the lavender dress."

Cavendish remembered how the blood-soaked dress had clung to her. "Have someone interview everyone she worked with. I'll talk to the husband as soon as he's ready. Maybe he'll talk to me."

"Yes, sir."

"Not much to go on. Could be a random murder. Just killing for the sport of it. Anyone that comes along at the right moment." He fished out another toothpick from his pocket. "I'm not so excited about that lead and the witness who got away. That the woman is a murderer. Bit farfetched, I should say. I don't think, Hollings, that a woman could have pulled all this off."

"Both murders, you mean?"

"Quite."

On Wednesday evening Lockey fell asleep in a chair and then woke up suddenly for no reason at all. She'd have to start dinner soon. The place needed a bit of air. Going to the window, she opened it and then said to her husband, who was immersed as usual in the telly, "She's off again."

"What's that?"

"She's carrying a suitcase and just now stepping into a taxi. How do you like that? She just moved in."

"She pay her rent in full?" he demanded.

Lockey didn't answer. "She didn't tell me she was leaving so quickly. After that nice conversation we had."

"Probably thinks you're an old busybody, which you are."

She closed the window. She'd see how busy she could be.


There was a two-and-a-half-hour delay on the TWA flight to New York. Maybe she should be using a travel agent to verify this for her, to make all the arrangements. But that would be such a bother. And all one had to do, really, was call in. She still would have had this wait.

She was sitting on a chair, her legs crossed, contemplating getting a soft drink or something, when a strange woman approached her. Barbara looked up. The woman stared down, studying her.

"It couldn't be," she said. "But I *never* forget a face."

Barbara had never seen her before.

"Don't tell me . . . I know." The woman was clicking her fingers, like she was about to come up with the answer to a quiz show question. She opened her bag and slipped on a pair of glasses. "I got it. You're . . . No, you're not her."

Barbara couldn't help but smile.

"No, I got it. Don't tell me. You're that child star that was on that soap. I recognized the face because I used to watch it all the time. But you're all grown up now. Wearing heels and everything."

Barbara nodded, still smiling.

"You know who you are?" she said, clapping her hands together. "You're Cookie! That's who you are. And the soap was *Search for Tomorrow.*"

"*Tomorrow Is Another Day,*" Barbara corrected her softly.

"That's it!" shouted the woman. "What are you on now? I still watch all the soaps, and I've never seen you."

"I've stopped working."

The woman's face fell.

"I'm a writer," said Barbara.

The woman opened her bag and rummaged around until she came up with a used envelope. "May I have your autograph?"

Barbara was clearly moved as she scribbled *Cookie* across the front of the envelope in small letters, almost jagged. It had been so long since she had done this. "Are you from America?" she asked, putting a professional tone in her voice, as she was signing.

"I go back and forth with my husband. He's a businessman. I have all the soaps videotaped, and when I get back I watch them. Wait until my friends hear about this."

Impulsively she kissed Barbara and then went off to find her husband, the businessman.

After she left, Barbara sat there almost stony faced watching the people. Waiting. And then it happened. Again. She swayed and leaned over as if she were going to faint.

"I say, miss, are you all right?" a gentleman anxiously inquired.

She couldn't answer. Everything was a blur. Then she sat up and put on her glasses. She looked around. What the hell was she doing in an airport? She glanced quickly over at the signs. Heathrow Airport. Good Lord. Well, she'd been in worse jams than this. Best thing to do was go back to the flat in Hammersmith.

She edged her way through the crowds, her head held high, her lips pursed together in determination. She handed her ticket to the woman behind the ticket counter, who started to process it.

"Oh, no, no. You see, I'm checked in. I want to check out. Cancel the flight. I've decided not to fly."

"Do you wish to book another flight?" the woman asked, looking up.

"Oh, no, that won't be necessary. I always travel . . . spontaneously."

# CHAPTER 9

Julia Davidson had never missed a plane in her life. And she wasn't going to miss this one. It was just that the flight was delayed for so long, and she had had those two whiskey sours and had to go to the ladies' room so badly. She couldn't wait until she got on the plane.

Julia couldn't remember when she'd felt happier, and it wasn't the liquor. Such rich times she had had visiting her daughter. To be there when she had the baby, that pink, precious bundle, brand-new Rachael. Three generations of women. If only her late husband could have been there. She sighed. How many times had she said that? But she had her own personal theory. That somewhere in the sky was a big television screen, and he was watching. She smiled at her silliness. Well, somehow she thought he knew.

She found a ladies' room and thought she could make it in a second. It was empty for the moment, so there was no problem. She had no carry-on luggage—only her navy bag. She was still thinking about her granddaughter and how all the other babies in the hospital nursery looked like red little monkeys except for beautiful Rachael with her satin blond hair. She smiled as she opened the stall door and turned, not really looking at anything.

When she felt the hands clamp down on her shoulders and sit her down, she began to scream in surprise. But all she had a chance to do, really, was open her mouth. As for the strangled scream, no one heard it. She felt a searing pain slide down her back and just for a second managed to turn her head around, squinting, tears spilling from her eyes.

She looked up in horror and saw a figure, two feet planted on the toilet seat, humpbacked over her. She saw her navy bag being taken. "Why?" she managed to choke out.

She brushed her hand over her victim's hair but didn't say what she was thinking—that the woman had graying hair and was very motherly looking. Because her mother had never looked like that. But the woman she got in the Underground had looked a bit like her Mum—had on a blue suit just like Mum had worn. And the lady in the lavender dress had the same brisk, no-nonsense walk Mum had had.

The blood that was spilling onto the floor was inching out in all directions. Julia Davidson died watching it and wondering if her daughter would have any more children. She died within ninety seconds of when she found the empty ladies' room.

The figure bent her victim at her waist, vaulted over her, and carried the navy bag, tucking her own bag under her coat. In her pocket was the knife. Just a kitchen knife. She felt good, satisfied, as if she had eaten a full meal.

Outside she opened the navy bag and found the boarding pass and ticket right away. Julia Davidson. Who was that? TWA. That sounded like a good flight. She'd take it and fly to New York. Better than hanging around Heathrow Airport.

Carefully, passing the nearest trash can, she disposed of the long thin knife. Walking fast, she found another receptacle and discreetly emptied the contents of her bag into the larger navy bag. No good. She couldn't close the navy bag. Hiding what she was doing, deftly she consolidated even more. One by one she threw out a gold and turquoise compact, a tiny brush, a small photo album, and a Charles of the Ritz lipstick. Now the bag closed.

Clutching the boarding pass, she ran for the plane and didn't

hear the screams coming from down the hall. She saw a flock of
bobbies seem to skid around the corner. A woman standing in
line ahead of her turned around and said, "I'm glad to get out
of here. Do you hear all the commotion? Someone said a
woman was killed in the ladies' room . . . stabbed. Can you
imagine? And wasn't there a murder in the Underground recently?"

She shook her head. "I don't know."

"Well, I do. London is unsafe. Just like New York. Can you
imagine, a woman murdered in a ladies' room in Heathrow
Airport?"

She stumbled backward a little. Everything became blurry,
and her face scrunched up with the pain of her headache.

The woman in front of her asked, her hand on her shoulder,
"Miss, are you okay?"

Barbara nodded. "Yes, I'm fine," she assured the woman.
"Just a little headache, that's all."

"Well, given that news . . ." the woman said, turning away
because they were moving onto the plane.

Barbara showed her boarding pass and was happy to see she
had a window seat. She looked down at her boarding pass before she stuffed it back into her bag. Then she felt a moment of
terror. It said Julia Davidson. Who was that? And the bag, that
navy bag, that wasn't hers.

It had happened again. The memory lapses. All she remembered was having to wait two and a half hours. And that
woman who had come up to her. Who had recognized her as
Cookie all grown up. That happened to her sometimes.

Angrily she took out her boarding pass. Then she slowly,
carefully ripped it into little bits and tucked it under the elastic
pocket for airline magazines attached to the back of the seat in
front of her. It must be some mistake.

As her eyes shut drowsily and she tuned out the hard-to-hear
stewardess's speech, she forgot about the strange name on her
boarding pass. Just like she forgot what had happened during
those memory lapses.

# CHAPTER 10

"You're doing this to punish me, Carolyn," Tammy accused.

"C'mon, now. You're doing fine. Just a few more feet."

"Yeah, I could use a few more feet."

"Honestly, Tammy, you were the one who complained about how out of shape you're getting."

"Yeah, but I don't think killing myself is the answer. Really, you try making your husband and kid breakfast, not having any, and then running all over Central Park in shorts."

They came, their fists clenched, jogging slowly out of the park on the upper West Side, and found themselves at Seventy-first Street.

"Well, he's a growing boy and your husband's a construction worker. What do you expect them to do—starve? Let's run over to the precinct, huh?" suggested Carolyn.

Tammy looked down at her knees, which were beginning to tremble. "I'm starving. I think I'll take a cab."

"Oh, no, you don't. C'mon, we'll run slowly. Let's talk about the case."

"Why do I feel, Carolyn," she said, breathing heavily, "like we'll never solve this one?"

"Because we have no motive, no suspect, no you-name-it, no

nothing. Keep running. It's good exercise. Sends the oxygen right up to your brain. Makes you think."

"I'm thinking, I'm thinking," Tammy said, almost running in place. "I'm thinking we got other cases."

"I hear ya."

"I hate to say it, but we need another murder just like that last one. Then it becomes part of a random mass murder killing."

"Bite your tongue," Carolyn replied. "That's all we need."

"But it does seem to be part of a puzzle, doesn't it?"

"You mean instead of one murder?"

"Yeah," Tammy said. "I have a hunch." They jogged along silently for a minute or two, and then Tammy spotted a small luncheonette with a sign in the window. Two eggs and bacon were only ninety-nine cents. "Hey, let's stop in here. I could eat a horse. I bet women in shorts are allowed."

Carolyn gave her a playful tap on the shoulder. "Let's shower and change first at the precinct. And, no, I don't think cops in shorts would be welcome, and I don't like your hunch either."

It was a little after ten that morning when Barbara opened the door to her apartment. Everything seemed so different since she'd been away, although in reality nothing had changed. It felt, though, like the bare flat in Hammersmith was becoming more her home than this beautifully furnished lonely apartment on Park Avenue. Maybe she should have stayed in Hammersmith longer. Why didn't she? She didn't know.

She looked at her answering machine sitting on the desk table. Blinkety-blink—blinkety-blink flashed the silent alarm. She could almost guess. A call from Eva and one, of course, from Jonathan. She didn't know too many other people. The machine had been purchased for her father in case a job call came in, and she had continued to use it. One day it would be gone. When she gave up the apartment. After all, she could visit Eva if she wanted to return to New York.

She pressed the rewind button, then the start button. She was right. The first call was from Eva. But the second call wasn't from Jonathan.

"Hi, this is Dr. Walters. I'd like to change your appointment from Monday to Friday, if I may. Please call and confirm."

Friday. Today was Friday. He must have called Thursday.

Reluctantly she dialed his office number. She expected to leave a message on his machine, and then she'd have to wait for a callback, which was so annoying. She wanted to get some sleep. She was surprised to hear his voice. He wanted to see her at twelve. That would mean little sleep. She would be caught off guard. But maybe she could go back to Hammersmith earlier and begin to settle in. She found herself agreeing somewhat cheerfully.

"Well, you sound in good spirits," Dr. Walters said.

"It's spring," she replied almost defensively. Barbara hung up.

It was spring, her favorite time of the year. But when she looked outside, it seemed to be just another dusty, humid day. She heard the sound of drilling in the distance but didn't let herself concentrate on it. The call wasn't from Jonathan. What must he think? She should call him. And she had never had that physical checkup for her dizziness.

Just as she thought of it, the dizziness swept over her. She shook her head trying to shake it away, but little dots danced in front of her eyes.

When she came to, she thought it was morning. But she wasn't in bed; she was on the floor. She couldn't remember what day it was. Looking around the apartment, she knew she was in New York. The sun stripes on the wooden floor around the carpeting told her it was later than morning.

Thirsty. She was so thirsty. Stumbling, she got up and walked into the kitchen. The refrigerator was almost empty except for one blessed frosty can of Coke. Was this what she was having for breakfast? She couldn't remember. She slammed the can of Coke down hard on the counter. Shit! She remembered. It was Friday and Barbara had an appointment with that witch doctor. At twelve. Her watch said eleven. Hell of a way to spend her time, but she supposed she'd have to keep it. Cause the little frump too much trouble if she didn't. Not that she cared. Might be interesting. Ha! Wait till he got a look at her.

Tearing into her bedroom, she swept the hangers aside until she found what she wanted. Tight pants and a low-cut cherry red top. As she was putting in red plastic bangle earrings she remembered she had to call Jonathan, too. What a pain. Next time she wouldn't do so many favors for her. It was just that if she didn't, she was afraid she couldn't come out.

He had moved from her branch to the Mid-Manhattan Branch on Fifth Avenue. She dialed from her bedroom, singing along with the touchtone melody.

"Jonathan Segal. No, I don't want the book about the sea gull! He's a librarian. This is Mid-Manhattan, isn't it? Well, try the fifth floor." There was a click and another click and finally Jonathan's voice. Did he know how hard it was for her to reach him? "Hi, Jonathan," she chirped. "I've taken a flat in London, so I've been away and couldn't call."

"Barbara," he said. He could feel his shirt collar against his neck as if it had too much starch. He was blushing, too. It had taken nerve to call her for a date.

"Jonathan, I'm in a rush. I'd love to see you for dinner. Say tonight at seven, my place?"

Jonathan blushed more deeply. He was partly embarrassed and partly grateful she had taken the initiative. He was by nature passive. Women were always making decisions for him, though. After all, they were friends. "I won't keep you then," he managed to say in the same clipped tones she had used. "That sounds fine."

"Fine," she echoed, hanging up.

Quickly she retraced her steps to the living room and grabbed her trench coat, which had been flung across the chair. Picking up the navy bag, she muttered, "Now where did I get this old-lady-looking thing?" But it was too late to change.

She flagged a cab, ignoring the doorman, and rode it until Seventy-first and Central Park West. In the high-rise apartment building she dashed past the men at the desk as if she lived there. There wasn't time to announce herself. She punched the elevator button a couple of times, and she felt as though she were commanding it down.

Getting off at the seventeenth floor, she knew she was exactly on time. Buzzing the door to the corner apartment, she found it already open. She had half a mind to turn around and go back, but this might be amusing. After all, she was the other half of the mind. And body. Still, headshrinkers. Just another way the frump kept herself from having fun.

There were tiny blue flowers floating around in water, and she found herself staring at them. Talk about creepy. They were artificial silk flowers. Why on earth did he keep fake flowers in a vase filled with water?

At that moment, she wanted to tear out of there and run. Get a cab going to Park Avenue and get as far away from him as she could. But it was too late. She looked from the wet flowers into his deep blue eyes.

"Hi!" he said, extending his hand.

Trying not to bend in any way, she took it and shook hands with him. Then as he stepped aside she let him follow her into the inner office with its clumps of plants all around. She wanted to ask him if he thought artificial flowers would grow in water, but she sat down almost sullenly and said nothing.

As he was trained to do, he noted her appearance. The extremely low-cut red top and the very clingy pants. The earrings looked sexy, too. Gone was the woman who fidgeted with the top button of her blouse, looking as if she wanted to unbutton it. Today she was a completely different person. Amazing. He was startled to see this aspect of her personality, but he couldn't let on. He smiled at her approvingly.

She traced the line of her lipstick with her tongue.

"So, what's happening in your life?"

"I didn't have time to get that checkup," she confessed like a naughty schoolgirl.

He shrugged. "You'll get it soon, I'm sure. What's happening in your life?"

She threw back her head and laughed.

"What's so funny?" he asked, laughing with her. He was good at reflecting the moods of his patients. It was part of his technique. He was like a talking mirror.

"Oh, a private joke," she said teasingly, tossing her hoop earrings with a finger.

"Between . . . ?"

"Myself and . . . you know?"

"Actually, I don't," he said, his voice suddenly a little more stern. "Do you hear voices?"

She laughed again. "Well, I should hope so. I hear yours."

The psychiatrist was trying to locate in his mind's eye the complete picture of the mousy, self-deprecating woman who had sat in the same chair last week. It was totally out of sync. He had had to make her feel at ease, and she had been stiff, very stiff. It was almost as if a twin had taken this session. Much as he might have helped her, surely his curative powers weren't that dazzling. "Let's go back to last week."

She was looking at him as if he were a tempting bargain in a boutique. It was very disconcerting. He loosened his tie.

"You left me someone else's business card. Did you know that? I have you on my books as Barbara Hargrove and—" Damn. He had thrown it away.

She interrupted him, "A lot of people make that mistake."

"What mistake?" He had an uneasy feeling that there was something wrong here, but he couldn't quite put his finger on what it was.

"Did you know your artificial flowers are floating around in water?"

He looked at her hard. "The cleaning lady must have done that. I'll fix it. About your mistake . . . ?"

"I gave you one of my other cards."

"You have more than one?"

She looked at him and her eyes seemed to be searching his face. She brought her hand to her forehead and then took it away. Looking more like the Barbara of last week, she slumped down into her chair. "What business card did you get?"

He thought for a moment. "Enid Thornton. Does that ring a bell?"

She stared at him, her face ashen.

"Enid Thornton," he repeated, this time more demanding. "Why did you give me a business card with the name of Enid Thornton on it?"

"Why not?" she answered.

His eyes were fixed on the skinny red hoops bouncing around her ears. "You're not Barbara Hargrove, are you?" he asked cautiously.

"Now you're getting the picture, kiddo."

"What *is* your name?" he inquired stiffly.

"I'm Enid Thornton."

"Not Enid Hargrove?" He heard the sound of his own voice and it sounded shaky.

"Nope."

"I see," he said slowly. But he had never seen anything like this in his career.

She smiled at him mischievously. "Have a radio? I like jazz." She began to click her fingers. "Say, maybe you and me could go out dancing sometime. You like to dance?"

He was nodding, beginning to understand.

"You do!"

Then he shook his head suddenly, as if he had been thinking about something bad, a nightmare perhaps. "No," he said firmly, trying to grasp control of the situation again. "No, I don't dance," he replied quickly. "You're not Barbara," he said again.

"Oh, *her.*" She leaned forward. "She's ruining my life. She's such an old stick-in-the-mud. I can never come out. Just before I came I had to talk to that boyfriend of hers, that creep, Jonathan." She elongated the *o* vowel so that it seemed to slip endlessly downhill. *"I* wouldn't be so interested that he called and asked for a date. In fact, he would have taken forever, so I asked him." She began to laugh.

"I thought they were going together. She said she had a relationship."

"No way. She doesn't do much. Never has much fun. Even with all that money she has. Now me, I like to buy pretty clothes and go dancing and have a couple of drinks. We're entirely different."

Dr. Walters nodded. Out of the corner of his eye, he was scanning his bookshelf for a certain book. He had read it once. He looked at his patient quickly. "Say," he said, "do you mind if I make a phone call? There's someone I'd like you to meet."

She shrugged and looked around the room. "Sure, I hope he's cute."

He could hear the phone ring in the next office. "Would you mind coming in here for a minute?"

"Alvin, I'm with a patient."

"I know, I know." He whispered, "For a minute. I have an emergency here."

He turned to Barbara. "I just want you to meet my colleague. It will only take a moment."

In one second, he heard the short rap on the door. Dr. Beth Belmont, the psychiatrist who rented the other small office in the suite, was standing in the doorway. She wore slacks and a silk blouse with a patterned scarf. She looked very peeved.

Alvin Walters held the door open, and she walked across the room, taking a seat on the beige couch.

Dr. Walters introduced the two and continued the session. "Now, Enid, I'd like to see you once a week but lengthen the session. Is that okay?"

"Am I gonna have a choice?" she asked sarcastically. She always looked as if she were chewing gum, but she wasn't.

"Of course," he said. "Will you tell Barbara that the session is at twelve on Monday?" He double-checked his book, swiveling around to get at it.

"I guess so," she replied, hanging her head.

"Is there something wrong, Enid?"

"I feel like I'm being punished."

Dr. Walters overlooked the comment as if it weren't important. "You'll tell Barbara, okay?"

"Oh, yeah. Barbara does anything she's told."

"Can I talk to Barbara about it?" he asked slyly.

"Why don't you try next time," she answered, her eyes meeting his in a half-challenging, half-flirtatious way, something Barbara would never dream of doing.

"Amazing," he murmured accidentally.

Beth was shooting him angry glances. Five minutes earlier than he should have he told Enid the session was up. He didn't think she'd know the difference anyway.

After she left, Beth started for the door. "Really, Alvin, I fail to see the emergency. I thought you had someone ready to go into the hospital, and now I have to make up the time with my patient."

"You didn't see it?"

"See what?"

He sat back down in his big black recliner chair. "That, Beth, was the case of a lifetime. My patient is quiet, sedate Barbara Hargrove. I saw her last time, and yet the woman sitting in that chair was called Enid Thornton and had the exact opposite personality."

"Alvin, I have a patient waiting. So your patient is manic-depressive. I have no idea what you're getting excited about."

"You don't?" he asked incredulously. "Oh, c'mon. Didn't you ever hear of *The Three Faces of Eve?* Haven't you ever read *Sybil?*"

"You mean multiple personalities?"

He nodded. "So far, there are only two."

# CHAPTER 11

It was the doorman's fault, actually. He had meant to warn her, but there was a group of people coming in the door all at once and they had to be announced. When Barbara walked down the long rubber streamer, she didn't see them at first. Then there was a squeal, and she saw, sitting on an apple green tufted love seat, both Jonathan and Eva. They seemed to be talking like two long-lost friends.

Barbara looked at her watch. It was late. She had lost time again and forgotten about her date with Jonathan. But she didn't remember making a date with Eva. Had she?

She stood there, her arms filled with packages, feeling embarrassed and awkward. There were tears in her eyes. She might have stood Jonathan up, without realizing it. Looking down at the two large white bags with gold lettering on them, she wondered what she had bought. Where she had been. She couldn't quite remember. These losses of time were starting to happen more and more frequently.

"Sorry, I'm late," Barbara began weakly.

"Oh, Barbara," Eva said enthusiastically, "it looks like you went and bought yourself some pretty new clothes."

Barbara instinctively brought the bags closer to her. She

didn't know what was in the bags. Recently she'd found some new things in her closet that she didn't remember buying. Now she'd done it again. "I'll take these upstairs," she replied quietly.

"Well, I'll be going," said Eva. "I didn't know if you were still in London, and we wanted to make plans to get together, so I thought I'd stop in. I didn't hear from you. It turned out Jonathan was waiting for you, too."

Barbara was touched to find that her friend had done that. "Say, why don't you join us for dinner?" Jonathan said impulsively. He realized part of the reason was that he would be less nervous on their date.

"Oh, no, I couldn't do that," Eva protested. She was almost as tall as Jonathan, what her relatives referred to as a "big girl." She shook her head, her orange-colored frizzy curls bobbing.

"No, *do,*" Barbara insisted. Leave it to her to botch up a first date, anyway. It was almost eight o'clock. If Eva hadn't been there to entertain him, Jonathan might have thought he had been stood up, and left. And the worst part of it was that she couldn't tell either of them. She really was reliable and responsible. It's just that she kept losing large chunks of time, and there was no way of explaining it.

Barbara took her bags upstairs, thinking that at least she knew she had been to some sort of boutique. Opening the door as quickly as she could, she ran through the apartment and crammed the bags into the back of her large closet as if she were ashamed to have anyone see them. She had no interest whatsoever in what they contained.

When she returned downstairs, Jonathan and Eva were engaged in a discussion of food and restaurants. She apologized again. "I'm sorry I'm so late. But I've been taking long walks lately, and then I stopped to do some shopping."

They both nodded sympathetically. They had both gone to her father's funeral not even a month ago.

"Walks are good," Eva said.

"Especially long ones," Jonathan agreed.

They were all silent for a while.

"Barbara, where do you want to go for dinner?" Jonathan

asked, realizing again that Eva was a good coverup for his shyness.

"Let's go down to Little Italy and find a restaurant. My father used to take me to a marvelous place on Mulberry Street."

"Sounds good to me," Jonathan said, glad the decision didn't have to be his.

"Perfect!" pronounced Eva.

The threesome passed the doorman, who nodded, and Eva raised her arm for a cab that was cruising by. Within a half hour they were walking through Little Italy, passing little family-owned restaurants just starting to put tables outside. They stopped at Paolucci's. Around the corner was Chinatown and its fanciful shops and colorful restaurants.

After they had ordered dinner, Eva asked, "So how is Hammersmith?" She was really dying to ask about Dr. Walters, but she couldn't in front of Jonathan.

"Oh, it's much like I remember it. Some of the shops have changed, but that's about it. And I have a maisonette, an upstairs and downstairs apartment. We had one of those."

"How long did you live in Hammersmith with your mother?" Jonathan asked.

"We came after I was fired—uh—stopped working on the soap. And I stayed until she died suddenly when I was fifteen. So that's three years in all."

"What did your mother die of?" Jonathan asked.

"A cerebral hemorrhage. She was never sick a day. Then she was just—just gone."

"I'm sorry," he said, and tried to twist the subject around to something more upbeat. "How's the book coming?"

"Oh, fine, fine," she said almost abstractly.

"I'm so impressed that you're writing a book. But why did you pick Hammersmith as a place to write?"

"I can think better. Besides, I had hoped to move back there. I—"

"That's going to be some book," Eva interrupted, her eyes shining. "For eight years Barbara was Cookie on that soap. I watched it every day. And I was so envious of her. We met at school."

"An actress *and* a writer," Jonathan replied. "I'm impressed."

Barbara made a circle on the tablecloth with her fingers, separating the bread crumbs. They didn't talk about what was in between. Coming back to New York, living with her father, who was well meaning but like a stranger. Going to New York University for a while and not making any friends. Sometimes not remembering what class she was supposed to be in or why she cut them. The endless typing jobs and the humiliation. When someone recognized her on the job, it was even worse. She always quit when that happened.

The decision to catch a cab was unanimous. They would drop Jonathan off first, who lived in Brooklyn, then go uptown to the West Eighties where Eva lived, then spin around to the East Side.

"It's worth the extra money," Eva said. "I always take cabs after dark. Good neighborhood, the West Side, but not always safe."

"Park Avenue isn't even safe," Jonathan remarked. "I was reading in the paper the other day about a woman who got stabbed. It was right near you, Barbara."

But Barbara wasn't listening. She was trying to figure out a way to see Jonathan again. What if he didn't ask her out again?

As they turned the corner of his street in Brooklyn, Jonathan said, "I hope this isn't too out of the way. Listen, I had a great time. We'll have to get together again. I'll call you, Barbara, okay?"

She nodded, allowing a thin smile to show.

Neither woman spoke as the cab went on. Finally Barbara ventured to ask, "Do you really think he will?"

Eva put her hand on Barbara's shoulder. "You should have more confidence in yourself. Look, you're a rich lady. You go to London to write. You can do anything you want. What does Dr. Walters say about that?"

Barbara looked away, out the window.

"You should talk to him about your lack of confidence."

Barbara was quiet and Eva wouldn't dare intrude on her therapy. It was private. But most people talked about it. Too much. Barbara never said anything. The cab made the second stop and Eva got out, kissing Barbara on the cheek and vowing to find someone like Jonathan for herself.

The cab crossed town at Eighty-sixth Street while Barbara was trying to remember if she had seen Dr. Walters that morning. There was that long walk and the shopping bags with the gold lettering. Before that, had she gone to his office? She vaguely remembered something about her appointments being changed. She hoped she had gone because she wanted to tell him about the memory lapses, the large chunks of time she lost. She was becoming aware of it more and more.

Somewhere in her purse was a card. She rummaged deep down inside the navy bag. The bag she didn't like, yet she was carrying. Her fingertips touched the card. It said there was a double session on Mondays at noon. Two times fifty minutes. Something told her she had to go because she couldn't remember his having done that.

She walked rapidly through the lobby, not even smiling at the doorman, and punched the elevator button. The elevator man said, "Good evening, miss," but she ignored him.

When she opened the door to her apartment, she felt engulfed by the large space. And the loneliness. She would have to get rid of this apartment and move to Hammersmith. That made her angry, very angry. How could she stay in Hammersmith if her week was broken up with stupid doctor's appointments. Why is it she could never do anything with her life without someone's ruining it?

She paced around the living room, scuffing her high-heeled sandals, feeling the fury, not knowing what to do. Tripping slightly over her sandal, she collapsed onto the sofa, blacking out for a second or two. The first voice she heard sounded like the roar of the ocean when you picked up a large seashell and held it against your ear. She clapped her hands over her ears, swaying a little. Fighting hard to come to, she blinked her eyes and put the room into focus. She felt the anger, but she didn't know why.

She looked at what she was wearing. A cherry red top and tan slacks? What an absurd outfit. And the sandals would never do. She must wear soft soles. Sneakers were what she needed.

She was calm. It was dark now. It would be darker if she

wore black. Somewhere in her closet was a black dress. She knew because she had bought it. For just such an occasion. A coming-out party.

She dressed quickly, purposefully. It was a thin black jersey dress with a sleeveless coat. Meant to be worn only once.

Lifting her knee and bending over, she tied the shoelaces on her sneakers. The dress would look good with black heels, but she wasn't going to a party.

The shifts had changed for the elevator operators, and this one just nodded, making no note that she was going out again. The doorman downstairs was busy hailing a couple a cab, and she walked right past him. At the far corner of Ninety-fourth she caught a cab but didn't know exactly where she wanted to go.

The cab was heading downtown, so she said, "Fifty-fourth and Lexington." She knew the neighborhood well. Disgusting, what had happened to the area over the years. High-class Hookerville. Prostitutes. That was one of Mum's pet peeves. Women who sold their bodies were the devil's daughters.

The cabdriver tried to make small talk, but she ignored him. As he babbled to himself, she checked her bag. Yes, it was there. She had changed to a black clutch bag. So much more efficient.

When she got out of the cab, her dress slid provocatively over her knee. A man was staring at her, but she saw him look away when she put her foot down and stepped out in her sneakers. It was a hungry neighborhood, she noted. Everyone seemed to be shopping.

She walked a few blocks downtown and then east, where the crowds thinned out. Here was where you could see the real action. She sneered. They were out like an army in the night. Standing in doorways waiting for a man to chance by and be suckered into it. They were all alike, the painted faces, the tall pencil-thin heels they wobbled in, the pushed-up breasts, the chubby fur jackets even on a warm night. If Forty-second Street was like a red-light district, this was a pink-light district. That was for sure.

Good girl, Priscilla, she whispered to herself. Her fingers reached inside the bag, and she knew it was time. The only way to quell the anger inside her, bubbling out uncontrollably, was to shed some blood. She could almost taste it. Then she'd calm down.

It was the pale blond hair that caught her eye first. She hated that shade of hair. The little girl who had ended up on the soap after they had said there would be no more little girls had that shade of hair.

And Mum.

She had dyed her hair that shade once. Flaxen blond. She hated that color. Hated it.

The whore with the pale blond hair was wearing a pale blue shiny dress and trashy-looking white heels that had skinny little straps that wound up her ankle and tied with little string bows. No bag.

No fun.

All Dressed in White had had a bag, and so had she. She switched them because she wanted to keep something of her to have for herself. But not this time. There was nothing she wanted to take from this slut.

Couched in the shadows, she overheard the conversation.

"Twenty dollars. I have my own room," the woman was saying in a husky voice.

"Sorry, lady, not interested. I'm a married man."

"Okay, fifteen dollars." Her voice got a little squeaky.

He walked away.

There were no people around. In a few seconds the man made a turn, and the street was empty. One thing she learned about the work was not to wait. There was a split-second timing to it when the moment was ripe. Unseen by the woman, she sprang out of the shadows. In her hand was a knife that she held low. Lifting her hand easily, she plunged the knife in right below that obnoxious yellow hair and slid it down the woman's back until it stopped just above the shiny pale blue sash on the dress. She wiped the blood off the knife on the still-dry shoulder of the woman's dress before the woman sank into a bloody puddle. Then she stuffed the knife inside her bag and began to run, her heart pounding, her legs alive with energy.

On Fifty-second and First Avenue she hailed a cab. She was out of breath.

"Sounds like you've been running," remarked the talkative cabbie.

"Yeah, I've been running," she said, slightly annoyed.

What did he know of the ecstasy she felt at the moment. The unbearable joy. The world was without someone who shouldn't have been in it, and she had the power to remove her. That hair. She smiled to herself, satisfied.

She settled back into the seat of the cab and then stiffened. Off in the distance she heard a siren. It seemed to be coming closer, getting louder. For a second the siren was deafening, and then they passed it and continued uptown.

"City's really something, isn't it?" the cabbie said amiably.

"Really something," she repeated, thinking someone had found the body and made a phone call. Or there would be another siren soon.

The piercing headache started in the cab. She paid her fare quickly, careful not to touch the knife, and got out. In her apartment she could feel time slipping away. Rapidly she peeled off her black clothes. She took the knife out of her bag and put it under running water in the sink. Changing into a flowered duster, she rolled up her black dress and sneaked out to the incinerator, dropping it into the chute. Then she almost stumbled into her apartment as the dizziness started. Bracing herself against the wall, she held on, her eyes shut.

A minute or two later Barbara stood motionless in the large living room. She forgot what she had been doing. She had come into the living room and forgot, literally, what she wanted to do next. When she came in, she had wanted to watch the eleven o'clock news. That's what she was doing in the living room. She turned on the television set. The *Tonight Show* was on. She had lost time again, and she couldn't remember.

The group of women were silent staring down at her. A few minutes ago a siren had wailed by, and they had all made themselves scarce, thinking it was a mass raid. But the noise had disappeared. That's when someone had spotted the body now almost buried in a pool of blood.

"My God," someone whispered, "that could have been me."

One of the hookers bravely put her hands in the slimy pockets, then gagged, and wiped them off on a piece of Kleenex. "No money in her pockets. No bag. Maybe she was robbed."

"Nah," came a voice. "I've seen her around. Green. She didn't make any money. A sicko man did this, that's what. And I don't think we should be standing around, asking for more trouble."

One of the women started to cry. "It's so sad. Look at her. She was so young—"

A shrill voice cut her off. "I suggest we split, vamoose. No more tricks here tonight. We'll all get locked up when they find this."

In five minutes the area had been cleaned of the high-heeled women who wore skirts above their knees. Some headed toward Eighth Avenue. Others headed toward the nearest bar to have a drink and thank their lucky stars it wasn't them swimming in blood, slashed by some sick John.

The sound of the phone woke her up. The *Tonight Show* was still on. She had dozed off. And she woke up with a headache that was like a hangover. She had dreamed about someone with pale yellow hair, but she didn't know who it was. Barbara stood up and saw that there were ridges from the fabric of the couch embedded in her arm. She had curled up and fallen asleep in front of the television. It wasn't twelve yet.

"Hello?" she asked, sure it was a wrong number.

"It's Jonathan, Barbara. It's late, I know. I hope I didn't wake you up."

"No, I was up," she lied.

"It's just that I remember your saying how you liked to take long walks. But I just heard on the radio that there was another stabbing. This one was in the East Fifties, another supposedly safe neighborhood. I wouldn't go for any real long walks. There seems to be a murderer loose."

"How frightening," she said. "Thanks for warning me." Her head felt like it had a tiny drum inside. Warm milk, that's what she needed. She would heat up some milk and go to bed. Barbara waited for Jonathan to ask her out again.

"I couldn't sleep for another reason," he continued miserably. "I guess if we had gone out alone I could have said something. But knowing me, I wouldn't have said anything at all."

Barbara was fully awake now and interested.

"Don't you think it odd that we never got together in all the months we've known each other except for the library?"

"You came to my father's funeral."

"But I never asked you out. All the time, I wanted to." She could detect a slight stutter in his voice now. "See, I'm taking an assertiveness-training course and that's how I can do it. This phone call is a big thing for me."

Barbara smiled. He should know how shy she was. But she would never have the guts to admit it. "It's very nice of you to say all this, Jonathan." He made it sound like she had the upper hand, and she hadn't thought she had. "Where do you take your course?"

"Oh, in the basement of a school in Brooklyn. I'm in a class with all women," he said.

She pressed the cool receiver of the phone against her forehead for just a second.

"It's good to know a real writer," he went on. "Maybe your book will come to our library."

"Maybe," she said wistfully.

"Well, I don't want to keep you. It's late."

"I'm glad you called, Jonathan, *really* I am," she replied, trying to put more enthusiasm into her voice because she sincerely meant it, but she had never had a high energy level. Now she felt as if she couldn't bear it if she spoke above a whisper.

When she hung up, she hunted in a desk drawer for a notebook. A journal. That's what she needed. Maybe if she wrote everything down, she wouldn't lose time. That's what was giving her headaches. She would tell that to Dr. Walters. She would have to, eventually.

"Dear Diary," she wrote. "Went out to dinner with Eva and Jonathan. Had a wonderful time. Lost about an hour and a half this afternoon, though. And I don't really remember what I did or said before that."

Angrily she ripped up the notebook page and crumbled it into her fist. Then she walked into the kitchen, threw the paper into the trash can, and took out a small saucepan for the milk. That's when she saw it in the sink.

She stood there alone, shivering, methodically stirring the milk in the pan even though the night was almost balmy. The dishes had been washed and dried, and the kitchen was spotless. Except for one thing.

There was a big, fat, gleaming knife in the middle of the white sink.

Why? How?

A tear spilled down her cheek, and she didn't bother to catch it with her fingertip. She just kept stirring the milk as if to calm herself.

What did she do when she blacked out? Put knives in sinks? Was anything else out of place? The milk was developing a thick top. She turned off the flame and got a glass from the cupboard. And then, in a flash, she knew about the knife and how it got there.

She was a sleepwalker. That had to be it. She had fallen asleep on the couch, crept in, and taken the knife out of its block.

She shook her head. Such a loss of control. And yet that's all she did. Thank God she never hurt herself or anyone else with it.

# CHAPTER 12

They had the early tour on Saturday. Eight to four. Tammy and Carolyn were sitting at their desks when the chief of detectives walked in, talking to two lieutenants and a captain of the precinct.

"Something's up," Carolyn said.

"Something's always up," Tammy answered, busy with paperwork. "How was your date last night?"

"Kept me up half the night."

Tammy smiled. "Well, that's good, isn't it?"

"No," Carolyn replied, making a face. "He was a drip, a bore. All he talked about all night were his cases and what a great detective he was. At one point I tapped him on the shoulder and said, 'Hey, I'm a detective, too, remember?'"

"And . . . ?"

"He didn't. Talk about sexist. You can't go out with anyone but a cop because you have nothing in common with anyone else, and when you go out with a cop they treat you like you're *not* one."

Tammy laughed. "Maybe you're being too tough on him. At least he was a first-grade detective."

"Yeah, that was the only thing first grade about him."

They were both looking at the front of the room being set up for a meeting. Someone was erasing the blackboard. A cluster of very important brass, including the chief, were in a corner talking.

"I don't think this is routine," Carolyn whispered slowly, enunciating every syllable.

"Okay, listen up, here. It's 8:05. We got a lot to talk about."

Tammy looked around. No, it wasn't routine. The room was suddenly standing room only. Men and women from other floors were lining up against the walls, their arms folded across their chests, leaning into one hip.

Flanagan was the chief of detectives. He wore a gray flannel hat pulled over one eye. His tie was loosened, his hands rested on an empty desk, and his ankles were crossed.

He had a thick South Bronx accent. That's where he was raised, and as he liked to say, he never forgot his roots. That's why he had become a cop.

"Awright, listen up, now," the captain repeated, as if anyone were thinking of doing otherwise.

Flanagan began, his voice monotone, each word coming like a bullet sailing into the room. "Late last night a hooker was found stabbed on Lexington Avenue and Fifty-third Street."

Everyone stared at him. That was it? Hookers were expected to be found murdered in the middle of the night. They waited for the kicker.

"As you know, according to the boundaries, the case would go to the Seventeenth Precinct."

They waited quietly.

"But this case is special." His voice became softer. There was almost a lilt to it now. All around the room you could hear the sound of cigarette lighters.

"This hooker was a young woman. Coroner says only seventeen. Just a kid."

There was a current of tension now as the anger connected throughout the room. A little girl, hooking, getting killed. They were there to protect little girls from those elements of society that sucked them in. It was close to kiddie porn, another pet peeve that made male cops, especially, trigger-happy.

"This kid," Flanagan went on, lifting the brim of his hat

above his eyebrow, "was not just stabbed. Her back was slit, slashed."

Tammy and Carolyn exchanged quick looks. They were sitting close enough so that their fingertips touched briefly, nervously.

"We are saying that this case belongs at the Nineteenth Precinct."

There wasn't a sound in the room.

"We are saying we want to set up a task force here because the M.O. is identical to a stabbing on the twenty-second of May on upper Park Avenue. A woman was also found, her back slit from neck to base of spine, in the same way."

"Oh, God," came a soft, involuntary response from somewhere back in the room.

"The weapon was not found. No traces of a skirmish were visible. In both cases the women were simply slashed, presumably taken by surprise."

Tammy took Carolyn's hand and squeezed it tightly.

"We think we have a serio-murderer here. It might be random; it might not be. A Son of Sam, if you will, but with a knife. But we're not sure, you understand. So we'll start out with a small force and if need be, we'll add. Now I understand the catching detective is Hank Patuto. What have you got so far on the stabbing on Park Avenue?"

Hank Patuto opened his mouth, and his cigarette, which was stuck on the corner of his lip, dropped off onto his desk. He picked it up quickly and stubbed it out in the ashtray. "Well, I've been working on a lot of cases lately."

Everyone was staring at him. His mouth felt like the Russian Army had marched through with socks on. It was one of his worst hangovers. He was just lucky he could sit there.

He cleared his throat. "Well, the thing is, most women carry bags, you know, and the fact that she was found without one makes me wonder, you know."

There were a few nods. Carolyn began biting her fingernails.

"That's what I'm working on. What happened to that bag," he said, gaining confidence.

Tammy couldn't stand it any longer. Her hand shot up. "Detective Flanagan, sir, if you don't mind?" Everyone turned to look at her. "We were helping Detective Patuto from his case overload, my partner Detective Kealing, and I." She pointed at Carolyn, then back at herself quickly. "We found that bag."

Hank Patuto slumped in his chair. Everyone else leaned in.

"The bag was found at the Transit Authority. It's a white bag like the victim's dress, and it had blood stains on it. Type O blood. Black hairs were swept up by forensics. Jay Street called us when it was found. After we had called all the I.D.'s in the other pages. It's our feeling—call it a hunch—that the killer didn't take the bag and kill her to get the money. No . . ." Tammy continued, speaking rapidly. "And now this case proves it. We think she was just killed"—she stopped, looking around the room—"and the bag was taken off the dead body by a mugger. The mugger ran with it, took out the cash, and left the bag on the trains. That's when the Transit Authority picked it up. The I.D. says the woman's name is Enid Thornton."

"And . . . ?" the chief asked impatiently.

"And we're trying to trace her. So far no luck." The last was said in a low voice.

"You don't *know* that that bag belonged to that woman or that her name was in fact Enid Thorsten," snapped Detective Hank Patuto.

"Thornton," fired back Carolyn. "And she has to exist. Everyone exists somewhere, sooner or later." Spoilsport is what she wanted to say. She was tired of sexist detectives. They had done a damn good job. It was his fault if he looked like an asshole, which he was.

"Interesting," said Flanagan. It was clear that he was impressed.

"Sir," Tammy went on, "we're going out of state now to find her. Also we're tracing if it's a married name or a career name. We'll find out who this woman was and hopefully get a lead on who killed her."

"Well, this young kid," Flanagan said, back to his safe monotone, "had no bag at all. There was no money found in her pockets. Maybe she turned it over to her pimp, or maybe she didn't turn any tricks, or maybe the killer frisked her. But there was no I.D."

It was getting close to eight thirty. Some officers in the back were yawning, trying to cover their mouths. Tammy and Carolyn were trying to look nonchalant. Tammy wanted to be on the task force so much she could taste it. She had a hunch about this case—always had. Carolyn was wondering if, after all, they would be passed over for the men. She had seen it happen enough. Between the two of them they couldn't even count the times they had been disappointed that way.

"You know what this is beginning to remind me of?" Hank Patuto asked. Tammy shot him a dirty look. He was angling for the case, too, and God knows he didn't deserve it even if it was his. "This reminds me of Jack the Ripper. Maybe the woman in white was a hooker? A high-class prossie. Jack the Ripper killed whores, didn't he?" He dwelled on the word—*whores*—pronouncing it *whooers*.

"The task force will be on the third floor," said Flanagan. "I'll be bringing in detectives from other precincts and boroughs eventually, if we have to. Right now I'd like to start with five men from the Nineteenth."

Carolyn winced. Tammy took out an emory board and started filing her nails.

Flanagan looked around the room. The people standing were shifting their weight. He took out the list from his pocket. Tammy's heart sank, and she looked sideways at Carolyn. The list had been made out before. The five detectives and officers had already been picked. Flanagan read the names. "Jackson, Mendez, Picard, Louigi, and . . ." He stopped and his eyebrows met. "No. Scratch Louigi. Make it Zuckerman and Kealing instead."

The emory board flew into the air, and a little squeal came from Tammy. Carolyn sat there grinning.

Hank Patuto was frowning. Had his name been on the list and those two broads one-upped him?

New Scotland Yard. He and his wife had covered all the sights like typical tourists when they had first moved to London. The Crown Jewels, the British Museum, Kensington Gardens, even Stratford-upon-Avon. No, they hadn't missed anything. Except they had never thought to pay a visit to Scotland Yard. Now they had no choice.

Their tour guide was a man with an irritating, nasal voice. In his two years heading up the British branch of a large American advertising agency, Kenneth Kline had learned to distinguish what part of Great Britain and what class the person was from by his or her accent. This man was flawlessly cockney.

"It's been called New Scotland Yard since 1890. They expanded to this building right on the Thames River."

Kenneth nodded and "ummed" politely. His wife paid the man no attention whatsoever.

"It was expanded further in 1939. The building we moved into in 1967 is still known as New Scotland Yard, although its proper title is the Metropolitan Police Office."

What if the man had remained silent while he was escorting them? Kenneth wondered. Would it have made much difference? Maybe the escort was afraid either he or his silent wife would become emotional. Maybe that was it.

"So, you see, we've come a long way since No. 4 Whitehall Place way back in 1829."

His spiel was timed exactly to the stopping place. In front of Detective Inspector Cavendish's office. Kenneth Kline found himself happy to see the man go. He wondered how the man would feel if there had been a murder in his family and he stood there and recited the "Gettysburg Address" for him.

Inspector Cavendish rose quickly and extended his hand to Kenneth and was about to shake hands with his pale-looking wife, but something in her eyes stopped him. "You must be Mr. Davidson," Cavendish said, motioning for them to have a seat. "How good of you to come."

"Oh, no," Kenneth replied. "I'm Kenneth Kline. She was my mother-in-law, my wife's mother. This is Annie, my wife. And you don't have to thank us for coming. We want to do everything we can to help."

His wife said nothing. The expression on her face was free of emotion. It was as if she had to remember to blink.

"My wife just had a baby," Kenneth Kline said by way of explanation for the mute woman sitting ramrod straight next to him. "Julia—I mean, my mother-in-law—came to London to help out." His voice shook a little. "She had made reservations for two days earlier, but we begged her to stay on. She had this idea she was intruding or something." He shook his head, not believing it. "She didn't have to be on that flight. We wanted her to stay on. Damn plane was delayed for almost two and a half hours. Even then when she called us, we asked her to come back and fly another time."

Cavendish nodded sympathetically.

Kenneth Kline's voice became high-pitched. "You know, Inspector, all these mother-in-law jokes you hear. They didn't apply to Julia. She was like a mother to me."

His voice cracked, and Cavendish thought for sure the man was going to break down. In contrast, his wife sat calmly, almost stoically.

Kenneth Kline took a large handkerchief from his pocket and blew his nose. "How can we help you find the murderer? Maybe if we could help correct this hideous injustice—not that it would bring Julia back, but it would help."

"Did your mother-in-law—or your mother, Mrs. Kline—have any enemies?"

Kenneth Kline answered that with almost a sputter. "Really, how could *anyone* dislike her! I don't think she had an enemy in the world."

"And you, Mrs. Kline, what do you think?"

"She might have had an enemy, but it would have been someone very unbalanced. Someone we didn't know about. But even that's a little farfetched, don't you think?" Only her mouth moved, and her voice was barely audible.

"You mean you think she was just murdered by a stranger?"

Annie Kline's voice showed the first signs of emotion. Sarcasm. "In the States the police solve the crimes, not the victims."

Victim, thought Cavendish. Very interesting expression. True in a way, but he had never heard it voiced that way before. "Oh, I do understand," he said. "I just wanted your opinion. There have been two other murders that fitted the same identical M.O. We are wondering if these murders are random or reason. So we have to determine if he knew your mother—"

"Wait a second," Kenneth interrupted him. "My mother-in-law was murdered in a ladies' room, and you think it was a *man?*"

Cavendish sighed. "Well, if we're thinking in terms of a multiple killing, we don't think a woman could have done it for a lot of reasons. Physical strength, of course, heads the list. To explain the ladies' room," Cavendish continued, "it could have been a man dressed as a woman. Or a man. They were alone. A bag and what we believe to be some of the contents of that bag were dumped into a trash can in the airport. The knife was found in another place," he said the last low, as an aside. "We'd like you to identify some of the things for us."

Cavendish took a tray from his drawer that held a number of objects. On it were a lipstick, a compact, a tiny brush, and a plastic photo album. Cavendish pointed to the small black snaptogether case. "That's where we were lucky," he said. "Inserted in the case we found an I.D. that she had filled out. Then we called New York, and a housekeeper or someone gave us your number."

Annie stared at the man, inwardly raging, outwardly showing nothing. What did they expect her to say: Good work? She didn't like the man. Something about his way bothered her. She said only, "I recognize the lipstick and the compact and the black photo case. But the bag is not the one my mother was carrying. She was carrying a rather expensive navy bag. I remember it well. Don't you dust for fingerprints?" Annie asked.

Cavendish didn't answer the American woman. Insolence. Of course they had. So far they had found nothing in the computer files.

Cavendish was almost relieved when the interview was over, and he thanked them for coming to Scotland Yard to identify the objects they had found. The woman reminded him of Stephen Knight, although she wasn't as openly hostile. Knight was still being followed for the time being.

Cavendish needed some time alone to think. So the bag didn't belong to the dead woman. But everything else in the same trash can had. He began to doodle, lines going up, down, right, left. Crosshatching. And an awkward rendering of a ladies' handbag. But not Julia Davidson's. He'd put a tracer on it. See if any of the shops in London carried the bag.

His pencil not leaving the paper, he scribbled a different kind of bag. The murderer was very clever. He would have had to be to have killed a woman in the Underground and a woman in a ladies' room at Heathrow. Maybe he stole another woman's handbag and planted it in the trash can to trick them. Maybe.

He drew a cartoonlike figure. The quintessential tourist. Luggage, camera, hat. Then he twirled his pencil around his fingers. Damned if there wasn't a pattern there. The first woman was a tour guide, the second was on the Underground, and the third in Heathrow Airport.

It could be a tourist. It was very bloody likely. As for the Underground, maybe only a tourist would attempt to pull that off. Cavendish thought of the extensive computer banks in Scotland Yard. They would need them if it were a tourist. He could picture him now, buried in the crowds, a camera in front of his face. One of those jolly Americans or a smiling German or an amiable Japanese who spoke not one word of English.

He ran a hand through his thinning hair. Three murders so far, and they hadn't a clue. Except one. A witness who they had lost who saw a woman get away. Well, he couldn't get excited by that.

On Saturday morning Lockey ventured downstairs and rapped lightly on the door. You never could tell when that one might be there. She wafted in and out like a ghost. Lockey knocked a little louder. She wasn't there.

Disappointed, she climbed heavily up the steps. So she had been right. She had seen her leaving, but it was hard to believe she would come and go that fast. She must be terribly rich, Lockey calculated. Better not tell the Mister, or the girl would find herself with a raise in the rent.

She was nice enough—but a bit odd, when you thought of it.

"Tea!" she shouted when she came in and got just a snore from her husband. Well, tea for one, then. She went into the kitchen and that's when she thought of it. Her little blue and white teakettle was missing. It annoyed her when something was gone from her kitchen. She knew the Mister never went inside. Couldn't fend for himself, no way. She began to take the pots out of the cupboard, and then she remembered. She had left that little teakettle downstairs a few days ago when she had carried down the tray of breakfast. It was downstairs. And there was no telling when Barbara would be back.

She walked into the living room. The Mister was sound asleep. But if she turned off the telly, he would wake up. She decided she didn't want him awake. She walked as quietly as she could into the kitchen. On a bit of pegboard hung all the keys. The key to the basement with the big boiler, the spare mailbox key, the key to the attic. And the spare keys to the downstairs flat, to be used in case of emergency.

She shrugged. A little teakettle left behind was a good enough emergency for her. She took the key and put it in her apron pocket, hearing the sounds of the telly even as she walked down the short flight of steps. She let her hand slide down the railing of the wooden balustrade and at the last step noticed how dusty her palm was. Wiping her hand on her apron, she stopped and looked around. It was quiet. The Mister was still snoozing. The mailman hadn't come yet. The front door was a solid block of wood. No one could see in.

Still, when she turned the key and the door opened, she found herself tiptoeing in and shutting the door softly behind her. The flat was quiet as a tomb. The windows were shut tight. Dust motes played in what little light was coming from the large kitchen windows.

She spotted her teakettle immediately. It sat on the stove as if it belonged there. Everything else was put away. Or had never been taken out and used.

Unable to stop herself she opened some cupboard doors. Empty. One small drawer had a plastic fork and a spoon, a straw, and a pair of chopsticks. The middle drawer. The drawer that had upset her so much was also empty. That knife was gone. She wondered where Barbara had tucked it away.

She had the teakettle now. Dare she go downstairs? What if Barbara turned her key in the door just then . . . What would she say? She smiled smugly. Checking on a leak. Don't want to drown you out now, do we? The Mister said it was coming from your flat. From downstairs.

She walked down to the first level, thinking what peculiar habits this Barbara had for one who obviously had money. At least more than they did. What did she say she was? Oh, yes, a writer. Shouldn't there be a typewriter or a desk?

Lockey stood in the small dark hallway with her hands on her wide hips. Neither room was furnished. There were a few toiletries and cosmetics in the bathroom. Some dresses hung in the closets. It was barren. Like no one lived there but rather had left a few things while passing through.

She turned to start back up the steps and, stubbing her toe, pitched forward, tripping over something. Angry, in pain, she looked down. Sticking straight up, its handle pointed toward the ceiling, was a knife. A big, thick knife.

Prying it loose, she studied it. A corner of the blade was streaked with red. She touched it and shivered. Dried blood. That's what it was. Suddenly the apartment seemed very still. Panicking, she dropped the knife. Then she put it back where she had found it. Sticking out of the wooden floor.

She clutched the little teakettle tightly as she ran up the steps and out of the apartment, pausing only to lock the door behind her. Out of breath, more out of fear than exhaustion, she started to run up the hall steps but slowed down. She mustn't give anything away.

As soon as she walked in the door, holding the little teakettle behind her, the Mister spoke. But he didn't take his eyes off the telly. "Just had a special program on the murders. Been three of them now. All slashed with a knife. Last one at the airport."

Lockey had disappeared into the kitchen. All she heard was that there had been a special program. She thought of the knife with blood on it stuck in the floor like a dart on a board. Peculiar. The whole thing was. But she'd best forget about it. She slipped the key back on the nail in the pegboard. If she told the Mister she had been snooping around in the new tenant's flat, she would never hear the end of it.

# CHAPTER 13

Detectives Zuckerman and Kealing were both sitting on the floor cross-legged. Their desks hadn't been put in yet. They were expected momentarily. The other three detectives were out in the field. The phones had been installed.

They were toasting each other with two damp cardboard containers of black coffee.

"Brilliant idea," Carolyn said.

"I came up with it first," Tammy replied.

"No, you didn't."

"We came up with it together, then," Tammy conceded.

"Yeah, we've got her name. There's just no person with the name. No history, no present," Carolyn replied morosely.

"Just a body in the morgue," Tammy added morbidly.

"That's disgusting."

"I know."

"No, I mean a roach just tried to crawl into my coffee."

"Shouldn't we wait for the computer printout?" Tammy asked.

"Nah, what's the difference? The yellow pages are the yellow pages. This is just as easy."

"This is what it's all about," Tammy said.

Carolyn laughed. "What's that supposed to mean?"

"Oh, the bookwork, the tracking, the tracing. Always on television, it's the charging down dark alleys, holding your gun with both hands, and getting the collar."

Carolyn grunted. "I'm on the *B*'s. I wonder how many hotels there are in New York City?"

"Let's just hope a woman named Enid Thornton stayed at one of them," Tammy said dryly.

It was after five London time when Inspector Cavendish got a little break. He had personally gone to the home of the second victim's husband. It was the usual interview. The man was out of shock but in deep grief. He wasn't much help.

Cavendish looked down at his desk. His doodles were showing. Sloppy of him. He turned them over and sighed. An epidemic of slashings, that's what it was. Jack the Ripper in the twentieth century. Only these were all nice girls. It depressed him to talk to the next of kin.

There was a knock on the open door. He looked up. Sergeant Hollings was standing there holding some papers.

"Yes, what is it, Hollings?"

"Checking out the airport again, sir. They've checked their records on the computer, and TWA has come up with something."

"Yes, Hollings, what is it?" The man's sense of drama annoyed him sometimes, especially on a bad day.

"It's Julia Davidson. They have a record of her flying out of London the night she was murdered."

Home for a year now was a large flat on Grosevenor Street in Central London. It was roomy enough for a wife and a new baby—and a mother-in-law anytime she wanted to visit.

Kenneth Kline walked into his home that evening to find his wife sitting very still and staring straight ahead. The baby was being fed by a nurse that he had hired after Julia . . . had left.

He walked up to her and kissed her on her cheek. She didn't turn. He ran his forefinger down the shock of blond baby's hair. She smiled toothlessly up at him. At least someone cared that he was home. "Would you like to go back to New York to live?

Would that make you feel better?" he asked his wife when the nurse had left the room with the baby.

She ignored his question. "This note came for us," she said tonelessly, then reached forward to hand it to him.

He read it quickly and started to rip it up.

She stopped him. "No! Don't do that." It was the most amount of emotion he had seen her show since they found out about her mother.

"But, Annie, these people are crackpots. You don't want to get mixed up with them. What good will that do?"

She became mute again.

"I have to take your mother back to New York. Won't you come to the funeral?"

She shook her head resolutely, and Kenneth had a sinking feeling in his stomach, a feeling of loss. "You're not planning to get in touch with Stephen Knight or Brian Harrington, are you? I mean hooking up with a vigilante committee when you have all of Scotland Yard on the case is absurd."

She shrugged.

"Don't you think, honey," he said gently, "that you should be paying more attention to the baby? I should let the nurse go." She got up and Kenneth noticed that she had lost weight in the last few days.

"I don't want the baby anymore," she announced flatly.

He winced.

"I want revenge."

Their usual tour of duty was forgotten with the demanding hours of the task force. In her spare time Tammy cooked endlessly, leaving roasts, chickens, and meat loafs for her husband and son while she was away from home. They were just as happy with Chinese food, but she felt guilty. On Sunday morning she arrived at work just as exhausted as if she had partied all night, which it was evident Carolyn had.

All the phones were installed, desks and chairs had been moved in, and the room was humming with voices.

"A, B, C, D, E, F, G," sang Carolyn like a child.

"You're still doing that, huh?" Tammy joked. "Whatsa matter? Educationally deprived?"

"That's the only way I can find a letter. I have to sing the whole alphabet."

Tammy laughed. "Well, what letter are you up to?"

"*L.* I'm about to dial the Lacey Hotel on East Twenty-third Street." Carolyn dialed. "Excuse me, sir. This is the New York City Police Department. We're checking to see if within the last two weeks a woman by the name of Enid Thornton checked into your hotel for any length of time." She waited. Why were hotel clerks always men? she wondered. "The woman was about five feet six with shoulder-length brunette hair and brown eyes. Did you see any woman like that come in at all? Possibly she checked in under another name? No, I know it's not much of a description to go on, but it's all we've got." She hung up the phone angrily. Maybe they should be walking from hotel to hotel with the sketch the artist had made from the corpse. She was well aware that the woman named Enid Thornton had checked into a hotel and maybe signed the book as Eleanor Roosevelt. But they had to make the effort even if there were no results.

The next hotel was Hotel Lincoln. Tammy was on the phone, going backward from the alphabet and not having to sing it. Somewhere around the middle they would meet. So far they had nothing.

"Hi, this is the New York City Police Department. No, this is not a joke. We're checking to see if a woman named Enid Thornton stayed at your hotel within the last two weeks. She was five feet six, shoulder-length brunette hair, brown eyes . . . Yes, I know the description is not exactly unique, but could you check the name anyway? You what! You don't believe this, you want us to come in person . . . No, by law you don't have to give any information over the phone . . . Well, you don't have to get nasty." Carolyn slammed the phone down. "Did you hear that?"

Tammy was just hanging up the phone. "Call back later. They have different shifts. Maybe someone else will be more cooperative."

At about one in the afternoon, they were moving toward the middle and still no luck.

"Wanna eat?" Tammy suggested.

"Yeah. Wait a second . . . I forgot one. Wasn't there one I was going to call back?"

"Yeah."

"But I didn't mark down the name. How stupid. One hotel sounds like the next."

"I think it was a president's name," Tammy remembered vaguely.

"No, like a car. Pontiac, Cadillac, *Lincoln!*" she screamed. "Well, here goes nothing," she said, picking up the phone.

"What do you feel like eating?"

"Pastrami on a seeded roll with celery tonic."

"Yeah? I feel like a big chef's salad."

"Funny, you don't look like one. Hotel Lincoln? This is the New York City Police Department." She pantomimed with her hands that it was a different voice. "We're checking to see if a woman by the name of Enid Thornton checked into your hotel and stayed within, say, the last two weeks."

Carolyn's eyes looked wide at Tammy as the man said without hesitating, "Oh, yes, Enid Thornton. How could I forget her? Tell me, was she a high-class prostitute, or what? I couldn't figure her out."

Carolyn slumped down into her chair, threw her pencil into the air, and let out a soft yell.

Detective First-Grade Hank Patuto gazed out over the top of the plastic cake pan in the coffee shop and through the backward lettering. He avoided the gaze of his partner, who was sitting next to him at the counter. He didn't want to admit to anyone how pissed he was. Damn it. He should be on that task force. It was his case. He was the catching detective.

He watched his partner point to a doughnut and turned away again to look at the people crossing in front of the restaurant's window. Nothing exciting had happened all day. Just routine and more routine and paperwork bullshit to go along with it. Everything was predictable—even his partner's sitting there for five minutes over coffee and then deciding to have a doughnut. The action was upstairs at the Nineteenth and he wanted to be there.

They had tricked him. Manipulated him. Those two broads

must have known, and they took the case away from him, right out from under his eyes. He looked down at the napkin folded under his coffee cup. He'd get even. Did they think he was stupid? He was a cop and he was vindictive. Oh, yeah, he'd get them. He was just waiting for a chance, one little mistake, one tiny slip—and he'd get them. And then those two broads, Zuckerman and Kealing, would be sorry they ever used him to get on the task force.

The Hotel Lincoln wasn't too far away. Just about thirty blocks down Lexington Avenue into the East Side's charming Murray Hill section. They got a parking space on Third and walked up.

"I've been keeping my fingers crossed so hard that I don't think I have any feeling in them," Tammy admitted nervously.

"Why, Detective Zuckerman, what if all the guys at the gin mill could hear you now? Could be a crank, though. We've been disappointed in crazier ways."

"There it is—your gloom and doom. What more could you want? He recognized the name."

She started to say, "Something could go wrong," but she stopped herself. She was just as excited as Tammy was. It was her way of showing it. And besides, all they were looking for was the history of a dead woman. They still had to find the killer. "Ritzy place, huh?" Carolyn commented as they approached the modern hotel.

"Doesn't fit the neighborhood, if you know what I mean. Pretty soon all these quaint little areas will be glass and chrome towers."

Carolyn took a deep breath, and they walked in over the rich royal blue carpeting, under the cut-glass chandelier, and up to the oak desk. They waited for the clerk to turn and notice them, and when he did they smiled and flashed their shields.

"We called about Enid Thornton," Tammy began.

"Oh, yes," said the desk clerk. His glasses slipped a little on his nose and he smiled.

Tammy noted that his maroon tie, white shirt, and navy three-piece suit were impeccably neat, and that he had a nervous habit of reaching up to pat his half-balding head.

"Ah, yes," he said in response to their shields. "You came to find out about Enid Thornton, or the lady in white."

"The lady in white—is that what you said?" Carolyn asked, feeling like her heart had skipped a beat.

"Well, that was my own private nickname for her. She had on this very attractive white outfit. It just screamed to be noticed."

"Do you have a record of her staying here?"

"Oh, yes, that I do." He motioned them to come to the middle of the desk, where the hotel ledger was kept. He flipped back the pages and let his finger trail down the names. "Here it is," he said, and turned it upside down so they could see. "I was on the desk from four until midnight. This week I'm on the desk from noon until eight. How fortunate for you."

Carolyn gave a silent grunt.

"Can you talk?" Tammy asked. "I mean, do you need someone to relieve you?"

"No such luxury on a Sunday. I'll do my best to help you." He looked at the ledger book. "Yes, she was some lady, that Enid Thornton. What's she wanted for?"

Tammy appraised him carefully and then said in a soft voice, "She's dead. We're trying to find out who killed her."

The clerk let out a small, strangled gasp. Then he composed himself and straightened his tie. In a low voice he asked, "You don't think she was murdered in our hotel, do you?"

"No, we don't," Carolyn replied. "She was found stabbed in the street on upper Park Avenue the night of the twenty-second of May—that was a Saturday."

"Good Lord." The desk clerk thought for a second about the vital lady he had seen, about life and death, and it occurred to him that no one here really knew his name. He knew theirs, if only briefly, but to the people who passed through the hotel, he was just a face. He found that very sad just then. "I'm Alexander Casey," he announced stiffly.

Tammy and Carolyn nodded in response.

"What can I help you with?" His eyes roamed the ceiling. "Oh, she was a flirt, that one, teasing. Even me. I guess it's no wonder."

"Was she with someone?"

"No, she checked in alone." He turned and ran his hand

through what was left of his hair. "Let's see," he said, studying the cubbyholes. "Oh, yes, how could I forget. She was in Room 712. There's someone occupying it now." He ran his hand through the empty cubbyhole. "That evening she was wearing this white outfit cut, uh, very low. Like I said, you couldn't help but notice her. She was that type of woman anyway. Provocative. Anyway, she had on this white . . . Oh, excuse me, I have to get the phone."

Tammy and Carolyn stood silently, almost mesmerized, watching him take the phone call.

"Madame, I can't describe the hotel. You will have to come in." He shot a glance at the two women detectives. "It's not a flophouse, and it's not the St. Moritz, you know? You don't have to buy it." He hung up and shrugged. "You get all kinds." He looked down, realizing just how true that statement was.

"Can you remember anything more about Enid Thornton?" Carolyn prompted.

"Yes. I remember she wore a rhinestone earring, but on just one ear. It dangled. I guess her hair was brushed in front of the other ear."

Tammy and Carolyn exchanged looks. No rhinestone earring. It could have fallen off.

"And her bag was white with a gold chain."

They nodded together. That was the bag they had found.

"And she was a flirt. She would have just as soon have flirted with a ten-year-old boy as she would have with an eighty-year-old man. She flirted with me. I thought she was a high-class prostitute, you know?"

"She may have been," Tammy replied softly, thinking of the young hooker who was killed. "We don't know. What did you talk to her about?"

"Oh, she asked me a good place to have dinner around here. I suggested several places, and she took me up on the restaurant across the street."

Both women turned around. Through the open curtains, they saw a tavern with lamplights, but they couldn't make out the name.

"Looks like a nice place to have dinner," Carolyn said, and Tammy immediately understood that she meant to do that.

"Oh, yes. The Tenderloin. Great steak house. Big baked potatoes swimming in sour cream."

"Expensive?" asked Carolyn.

"Moderate," answered the desk clerk.

"So she went to the restaurant and then what?" Tammy asked impatiently.

"And then she didn't stay long. Must have just had a drink or something because I saw her come through the door. Alone. She disappeared upstairs. I remember thinking it was odd that she had returned alone. She looked like she was out for some action. But then a gentleman came after her. In fact, he made a big fuss and we had to call security and have him . . . removed."

"What did he do?" Tammy asked quickly.

"Oh, he was pounding on her door. Annoying the people on that floor. Screaming for her to come out."

"Maybe she wasn't in there," Carolyn suggested.

"But she came down after that. She didn't give me her key, but I saw her walk through the lobby," Alexander said. "Oh, but he was yelling some terrible things. Calling her all sorts of things. I couldn't repeat them to women. Oh, but then, you're police officers."

"Detectives." Carolyn couldn't help correcting him. "What time was he removed?"

Alexander put his forefinger over his mouth and scrunched up his forehead. "Let's see, I think she came in around ten, and he came after her at about eleven and then left fifteen minutes later."

"So she must have gone to dinner late?"

"Yes, it was close to nine o'clock."

"And you didn't see her leave again?" Carolyn asked very carefully.

"No, I didn't. And I don't miss much. You develop eyes in the back of your head on this job."

"But you do turn around?" asked Tammy.

"What kind of watch do you wear?" interrupted Carolyn. "Is it a digital or a self-winding?"

"Self-winding," he answered automatically, touching his watch.

"And you say she came in around ten, he came at eleven, left at eleven fifteen, and then she went out again?"

"That's correct," he replied. "At approximately eleven thirty."

Nobody said anything, and finally it was Tammy who turned to Carolyn and asked, "What are you getting at?"

"That his watch may have been running fast. That Enid Thornton had dinner earlier, came in earlier, left earlier, went uptown, and somehow was murdered."

"Is that possible, Mr. Casey?" Tammy asked.

"I thought my watch was working, but maybe I was wrong."

Tammy and Carolyn nodded to each other.

"What did the man look like?" Tammy interrogated.

"Oh, he was very tall, sandy-haired, ruddy complexion, medium build. Well dressed, as I remember."

"No beard or mustache?" Tammy asked him.

"No. Clean shaven. Good-looking man."

"And you say she ate where?"

"She went across the street."

Tammy was recapping. "So, she met that man in the restaurant across the street. Are there plenty of cabs around here late at night? Could she have gotten uptown about sixty blocks before twelve, which is when the medical examiner set the time of death?"

He shrugged. "I never timed it."

"We could double-check the time from the Medical Examiner's Office. Everything checks out, but the time bothers me," Carolyn said.

"I wonder if he killed her?" Alexander suggested wide-eyed. "Maybe he chased her all the way to upper Park Avenue!"

Tammy and Carolyn exchanged glances. They were wondering about the man from the restaurant, too. It made sense. Up to a point. Because they were on a task force and there were now multiple murders. A crime of passion was not a random killing.

Alexander went to register a couple, and Tammy took the opportunity to speak openly. "She was probably running away from him and got stabbed by someone else."

Carolyn shrugged. "Maybe he saw someone run away and is afraid to talk to the police."

"We'll have to question the manager and see where we can reach him."

"And we'll have to have dinner in that restaurant later on. Did you hear what he said about the food? Big white baked potatoes, flaky soft, swimming in a creamy sour cream teased by the juices of a sizzling steak . . ."

Tammy laughed quietly behind her hand. "You know, you missed your calling."

"What should I have been that I'm not?"

"You should write the copy for menus," Tammy whispered just as Alexander Casey finished registering the couple.

This was by far the most interesting thing that had ever happened to him on any hotel job he had ever had.

Tammy looked at the ledger book where the couple had just signed in. She looked up. "Wait a second. If Enid Thornton was murdered, how did she check out?"

"But I thought you already knew," Alexander said, surprised. "She didn't check out. She didn't pay her bill. She just disappeared!"

"And the key?"

"She never returned the key."

# CHAPTER 14

The first thing she noticed when she walked into the office at noon that Monday were the lovely gladiolas in the long-stemmed vase. She didn't know that he had bought them especially because she would be there. And that behind the vase was an extension cord that connected to a tape recorder, already rolling, under the desk with the volume turned on loud.

He had spent the whole morning wondering who would walk in, Enid or Barbara. The first thing he noticed was that she was wearing tortoiseshell glasses when she sat down in the chair. He hadn't noticed she wore glasses before. Interesting.

The whole case was. He had already approached a writer about doing a book, but she had said she couldn't do it until the patient was realized, or cured. He'd look for another writer. Meanwhile he'd have the tapes as proof.

"Hello," he greeted her.

"Good afternoon, Dr. Walters," she replied.

He nodded. There was a pause. "So, what's been happening in your life?"

"Oh, the same old thing. We went to Hammersmith."

He frowned. "That's where your other apartment is."

"Flat," she corrected him. "It's a maisonette with a garden on the lower level."

"What do you do there?" he asked.

"You mean, what exactly do *we* do there," she corrected him.

She was aware that she had more than one personality? he thought, confused and astounded at the same time. Behind him in the tall bookshelves covering the wall were books. Freud, Jung, Adler, Karen Horney. And some new books. On the multiple personality or, rather, disassociative personality disorder. Reading about the disease was so remote. But having an actual patient with it—well, it was worth ten other patients with simple neuroses. Fascinating. According to his readings, she would just switch personalities. No reason needed.

He cupped his hand under his chin. "Does Enid know about you?" How different Barbara was today. How much more confident and authoritative.

"Not really," she said very crisply. "Enid knows about Barbara's existence, though. Enid, of course, is self-centered and cares only about freeing herself from Barbara, whom she resents."

Dr. Walters smiled as if the joke were on him, but he had suspected it all along. "You're not Barbara, are you?"

She smiled back, patronizingly. "No, I'm Dana, the keeper of the personalities. I've been here, but I haven't been here, if you know what I mean." She stood up, walked over, shook his hand, and then returned to her chair.

There was a pause. He wondered if the tape recorder were running smoothly, but there was no way he could stop and check. Again he was struck by the fact that it was the most fascinating thing he had ever witnessed in all his years of practicing psychiatry.

He cleared his throat and looked directly into her glasses, wondering if they were window glass or if she actually became nearsighted when she was this new one, Dana. So there were three personalities. He had read of a case where the woman was allergic to nylon with one personality and not allergic with the other. "Do you think, Dana, we could begin to summon the others?" Good Lord, he thought, this wasn't enough time to work with her. He was going to need more time.

"I can try to help you, but I can't make any promises." She smiled at him, peering over her glasses.

He sighed. "What is it that happens in this Hammersmith? That's quite unusual, flying back and forth to London during the week."

She looked at him through narrow eyes. "Barbara works in Hammersmith. She feels comfortable writing there. It reminds her of her adolescence when she was very close to her mother. Other businesspeople commute back and forth to get *their* work done."

"You mentioned Barbara's mother. Do you remember her?"

Without warning, Dana's head rolled back to the side and then around. Her glasses slipped off one ear, then fell onto her lap. Her eyes were shut tight, as if she were on a speeding roller coaster and couldn't take the turns. Her fingers flew to her blouse, fumbling with the top button. Then she removed her bead necklace and began swinging it flippantly. He watched, wide-eyed, wondering if the coquettish personality wanted to come out. He had always as a psychiatrist maintained a distance or a detachment from his patients as a matter of professional good form. Now he felt as if he were going through the personality changes with her. It was *happening* right in front of him!

He was right. It was the flirtatious one who came out next. The change was unbelievable. It would be only partially captured on the tape recorder. Too bad he couldn't get it on videotape. Maybe later he would do that as part of the session.

"And who is this charming lady?" he asked, playing into the new personality.

"Enid," she replied, giggling. The glasses had been folded into the bag at the side of the chair, her hands were pushing her hair up off her neck, not one but two buttons had been opened on her blouse, and her skirt was way above her knee on the leg that was crossed. She was smiling at the doctor, but there was nothing demure about it.

"So what's been happening in your life, Enid?" he asked, still smiling.

She stared at him. "Are you crazy? I don't have any life. She keeps me locked up, never lets me come out. I can't wear my pretty new clothes. I can't go dancing. Geez."

He stared at her pleasantly, all the while thinking that the Enid personality would be the one to die first. Her time was limited because she couldn't possibly be of any use. The promiscuity Barbara couldn't ever express . . . Was it rebellion or what? He needed to know more. "Enid, could you bring back Dana?"

"Who the hell is Dana?"

Amazing. So Enid knew Barbara. Dana knew both. Barbara didn't know anything. "I'm sorry," he said, and bit his lip. Since when did he ever apologize? "Do you go to Hammersmith?"

"I don't have a choice, do I? But I don't have any fun. Barbara's writing her memoirs."

"She's writing a book?" he asked incredulously. "Could you tell me more about that?"

"There's nothing to tell," she replied flippantly. "Barbara used to be a child star." She looked at him. "Oh, don't get excited. Just a soap opera star. Cookie, they called her. Doesn't that nauseate you? From when she was four until she was twelve, and then they moved to Hammersmith." She flung her arms out. "Whatever happened to Cookie?" She leaned in. "I'll tell you. She became a bore, a frump, a shy woman with hardly any friends. So much for the big television star."

"Why didn't you—I mean, she—continue with that career?"

"They killed her. Wrote her out of the script. Or that's what they said. They actually replaced her. See, even at twelve she showed signs of being the miserable wretch that she is now."

"Tell me about your . . . Barbara's mother."

She stared at him. The strand of beads slipped from her hands. Her legs uncrossed and then recrossed. He watched, waiting. It was happening again. Now he could see a pattern. It had something to do with the mother. Whenever he brought her up, she would escape into another change. Remarkable.

She shivered and blinked her eyes several times. Then both hands flew to her forehead, and she looked for a second like the woman in the headache commercial who rubbed her temples and looked as if she might cry. Then she blinked rapidly as if she were trying to put the room into focus.

"Barbara?" he asked.

She said nothing. She just looked around as if she couldn't figure out how she had gotten there.

"I'd like to talk about your mother . . ."

She stared at him, baffled. "I blacked out again, didn't I? I—I —don't remember what you were saying? We should talk about these attacks I've been having."

"I'd like to talk about your mother . . ." he persisted. If she kept changing personalities on him everytime he brought up the subject of her mother, he'd never be able to solve her problem.

"My mother's dead," she said flatly.

"And that's very painful for you," he encouraged, determined to get the work done.

"Not really," she admitted.

"You and your mother didn't get along?" He was quite comfortable with Barbara when she was Barbara. She was like most of his women patients, repressed, compliant, eager to please.

"My mother was a backstage mother. I was Cookie. I was her creation. And after, when I wasn't Cookie . . ." she looked down, unable to finish.

"The cookie crumbled?"

Her lips worked, but she didn't say anything.

He looked at the clock he kept at eye level on the little table directly across from his chair. Damn, the session was almost over. And what had he accomplished? "What's happening in your life?" he asked almost wearily.

"Well, today's Monday. Tomorrow's Tuesday, and I'm off to Hammersmith. I guess I'll stay until the night before my next appointment and then zip back."

"I don't think all that traveling is a good idea. In fact, I would like to suggest you give up your flat in Hammersmith until you're, uh, feeling better."

Barbara glared at him. She wouldn't dare say anything, but her face was tinged with pink. She was angry. "I write in Hammersmith. I'm writing my memoirs. I did tell you I was a child soap star, didn't I?" He said nothing. "A lot of people remember me. They stop me in airports. Why, just the other—When was it?—someone—"

Dr. Walters interrupted her. "That's not the point. It's that you are in treatment now, and it's not advisable. All this rushing back and forth agitates you."

She stared at him and met his gaze directly, throwing him off guard.

"What is it that's wrong with me?" she demanded.

He looked away. A patient was no doubt waiting out front. There were only two or three minutes left to the session. He opened his mouth to say something and then closed it.

She had reached for her bag. There was a slight tremor in her body. Her fists were clenched, and her mouth was set as tight as her fists. Then she put on her glasses and looked up at him sternly. He was transfixed.

"How dare you tell her not to go to Hammersmith," Dana scolded.

Amazing. Barbara couldn't tell him herself, but she could summon Dana to show anger. "Do you know what her mother did to her?"

"I'm trying to find out," he replied dryly.

"She kept her from living. And she tried to take her money, too. But now Barbara has it, and for the first time in her life, she's doing what she wants to do. She wants to write."

Dr. Walters shook his head. "You misunderstand. I'm not saying she can't write. I'm just telling her not to make so many transatlantic crossings." He shook his head. This was unbelievable. Here they were like two parents arguing about a woman who occupied the same body but was being referred to in the third person. "You forget, she doesn't know she's . . . many people."

"Why don't you have her read *The Three Faces of Eve* or *Sybil?*" she suggested sarcastically.

"You mean I should tell her outright?"

For a minute their roles were absurdly reversed. "I won't tell you what to do, but you might get her to talk about her mother if she knew what her problem was."

He seemed lost in thought.

"Just remember the mistake in *The Three Faces of Eve.*"

He looked up sharply.

"There were more than three personalities. Twenty-two, I believe, after the book came out and the doctor claimed she was cured. And Sybil had, what was it, sixteen?"

"What are you getting at?"

"The problem is not whether she's going to go to Hammersmith. Barbara's stubborn. She'll go anyway. The problem is that you should tell her what's wrong with her. All she knows is that she has blackouts and loses track of time. Do you think that's fair?"

"Are you afraid of what will happen to you if I cure Barbara?"

"Touché."

He smiled at her. "Actually, what I plan to do is kill Barbara and have you be the dominant personality." Truthfully that wasn't the case at all. He planned to eliminate this Dana and have only the personality of Barbara remain. Then he'd put her in treatment the same way he had all his other women patients. Barbara was merely neurotic. But he needed Dana's help, so he told her a little white lie. She wasn't a real person anyway.

"I believe our time is up. Can you convey to Barbara that I want to change our schedule? I want to see her twice a week in double sessions." He reached over for his appointment book. "What about Tuesday and Friday . . . at nine o'clock? Is that okay?"

Dana smiled confidently. "Yes. I'll see that she keeps the appointments. But she'll still go to Hammersmith in between."

Dr. Walters smiled back at her as if he understood the deal. He was really thinking that the sooner he got rid of Dana, the better. She was getting in the way.

When the cab let Barbara off in front of her apartment building, she felt the panic rising. Her beads had broken, so all that was left was a string with a bead or two. Her hands were dirty. Her right sandal had a strange cluster of tiny dots of blood on it. Had she been running and fallen somehow? She didn't feel especially out of breath, but then again, how could she know? Her watch had moved ahead five hours.

She remembered having the appointment with Dr. Walters.

After that, she had blacked out, done something, been somewhere . . . been someone . . . She shuddered. It was frightening, grotesque.

And then she remembered something else. The anger, the
rage. And then nothingness. She was nothing now. A used
sponge, a dried-out dishtowel. Why couldn't God be kind and
let her just die?

She tried very hard, her head down, her broken beads in her
smudged hand, to be invisible as she walked quietly through the
lobby of the Park Avenue apartment house.

There was that sinking feeling again. After the anger was the
depression. For some reason, she thought a shower would cure
it. What is it that Dr. Walters said during those sessions? She
couldn't remember all of it. Just couldn't remember.

The elevator operator took her up wordlessly. She hung her
head. Wouldn't it be great, she thought, if I were invisible? And
then she gulped. In many ways she was. She kept losing herself.

No one was in the hall. Good thing. Because Barbara was
standing in front of her door, weeping uncontrollably. In her
hand was a big, ugly knife. It had been in her bag. As her key
turned in the door and she opened it she felt the room spin, and
she whispered, "Oh, God, not again."


People strolling the West Village could hear the sirens
screeching for blocks away. Four turquoise and white cars from
the Sixth Precinct parked at angles sealed off Waverly Place
from cars and passersby. On the little side street between Bank
Street and Charles Street, in the late afternoon sunshine, lay a
woman who had been ripped apart by a knife. The sidewalks
were shiny with blood.

It was hard to detect, but the woman was dressed in sneakers
and socks, a peasant skirt, and a man's shirt and apparently had
not been carrying a handbag. After close inspection, a five-dollar bill was found in the heel of her sneaker.

The call had come into the Sixth that there had been a stabbing on Waverly Place. This precinct's cops saw everything.
The safe, middle-class neighborhood that was once old Bohe-
mia was also a haven for every crazy, drug addict, and stray in
New York. Six officers stood there and looked at the murdered

woman. "Someone should call the Nineteenth, the task force," a woman officer said. "It's their case."

A black cop, not able to take his eyes off the blood-soaked body, said, "Sure fits the M.O., doesn't it? We got ourselves a nice mass murderer loose here. Killing in broad daylight. Shit, if I were a woman, I'd lock myself in the house and stay there."

Shaking, Barbara realized she was awake but on the floor. She looked at her watch. She had passed out again but only for a few minutes. He had told her to get a physical examination, and she hadn't done it. She felt angry, but she couldn't quite figure out with whom. Perhaps at herself for not doing it. Perhaps at Dr. Walters because he thought it was part of her problem. It was her anger that propelled her up off the floor and to the telephone.

It was six o'clock, and she didn't expect him to be in. She would just leave a message on his answering machine and wait for him to call her back. When he picked up his phone, she was surprised.

"Dr. Walters? This is Barbara Hargrove. I'm sorry to bother you. It's just that I had a memory lapse . . . I don't think we talked about that, did we? You see, time just goes by and I can't account for it. And then just now I passed out and I think, really, it has nothing to do with having a physical examination, and I wondered if I could drop by and just talk to you now for a few minutes? Or are you busy?"

Dr. Walters smiled. First, at her naïveté. Drop by. At ninety dollars per fifty minutes every minute was booked. Second, he was pleased and saw it as a major breakthrough in the transference that she had called to talk to him and tell him her troubles. Anyone else would get a few kind words, some hasty therapy, and know that they had to wait for their appointment to work things out.

"Okay," he said. "I'll see what I can do and call you back."

He looked up at his patient, who was sitting there biting her nails. "I have an emergency," he explained apologetically.

He dialed the phone quickly. Thank heaven the seven o'clock was still home, getting ready to leave. "Hi! This is Dr. Walters. Can I reschedule your appointment? I know you were just getting ready to leave. Can I see you at three on Wednesday instead of seven tonight? Okay? Fine."

He hung up the phone and dialed again. This time it was clear to his patient that he was talking into a machine. "Hi! This is Dr. Walters. I was wondering if I could change your appointment at three on Wednesday to, say, four on Thursday? Could you call my office to confirm? Thank you."

He dialed once more. "Hi. This is Dr. Walters. Yes, you can come by at seven o'clock tonight, and we can have a session." He was almost breathless.

"Oh, I don't know," Barbara demured. "I'm creating too much trouble. Maybe it isn't necessary. Maybe I can handle everything myself."

Like a headmaster to an errant child, Dr. Walters said only, "Be here at seven tonight."

The blackboard in the task force room was largely ignored now by everyone. Before they left for the Village, Carolyn and Tammy passed by it. In crooked block letters Captain Fulani had written: Enid Thornton, Hooker, Woman in Village.

"This is the headline breaker," Carolyn said as they approached their car.

"Yeah, and when they get through, this is the murder that will make every woman afraid to walk down the street alone at night."

"This one happened in daylight," Carolyn reminded her.

"I guess we won't eat until later," said Tammy.

"Yuck," said Carolyn. All she had been thinking about was going back to that restaurant, interviewing the manager, and asking after the man who had been with Enid Thornton. And in the back of her mind she could feel the knife slicing through a medium rare slab of prime rib, her favorite dish. Now all she could think of was a knife slicing through flesh somewhere in the Village while the sun was still shining and knowing that they were driving to see a woman, with no name, who was the victim of some man who had to be stopped.

When she stepped out of the shower, Barbara had the distinct feeling of wanting to look nice for Dr. Walters. Though she didn't know why. She decided to wear her beige suit. Then she selected a short-sleeved floral blouse and a gold circle pin. She slipped into high-heeled sandals.

He wasn't such a bad-looking man. Not at all. In fact, he was kind of cute with his wavy black hair and his dimpled smile and those clear blue eyes.

Mum had had sapphire blue eyes like that. Sapphire was her birthstone. She was born in September. Mum had once given her a half-birthday party in March. Not in Hammersmith, of course, because she had no real friends. But on the set one day for the cast and the crew. There was half a cake that said ". . . kie." Half sandwiches, half gallons of ice cream, and they sang half the song. Mum was such a lark! She had gotten a photographer, and a picture and a caption appeared in a fan magazine. Cookie's Half-Birthday Party. Then she got fan mail from other little kids saying they had the same kind of party. Mum was like that.

It was six fifty when she got out of the cab and walked into the large lobby of the building.

At exactly two minutes after seven, according to her digital watch, Dr. Walters walked in, greeted her with his usual enthusiastic "Hi!" as if they were meeting at a party after not seeing each other for a long time, and stepped aside to let her lead the way. She sat down.

"I came home today, and I couldn't remember where I had been after I had seen you."

He nodded. "And how did you feel about that?"

"I felt angry, depressed, frustrated. I lost about five hours. And it's been happening more and more since my father died."

"What do you think causes that?"

She stared at him, uncomprehending. She had thought he was going to tell her. "I don't know. I just can't remember where I've been or what I've done."

"You say this began happening after your father died. Could you talk a little about him. Did you have a good relationship with your father?"

She glared at him. "What's that got to do with it?"

It was the first time he had seen her on edge. Above all, he wanted to do some work with the Barbara personality before she changed, if she was going to, into one of the others.

His hands were joined in a church steeple pose. "Well, I'm trying to get at the root of your loss of memory. This is the first time you've told me about that."

"It is?"

"We've just spoken about the dizzy spells," he said, knowing full well he was manipulating her.

She squinted at him. "Then what have I talked about when I've been here? I don't remember a lot of that, either."

He chose to ignore that. "What about your father?" he inquired instead.

"I don't remember a thing about him. He wasn't very memorable," she said, her lips pursed tightly together.

"So you resented your father."

"I didn't say that. I felt sorry for him."

Dr. Walters shook his head. "Why? He was your father. Father's are all-powerful creatures to a little girl."

"He was a drunkard," she answered simply.

Dr. Walters sighed. He looked at his watch and realized that this session could slip away from him like all the rest of them had. He made a quick decision, although he had been debating it over and over. It wouldn't be fair to her to continue this way. He also had no faith in the deep psychoanalytic approach. He was a short-term therapist, and he was positive she could be cured much the same way.

"There's something I think you should know—" she began. She wanted desperately to tell him about the blood-stained knife she had found in her bag this afternoon.

"Well," he smiled, interrupting her, "actually, I think there's something you should know first before we talk any longer." And then his smile vanished. "There's a reason for your memory lapses."

Barbara leaned forward, anxious for him to go on. Good, he thought. He had sensed all along her resistance to treatment. Imagine not remembering your parents? Everyone remembered something about their parents. They talked for hours about them. They cried until tears rolled down their cheeks, and he helped them with that. He became their parent so that they could get over their difficulties. They could transfer the parental feelings to him and he became a good parent, where their parents had been bad to them. He thought about it then because he would have liked to have waited until he was more of a parent to her. But she had to know. She had to live in the real world with it.

"Barbara, I'm going to level with you."

Almost sensing she didn't want to hear what he was going to say, her body began to stiffen.

How to begin, he thought, then plunged in. "Barbara, you have a rare psychotic disease. Not many people have this, and the cure is arduous and requires the complete cooperation of the patient."

Barbara's blouse felt sticky, and she would have removed her suit jacket had she not felt immobilized. She couldn't take her eyes off the doctor's mouth.

"You have these memory lapses for a reason. I don't want to get too technical here, but they are called *fugues.* You lose your memory because you become a different personality. You have what is called a disassociative personality disorder. When you were very young, you couldn't cope, so you found a hiding place. You began to become different personalities."

She was staring wide-eyed in horror at him.

He put up his hand like a referee. "I know. I've seen you in this office. That's also why you can't remember. Because you haven't always been yourself. Sometimes you're Enid, the flirtatious one."

"Do I flirt with you?" she asked in a small voice, astounded.

He smiled and nodded. "Yes, you do."

Her mouth fell open.

"And then there's Dana," he explained as if he were reading a picture book to a child. "She's very smart, very analytical. If you check your bag, you'll find a pair of eyeglasses you've probably trained yourself to overlook. Dana's nearsighted. When I'm talking to her, she wears glasses."

Barbara looked like she was going to cry. "I used to wear glasses for a while," she said, but she couldn't bring herself to check her bag.

She looked up at him, then rolled her eyes frantically around the room. He thought for a moment that she wouldn't be able to handle finding out about her disorder, that she would have to escape into another personality. He expected Dana, the keeper of the selves.

But she remained Barbara. "It's bizarre. That accounts for everything. I've heard about this."

He nodded. "Yes, *The Three Faces of Eve . . . Sybil.*"

"Are you sure I only have three personalities?"

He nodded his head emphatically. "Positive. But others may spring up." Not if there was any way of stopping that, he thought to himself.

She searched his face hungrily.

"How do you feel about this?"

"I feel"—her voice cracked and she swallowed—"I feel . . . like a freak," she finished, then put her head in her hands and sobbed.

# CHAPTER 15

The wallpaper was red file with a black velvet pattern superimposed. The booths were red tufted leather.

Carolyn dipped a clump of baked potato and slathered it with sour cream, but her eyes never left the door. "Think he'll show up?" she asked Tammy.

"The bartender said he was expected. This is his hangout."

"No I.D. on the woman in the Village. No fingerprints either. Can't help thinking that's a pattern," Carolyn suggested, spearing a piece of steak.

"But there was I.D. for Enid," Tammy replied, her mouth full of food.

"Only when we found it. Do you think the others had I.D., but it got taken?"

"Just for now, can we cease and desist talking about the latest body? How often do we get to eat a *real* dinner?"

"Wait a second," Carolyn said suddenly. "Don't turn. I think there's our man. Just walked in. Tall, sandy-haired, not bad-looking at all—my type. And he's heading toward the bar. That's our man."

"Eat fast," Tammy lamented, "cause that's the end of this dinner."

"I'll bet he won't be so quick to pick up a lady like Enid Thornton again and go banging on her door," Carolyn observed.

"Yeah, especially if he killed her," Tammy replied, scraping the skin of her baked potato.

Uptown in a little coffee shop between Park and Lexington Avenues, Barbara sat with her childhood chum, Eva, in a tufted booth. Only the tufts had little threads that were becoming unraveled, and someone had carved in the corner of the table "Jesus Loves You."

Eva poured catsup all over a plate of french fries, almost drowning them. "When I get nervous, I eat," she said.

"I know," replied Barbara, staring down at a now cold cheeseburger with one bite taken from it.

"I never knew . . . I never knew," Eva repeated almost unintelligibly.

"I know," Barbara replied. "You're not still going to him, are you?"

"Dr. Walters? No, I can't afford it anymore."

"I could lend you the money," Barbara offered promptly.

Eva shook her head. "No, thank you, really." She looked up sharply. "We were talking about you, not me."

Barbara sighed. "I spent hours walking around the city, sorting it all out, thinking about so many things. And then I just called you."

"Thank you for that," Eva returned as if she were saying "Amen."

"I guess it isn't your everyday problem, huh? Guess what! I'm three different people!" Barbara started to laugh but found she was crying. God, it was incredible. But now at least there was an answer. She brushed her tears away with a clenched fist.

Eva reached into her bag and handed her some Kleenex.

"Have *you* ever seen any of the other personalities?" she demanded of her friend.

"I don't know. There were times you acted strange, but . . ."

"Even when we were little?"

"I guess so," Eva admitted reluctantly. She was playing with the catsup on the plate, making designs with her fork. The french fries were gone. "The thing is, the women in *The Three Faces of Eve* and *Sybil*—they got better. And Dr. Walters will cure you, too, you wait and see. And then your whole life will come together. And just think, the book you're writing now about being a soap star as a child can have a sequel about your having multiple personalities."

Barbara couldn't help but smile at Eva. She was such a good friend. Even now she could make everything seem rosy—like there was nothing but a happy ending at the end of the rainbow. Eva had been her best friend—most of the time, her only friend —over the years. When they had gone to that private girls' school together, the other girls never made friends with her because she was a soap opera star. And because she wore long curls and pinafores and high socks. She had felt alienated except for Eva, who was her friend despite what the other girls thought. And then when they moved to Hammersmith, she and Eva wrote once a week. When she came back to the States to live, her friend was the only person she was looking forward to seeing, and Eva had never disappointed her.

"I'll always be there for you," Eva said now, placing her hand over Barbara's.

"I know you will," Barbara replied in a choked voice, holding back the tears. "I guess I'll have to tell Jonathan—only I don't know quite how to do it."

"Oh, *no,* don't do that." She smiled. "He likes you, Barbara. You're not far enough along in your relationship with him to tell him something like this. Besides, he might not understand. I mean, everyone in New York is seeing a shrink, but this is a little different."

Barbara nodded. "I guess you're right."

"When are you going back to London?"

"Tomorrow. Dr. Walters doesn't want me to go. He wants me to give up the flat."

"Then that's what you should do."

"I can't," Barbara said simply.

Eva smiled. "It takes awhile to get used to a psychiatrist, but in the end, you do what they say."

Barbara felt guilty. That made her somehow angry. An emotion she rarely felt.

"Don't look now, but look," Carolyn said, dabbing her mouth with a big red cloth napkin.

Tammy turned. The tall, sandy-haired man was walking toward their table. His complexion was ruddy. He had a vague smile on his face. When he got to their table, he borrowed a chair from a table nearby, put it on the side, and sat backward on it.

His smile turned into a sarcastic smirk. "Cops, huh?"

Carolyn decided he was nervous and this was the best way to bluff it out.

"I don't believe it. Two lovely ladies like you. I thought Joe was pulling my leg. Can I buy you two a drink?"

"No, thanks," Carolyn replied. Her expression said that the joke was over—they were taking charge.

"Nice of you to be so helpful," Tammy added.

"Don't mention it," he said, but some of the swagger had gone out of his attitude. "Mike Holler." He held out his hand.

Tammy was nearest. She shook it. "How well do you know Enid Thornton?" Tammy asked. Both women had stopped eating and had turned their attention to the impromptu interrogation.

The man let out a low whistle and shook his head.

"Does that mean you knew her?" Tammy demanded.

"You might say that. But no one knew Enid Thornton is my guess. She's what we used to call in high school . . . a cockteaser." He looked from one woman to the other. "Oh, excuse me, ladies. Wait a second . . . You're cops. Anything goes."

"Did you spend some time with her on Saturday, the twenty-second of May?"

"Yeah," he said. "That was the last time I was in town for business. Why? What's she wanted for? Armed robbery?"

"She's dead."

His mouth dropped open for a second in shock, and then he tried to cover it up. "What am I supposed to do . . . cry? She probably drove some guy crazy—drove him to commit murder."

"Well," Carolyn said, "it would have had to have been a very fast argument." She pulled her notebook out of her bag. "The desk clerk saw her come in alone around eleven. Then the hotel had some trouble with"—she looked into his eyes—"you trying to pound your way into her room after eleven. Then you were asked to leave. And then the desk clerk says she left after that. Were you the guy she drove crazy who was waiting for her?"

He shook his head emphatically. "I went back to the bar after . . . that. I thought she wanted me to run after her, that's all. I'm not some kind of masher."

"But you're a heavy drinker," Tammy added.

"I'm *not* a killer," he retorted quickly. "Ask Joe where I spent most of the night. Ask the rest of the guys who were sitting around the bar, the regulars here."

"She was killed at Ninety-sixth and Park. The time of death was around twelve."

He looked from one to the other. "Who says?"

"What? That she was killed?" Tammy asked carefully.

"No, the time of death. That shit."

"The chief medical examiner. And the body was reported found at around twelve thirty."

He leaned in, gripping the back of the chair, which pushed against his chest. "I can tell you this, and Joe and all the guys can vouch for it. The little lady, Enid Thornton, sauntered back into the bar after me at around twelve thirty. So you're wrong unless she has a twin or it was a ghost."


It was around nine thirty when Barbara came back to her Park Avenue apartment. The two-bedroom apartment seemed to overwhelm her, and as she sat on the sofa in the living room she thought she heard voices from the past like soft whispers about her. When the headache rippled across her forehead, the voices crescendoed and she had a vague awareness that she was changing. But it didn't matter. She shut her eyes against the rush of wind she heard in her ears and pretended it was just that she was on an airplane that had touched ground and was whooshing down the runway.

Slowly she opened her eyes and looked around. Then she ran into her bedroom, opened the door to one of the closets, and yanked out two white bags with gold lettering. She hadn't even taken the outfits out yet. Ripping the boutique bag, she lifted out one of the new dresses she had bought. It was red with one strap and layers and layers of shiny fringe. Outrageous. Every time she danced, it would shimmy.

The other dress was even better. A deep but bright blue, it was very low cut, with a sequined collar. She whirled around with the dress pressed to the front of her and sang a tune she made up. Oh, it was so good to come out. She was locked inside for such long periods of time. And as Enid it was the only time she ever had any fun.

When was the last time she had fun? Oh, yes, the Hotel Lincoln. And that man—she had forgotten his name. They hadn't gone dancing, though. But they had had drinks. She giggled. He had been so angry when she hadn't let him come up. The truth was she liked to have fun, but she was afraid of men a little. She liked to lead them on and then throw them out. And the gentleman had been too forceful. No gentleman at all.

She lifted out a gold jumpsuit made out of shiny cotton material, a white sweater with a plunging neckline dotted with pearls sewn on, and a shocking pink dress with crisscross straps and a flared skirt. *That's* what she would wear.

She would find a disco and dance and dance and dance. There'd be no problem getting a partner—there never had been. And she'd dance all night and then like Cinderella leave one slipper and then vanish into the night.

She laughed and found in the back of the closet some black high-heeled ankle-strapped shoes with rhinestones running down the heel. She picked up the hot pink dress again. Pity she didn't have pink shoes to match. She knew there was no way she could trick Barbara into buying some, but the next time she came out she would go shopping and get some pretty new shoes.

She flipped on the clock radio next to her bed, snapping her fingers to the jazz-rock song and dancing around the room. First, she'd take a long, sensuous bubble bath, then she'd get dressed and put on her makeup very slowly. That was half the fun—like packing for a trip. Outside she'd find a friendly, flirty cabdriver to take her to the jumpingest disco in town. And after that . . . There was no telling what would happen after that.

As she was running the bath water and sprinkling bubble bath into it, the phone rang. With a soft "Damn," she padded out to the bedroom wearing nothing but her panties. As she answered she flopped down on the bed and lifted a corner of the pink dress with her toe. "Hellloooo?" she sang into the phone.

"Barbara? It's Jonathan." His voice sounded tentative, as if he were afraid he was intruding. "I haven't talked to you for a while. I had hoped you would have called. I'm not sure of your schedule." He waited. Maybe he should have called her.

It's that creep Barbara likes, thought Enid. Well, I suppose I'll have to be nice to him. "I guess I lost track of the time," she answered sweetly, then giggled a little as her toe lifted the strap of her black heel. "I sniggled my toe. Did you ever hear of a sniglet, Jonathan? It's a made-up word, not in the dictionary. I sniggled my toe." She began to giggle again, liking the sound of it.

"Have you been drinking?" he asked innocently.

"No, honey." She couldn't help herself. It had just come slithering out. But it was barely audible.

Jonathan was confused for just a minute. He decided she had taken a nip or two. After all, she was a writer, an artistic type. She was entitled to her moments of frivolity.

"I was thinking," he continued boldly, "that I could stop over tonight. It's such a beautiful evening. Maybe we could go out somewhere for a drink." He felt like saying that she had already gotten a headstart, but he didn't.

Oh, *rats,* thought Enid. But the night was still young.

She could go out dancing after he left. She was certain he wouldn't want to go. He was so dull. She just didn't know what Barbara saw in him. But then, Barbara was such a creep herself.

She said yes, hung up, and then began to pout. As she was going back into the bathroom a thunderbolt of dizziness swept over her and she fell to the floor. Holding her naked shoulders, she began to cry.

And then it was gone. She was dazed, but she could get up. Dashing into the bathroom, she turned off the water. But it was too late. The bathroom had about a quarter inch of water with bubbles in a pool on the floor. She had had another spell. So she must have been one of her other personalities. She shivered, ran for her bathrobe, and went into the kitchen for a mop. She cleaned up the bathroom and took a bath in the water that was left in the tub, the bubbles having popped and melted long ago.

Back in her bedroom she noticed all the clothes laid out on her bed. The colors hit her first. Hot pink, gold, sparkling blue. And those ghastly shoes. They looked like something those girls who worked in Times Square might wear. How disgusting. What if Jonathan ever found out about her secret?

It was well after ten when the doorbell rang. Barbara was sitting in her bathrobe, watching television. She couldn't imagine who it might be. But she pressed the intercom button and heard the doorman announce, "Mr. Jonathan Seagull."

She thought a moment and then said, "Fine. Send him up." Then she tore into the bedroom, slipped on a beige shirtwaist dress, and then stood in the middle of the floor, wondering what to do next.

The doorbell rang. She ran a brush through her hair and went to answer it. The doorman's pronunciation of his name made her smile. Jonathan Seagull. Like the book. It was Jonathan Segal. He had probably been walking in the neighborhood and just decided to drop by. She wondered why he hadn't called, but this losing of time had her confused.

Instinctively she buttoned the top of her dress and then opened the door. The first thing she saw was Jonathan's half-balding head and horn-rimmed glasses peeking out over a bouquet of red, white, and pink carnations he was holding in front of his face. Barbara couldn't help but smile.

"For me?" she said stupidly, realizing that of course they were for her. They weren't for him. She never knew the right things to say somehow.

"I hope I'm not too late. The subway got delayed."

She looked at him curiously. Then he was expected. She would have to pretend she knew all along. "I'll get a vase to put these in," she announced.

He sat down on the couch, admiring her big apartment—

nothing like he'd ever lived in—and thinking that if she was drunk, she sure did sober up fast.

She put the flowers in a milky blue vase and set them on the dining room table, which was in the large living room.

"Would you like to go out for a drink?"

She looked at her watch. "This is a funny neighborhood to find a bar in. I have liquor and wine. Why don't we stay here?"

"Okay, if that's what you want to do."

"What can I get you?"

"White wine, if you have it. Though red is okay. Or maybe it's less trouble to have vodka. But then, you might not have orange juice. Oh, dear, I'm not being very assertive."

"I have white wine, Jonathan," she said.

"I'll have that, then."

Jonathan put his right arm across the top of the couch. Barbara came back with the two glasses of wine and sat on the left side of him about two feet away. Awkwardly he left his right arm where it was and sat sipping his wine.

"How long are you in town for?" he asked.

"I'm going to London tomorrow morning. I guess the jet lag will come at night." Dr. Walters didn't want her doing that, she recalled, but she didn't want to think about that right now.

"And how is your book coming?" he asked.

"Oh, you know how hard it is to write." She didn't want to talk about that. It was so hard she wasn't doing it.

He cleared his throat. "Would you like to go out for a walk? It's a lovely night."

She thought it over for a second. "Not really, Jonathan."

Jonathan laughed. "Oh, I see what I'm trying to do. Arrange to talk to you when you can't see me. When it's dark out."

"I beg your pardon, Jonathan?"

Boldly he maneuvered to switch his arms. The right arm fell into his lap, and his left arm rested on the top of the couch without touching her.

"I guess what I'm trying to say is that I want to start seeing you, seriously. I mean, as much as I can because I know you go back and forth to London and how important that is to you. That is, if you want to see me."

She looked into his light blue eyes.

"Maybe you don't," he added. "I mean, I might be presuming. Oh, dear, there goes my lack of assertiveness."

"I do want to see you, Jonathan," Barbara said directly.

"You know you're making it easier for me, Barbara."

"I know."

"It's just that you know how we both like to read historical sagas. I'm so unlike those swashbuckling heroes in those books, and that's the very reason I like to read them, I suppose. To escape. Because I don't feel I belong in this generation at all. That's why I'm so dull and boring. I was born too late."

"Oh, Jonathan, you're not dull and boring. But I've often had the same thoughts. Everything seems so fast and loud that I can't keep up with it. I wish I could walk slowly down Park Avenue in a long dress and carry a ruffled parasol."

"Well, I guess what I'm saying is that we're alike in so many ways. I think we kind of belong together. I don't mean to insult you."

"No, Jonathan, I think we are, too."

"We would be better able to survive if we banded together," he declared firmly.

A dull, thumping headache began to press at her temples. She sipped some wine, hoping it would go away, knowing somehow this one wouldn't.

"Jonathan," she said abruptly, "it's getting late." She didn't care really how late he wanted to stay, but the emergency of that headache worried her. What if she became another person in front of him? How could she handle that?

Jonathan stood up. "Yes, I'm sorry. I should have been more considerate. You have to travel tomorrow. Perhaps when you come back, we can spend more time together."

"I'd like that," Barbara replied, feeling the onset of the dizziness. She began walking to the door so that he had no choice but to follow. "Jonathan, I can't make any definite plans for the future." It was all she could do to keep her hands from her forehead.

"Of course, I understand," he said, nodding.

"But I do want to see you."

"Of course," he said, still nodding.

She had opened the door. He was halfway out, his hand still keeping the door open.

"I'll call you when I get back, Jonathan," Barbara said weakly.

"Of course. I understand," Jonathan replied as if she were rejecting him when she wasn't doing that at all. She felt the kiss on her lips before she saw it. And then it was gone. And the door was shut and he had gone.

Her headache was steady, persistent. She wanted to open the door and invite him back in. She wanted a second kiss. But it was almost all she could do to stagger over to the couch and clutch it as the waves of dizziness washed over her.

She blacked out for about five minutes. When she awoke, she got up uncertainly. Then she found her bag and dug out her glasses. Underneath the catercorner desk in her bedroom was an electric portable typewriter in a case. She pulled it out and set it beside her suitcases, where she wouldn't forget it.

# CHAPTER 16

Barbara woke up before her alarm went off, and she thought she heard birds chirping outside her window. But the reality was that the window was closed and the air conditioner was on low. She looked around and saw that all her bags were packed and her typewriter was next to her suitcases. She couldn't remember doing that. She closed her eyes and smiled, sinking into the pillows. She was all packed. She must have been one of the others after Jonathan had left. Maybe there were some pluses to being many personalities. Private joke. Bad joke. She brushed a tear away.

Thinking of Jonathan, she realized he had been on her mind ever since she woke up. He wanted her. No one had really ever wanted her in her whole life. And he was right. They were so very much alike. Maybe he wasn't everybody's idea of Prince Charming, but he was so gentle and so understanding. Not like the other men she had known. The married man that went back to his wife. The man who got away. She had almost been engaged, but he changed his mind. Well, they had all gotten away. But now there was Jonathan.

He had the most potential for a real relationship that would last. Rolling over, she buried her head under the pillow so that it looked like she was wearing a fat bonnet. How long could she ignore her problem with Jonathan? It worried her, but she didn't want to put a dent in her good mood.

In the shower, singing merrily, enjoying the feel of the spray massaging her back, it didn't seem like she had any problems. She felt good, whole. Jonathan had seen to that.

Toweling herself dry in the bedroom, she looked out the window and saw the sun speckling the flower buds just blossoming on the strip of grass that divided Park Avenue. It was almost six. New York was still asleep. Funny, there were more newspapers in London. She was so busy that she had even forgotten to read the *Times*. She must get around to it. Jonathan was such an intellectual.

On that Tuesday morning, the small task force on the third floor of the decrepit Nineteenth Precinct was as active as an ant hill. The line set up for people to call the task force with leads sounded like one continuous buzz.

Carolyn had put Erase under her eyes this morning, but she knew it didn't cover the bags. She had tried to sleep but had gone over and over the problem in her mind. How could Enid Thornton have been murdered at twelve and been seen in the bar by Mike Holler at twelve thirty? He then claimed he went back with her, she rebuffed him again, and she went up to her room. "Anyone hear from the Medical Examiner's Office yet?" she shouted across the room. All she heard was noise and then, "No, not yet."

Tammy came into the room, looked at Carolyn, and shook her head. She had made one more stop alone the night before to talk to the night clerk at the Hotel Lincoln.

"I would have called you late last night, but I was afraid you wouldn't sleep."

"I didn't anyway," Carolyn replied.

"The night clerk, the guy on after midnight, says that around one or one thirty this Enid Thornton came to the desk and said she lost her key. So he had to give her one of the extra ones."

They heard the shout across the room. "Medical Examiner's Office."

"It almost doesn't matter anymore. Unless they're about two or three hours off," Tammy said.

Carolyn took the call, nodded her head, grunted, and hung up. "Time of death was twelve. There's no mistake. Better tell the captain. Have any aspirin?"

"You're going to need it," a voice said. "Anyone seen this?"

Tammy and Carolyn turned as another detective spread out the latest edition of the *New York Post* on Carolyn's desk. "BLOODBATH," he said.

"I can read," Tammy replied.

"I don't believe it," Carolyn moaned, reading the copy underneath. The headline for the *Post* covered almost half the page in big black block letters—a headline meant to shock.

"Believe it," Tammy said. "They didn't have a kidnapped baby available, so they picked our story. And the first stabbing you couldn't even find."

"This is the cover?" someone else who had come over said. "BLOODBATH? It sounds like the French Revolution."

"Shh, I'm concentrating," someone else said, trying to read. " 'These women stabbed as blood rains down on the streets of New York City' . . . Whew."

"Don't they talk about how attractive the women were? It's always 'A beautiful blond found stabbed.' "

"Makes for good copy," Tammy said. "Come to think of it, sometimes I think they stage things. Like they kidnap babies so they can write about it. Anything to sell papers."

"Well, this is going to sell papers," a voice behind Tammy's shoulder said loudly.

"For a long time," chimed in someone else.

"Listen to this," Carolyn said, tracing the newspaper print with her finger. " 'Just ten days ago there was a similar slashing that took place on upper Park Avenue. Police are hunting for an attractive brunet known as Enid Thornton, who was a resident at the Hotel Lincoln.' "

There was a silence.

"Someone leaked," Tammy said softly.

No one said anything. In every major case there was usually a piece of information the police kept to themselves. It was not let out to the newspapers and was often used to trap a suspect.

In this case it was the fact that Enid Thornton was a resident of the Hotel Lincoln. And even that fact wasn't reported correctly. She had only stayed there overnight.

"Maybe they have a hotshot reporter at the *Post* who does his job well," someone said to break the tension.

"Impossible," Tammy pronounced.

"And now the media will be on our back and so will the mayor and maybe the governor." Everyone looked up, listening to this new voice. It came from Captain Fulani, a captain from Manhattan South who was heading up the ever-growing task force being stuffed into the small squad room.

Captain Fulani had no glamorous bluster about him. He looked to some, although they wouldn't dare voice it, a lot like Humpty-Dumpty. He had a roly-poly belly, thinning hair pasted across a pinkish scalp, blond eyebrows, and a fat lower lip. He also possessed a slight speech impediment, which gave him the aura of an Alfred Hitchcock. In fact, his nickname to a closeknit circle of buddies was "Cock." Captain Fulani was one of the most respected men in the department, both for his record and his integrity.

"That's right," he said. "We're going to get plenty of flak on this. The feminists, the Village Independent Democrats, the Park Avenue Association, if there is one. And we'll hear from the city because, my friends, we have a demented murderer on our hands. We knew this, but now the papers are articulating it for the benefit of the already frightened citizens of our fair city. I'm going to double the force."

Everyone had now turned to Captain Fulani and knew suddenly that they were in a meeting.

"From now on we have to do some switching. I want Zuckerman and Kealing to stay on top of the Thornton case." He was pointing now like he was choosing a ball team. "You two on the new murder. You, you, and Davis bum around Eighth Avenue and see what you can come up with on the hooker. You four stick to phone work, do anything the other teams tell you to do, and man the calls coming in. Anything that's not an obvious crank, mark down—and some of those, mark down just in case. We'll do more when we have more men."

If there had been a sound in the room, which there wasn't,

they would have heard it. The phones were off the hook, and the busy signal had died a long time ago. Every single person in that room knew they were working on the most important case New York City had seen in a long time. And now the city knew it, too.

Captain Fulani gave no closing statement or peptalk. He just turned and walked to his small adjoining office to the side of the squad room.

Tammy and Carolyn looked at each other. About five headaches back they had wanted to tell the captain about the discrepancy in time on the Thornton case. " 'Stick to the Thornton case,' " Tammy mimicked, not disrespectfully. "Where do we begin now?"

Carolyn shrugged.

Captain Fulani was on the phone with One Police Plaza when the loud knock on his door came. "Come in," he said. The knocking grew louder. "I said, come in!" he shouted.

It was an officer but not one from the task force. "There's a woman, been making a scene downstairs, demanding to see someone. Says she knows something about the lady from the Hotel Lincoln."

Captain Fulani sighed and finished his phone call. "Next time, send no one *up*. Got that? We'll come down. But send her in."

A young woman, very plump, her hair piled on top of her head in a cap of dirty blond braids, came into the office. She was holding a shopping bag and wringing her hands together nervously.

She looked at the uniformed officer and at the man with the fat cheeks and big lower lip. They stared at her. "My husband made me come," she blurted out. "He's waiting down the street. He don't like police stations, but he said what I did was wrong. He wanted me to give you this." Carefully, lovingly she lifted from the shopping bag something wrapped in white tissue. She folded back the tissue, and there was a white leather bag with gold snaps. "I used to work in the Hotel Lincoln. I was a chambermaid. I found this in Room 712 and took it. It was the room of that Enid Thornton. My husband read it in the paper."

Captain Fulani picked up the phone and barked, "Send Zuck-erman and Kealing in here right away!"

Tammy and Carolyn were in his office in less than a minute.

Captain Fulani lighted a cigar. "These are Detectives Zucker-man and Kealing, and this is . . ."

"Olga," said the young woman almost defensively, "Olga Grunwald."

"She was the chambermaid in the room Enid Thornton occu-pied," Fulani said.

"Room 712," Tammy said.

The woman nodded and then appeared to be almost sizing them up. Women police officers were beyond her experience, let alone women detectives who wore beautiful clothes. She handed the women detectives the bag. "I took this out of the room."

Tammy took the buttery white leather bag. She looked inside and took out the little leather case full of credit cards. Then she felt immediate disappointment, as if she had been stabbed by a knife.

"All these credit cards say Polly Manklin. Not Enid Thorn-ton."

The woman shrugged as if she didn't understand English, but everyone knew she did.

"You found this bag and took it out?"

Olga interpreted this to be a criminal accusation. She looked around at the drab ugliness of the precinct room. In one corner olive-colored paint was hanging in curls ready to fall off the wall. She looked at Carolyn like a trapped animal who knew it was caught and was looking for a way to escape. She looked at everyone who was staring at her. "I took it. I wore it with my wedding dress. Then my husband, he said I have to give it back because he read about the murder of the lady in Room 712."

"But her name was Enid Thornton, not Polly Manklin," Car-olyn reiterated. "Was there anything else in this bag that you took out?"

Olga shook her head desperately. Her husband had told her to tell them about the money she had taken, but she was afraid they would arrest her. Easy for him. He was waiting around the corner in a coffee shop.

"When did you find this bag? Do you remember?" Tammy asked. "What was the date?"

"Date?" repeated Olga. "I don't remember. I left the hotel shortly after. But"—her voice was so small and shaky they had to listen very carefully—"I found it in the back of the bottom drawer of one of the dressers. Most people in hotels don't pack their things in the drawers, you know. There was nothing else in this drawer but the bag."

"Can I use your phone, sir?" Tammy asked.

Captain Fulani pushed it toward her.

Tammy dialed information, got the number of the Hotel Lincoln, and dialed it. Since the case was in the newspapers, the desk clerk on duty treated her more respectfully this time.

"I want to know if after Enid Thornton left Room 712 a woman by the name of Polly Manklin checked in."

A male detective had come into the room and was waiting to speak to the captain. They all waited for the desk clerk at the Hotel Lincoln to check the book.

Finally she nodded, answering, "I see. Thank you." Then she hung up. "No woman named Polly Manklin stayed at the hotel. The next occupant of the room after Enid Thornton was a man." She shrugged slightly. "Who the hell is Polly Manklin?"

The detective who had come into the room and was waiting scratched his head and said, "Wait a second, wait a second. I've heard that name. I was having a drink last night at Mario's with some of the guys from the precinct, and somebody had a missing person case where the relatives were a real pain in the ass. Rich lady. The name was Polly Manklin. We kept ribbing him about it all night." He cocked his head. He wasn't going to repeat some of the dirty jokes. "Detective Goldstein. That's who it was. Lady was missing since Saturday, the twenty-second of May, and they were calling him every hour on the hour, driving him crazy. Yeah, the woman's name was Polly Manklin."

Tammy, Carolyn, and Captain Fulani exchanged glances.

"The twenty-second of May was the night of the murder," Tammy said. "Enid Thornton was murdered at twelve," she continued, addressing Captain Fulani. "But our witnesses say she came back to a bar after twelve. So she would have to have been a ghost or a twin."

"The witnesses are reliable, sir. That's what didn't check out," Carolyn chimed in. "So doesn't it stand to reason that she wasn't murdered?"

The room was quiet.

"That the body was Polly Manklin's?" Tammy added.

"Goldstein will have to bring the whole family in for an I.D. I'll tell him," the detective in the back said. "Huh, so she *was* really missing. The famous Polly Manklin."

"What about this Enid Thornton?" Fulani wanted to know.

"Don't you see, sir?" Tammy spun around. "She was the *murderer.* Not the murdered. She must have swapped bags with the victim, who was really Polly Manklin."

"What about the white bag with blood stains belonging to Enid Thornton?" a voice asked.

"What about it?" the detective in the back said. "They turn up on the subway all the time. So the Transit Authority found it. So what?"

"Something else," Tammy said. "When we checked with the night clerk, he said Enid Thornton disappeared without returning her key."

"How could she have returned the key if it wasn't in her bag?" Carolyn said.

Captain Fulani scratched his balding head nervously.

The detective at the door cleared his throat. "I'm missing something here."

"Oh, it's very simple," Carolyn explained. "The woman who was murdered is not who we thought it was."

"Not Enid Thornton," Captain Fulani supplied.

"Right."

"So we'll check out Polly Manklin."

"That's probably who it is. But it doesn't matter *who* was killed . . . Don't you see? The woman we were looking for as the victim is the murderer!" Tammy exclaimed.

They were sitting in the garden. It had rained the day before, and all the wet surfaces glittered in the sun. Barbara's plane had landed in the evening, and she had rested well the night before.

Today she had written two chapters in her book.

Then she had gone shopping on Oxford Street, stopping at Selfridges and Marks and Spencer to pick up some dishes and some silverware and a big comforter. She couldn't carry them home and she didn't want them delivered, so she thought of calling Lockey for a ride. By a stroke of luck, Barbara thought, she was home. Now they were sitting chummily, having tea in the garden. Barbara thought, looking at the lush garden greenery, that it had been a good day. One of the best she could remember in a long time. She found herself thinking of Jonathan again and again.

"You seem pleased, ducks," observed Lockey.

"Yes, I was rather happy today."

"Shopping does that to you," Lockey replied, nibbling on one of the cucumber sandwiches she had made. She studied Barbara's flushed face. "Either that—or a *man.*" She laughed.

"Why, Lockey, you're a witch," Barbara answered.

"Tell me about him, then." So, this Barbara Hargrove, the rich lady from New York, had a beau. That was good to know. Barbara had made her a confidant and she could manipulate her now. It was like pressing a weakness button. And soon she would know more. Like why this woman bounced back and forth between two continents. And what she really did. "Tell me about him, love," she said, licking her fingers. "I'm all ears."


Later that evening Barbara decided to go for a stroll after dinner, the perfect capping to an almost perfect day. She was coming down the steps when she heard a voice from behind. Looking up, she saw that it came from above.

"Going out for a walk, are you?" Lockey yelled down.

Barbara looked up. She wondered if Lockey kept a chair by the window and just watched the action in the street. Mum had used to do that. "Just a short one. It's such a nice evening." The first streaks of violet were just starting to tinge the sky.

"Well, you don't want to go too far now, love. You heard about all those murders of young women in London."

Barbara didn't say anything. She had no television yet or

even a radio. She had always been very bad about reading the papers.

"Slashed with a knife. Three of them. You remember the first one. You had just taken the flat. It was right near your hotel. But it might not be such a good idea to go traipsing around Hammersmith after twilight. You can't be too careful when there's a maniac like that loose. And nobody knows what he looks like."

"I won't go far," Barbara assured her.

Barbara walked to the edge of the park. It had gotten progressively darker. Twilight had turned to a shadowy dark purple. It would be night in a short while. A murderer could strike with a knife in the park under a tree. She shrank back. No one was walking. Did everyone know of the murders? She turned and began walking fast. She wondered how the young women were murdered. Lockey didn't say. Did the man rape and strangle his poor victims? Her ankles began to throb as she walked faster. She wouldn't run. This was London. She stumbled over a crack in the sidewalk, and as her throat constricted she took her midheels off and began to run.

The next morning Barbara packed a small case, tidied up the papers near her typewriter, which rested on a small table Lockey had loaned her, and left London. Two chapters had been completed. She could remember everything she had done since she had gotten there. There were no lapses of time she couldn't account for.

The first thing she did when she arrived home that night was to call Jonathan. She wondered when he picked it up on the first ring if perhaps he had been waiting by the phone. She was touched by that.

"I'm back," she announced cheerfully without even saying hello.

"How did the work go?"

"Better than ever." She bit her lip. She didn't want to say something was better than nothing. And she didn't have the nerve to tell him she thought her progress was because of him.

"Let's have dinner," he suggested. "Are you too tired after your trip?"

She could tell he was pleased she had called. "No, no, I'd love to go."

"There's an Indian restaurant I love on East Twenty-third Street. It's a lovely little restaurant if you like that kind of food."

Barbara wasn't sure she did. "Sounds wonderful, Jonathan. And at dinner you can tell me how *you've* been."

It was close to nine when they were seated at a little table in the back of the dimly lighted restaurant. She noticed it immediately.

"Jonathan, you seem a little upset tonight."

He was flipping his fork back and forth between his thumb and forefinger. "How astute you are. I am."

"What's wrong?"

"Oh, remember our conversation about not belonging in this century, not fitting in somehow?"

She nodded.

"Today in the library there was a woman who really irritated me. I can't quite forget it. She wanted this book and then that book, and she kept coming up to my desk. Finally she arranged it so that I had to get up and point her toward a stack of books. She chucked me under the chin and said, 'You're a cute one. I'd like to see more of you.' I rushed back to my desk and never left the whole afternoon. Now, don't get me wrong"—his fork was turning faster and faster—"I'm all for women achieving and everything, but I can't stand aggressive, flirty women who treat me like that. I feel like a sex object! It ruined my whole day."

Barbara's throat felt constricted, although she wasn't exactly sure why. She also felt a tiny pang of jealousy that such a horrid creature should feel that he was available for the asking.

Just talking about it made Jonathan feel better, and being with Barbara was always so wonderful. She was one of the nicest, most stable women he had ever met.

It was close to eleven when they finished their long, leisurely dinner.

"Shall we go for a walk?" he suggested.

"Oh, not tonight. I have a busy day tomorrow. I'll take a raincheck on that. Maybe for tomorrow night."

"Writers," he said, "they march to a different drummer. Do you write when you're in New York as well?"

"Research," she said softly. She would be in London all the time if it wasn't for Dr. Walters. But maybe coming back wasn't so awful now, since she got to see Jonathan.

Jonathan hailed a cab for her and then kissed her on the cheek. His hands in his pockets he walked toward the nearest subway entrance.

In the cab, Barbara leaned her head back against the seat. Perhaps she should have taken that walk with him, but she could feel the jet lag. And tomorrow was the nine o'clock double session.

Alvin Walters waited for Barbara, feeling especially good about himself. This was a dream case. It made his whole practice worth having. The others just paid their ninety dollars an hour and got treatment, but she would become one person again.

He twisted his gold wedding band around his finger. He had been divorced for two years, but wearing it saved him a lot of trouble. His female patients got crushes on him. It was part of the transference. And then he would have to make them see that it was a fantasy attraction. Without the wedding ring, his practice would be unmanageable, since most of his patients were women.

He looked at his watch and paced around the office. It was about three minutes to nine. But Barbara Hargrove was always punctual. The excitement was unbearable.

At nine exactly he heard the chime that sounded when someone came into the office. He wondered which personality would manifest itself today.

Walking into his waiting room, he said, with his usual energy and enthusiasm, "Hi! How are you today?"

"Never felt better," she replied.

He stepped aside and let her lead the way into his office. She sounded so up that for a moment he thought it was going to be Enid. But when she sat down in the chair and he studied her blouse buttoned up to the top button, her blazer with the circle pin, and her flat shoes, he knew it was Barbara. In a good mood. "Well, what's happening in your life?" he asked.

"I wrote two chapters in my book and I shopped for some things on Oxford Street and I had a lovely stay in London. I remember everything I did," she said, her eyes shining.

He frowned. He wished she would give up the childish notion of acting out her fantasies in Hammersmith and get down to work.

She went on, her good spirits carrying her. "And . . . I'm going with a man," she continued, pleased with herself.

"The man you told me about. Jonathan."

"I don't remember telling you about him."

He smiled. "Oh, but you did. Enid talked about him. She doesn't like him."

Barbara started to stutter. "J—J—Jonathan's a fine person." She felt Dr. Walters didn't like him. She sensed his disapproval, and for some reason, she wanted desperately to please him.

"This isn't the best time in your life to have a relationship. I mean, I'm not going to tell you to give it up, but there are obviously serious limitations. What if you became another personality in front of him?"

She stared at him. She wasn't in good spirits anymore.

"Now, let's get on to something important. Have you ever been hypnotized?"

Barbara kept staring at him, nodding her head slowly.

"Well, it's the way cases like yours are treated. And I'm very excited about it. We just go deep into your past. And if the past is so painful to you that you had to hide out in several different personalities, then the treatment must be done through taking you back to find out why this happened. And the only way to do it is through hypnosis. Do you understand?"

She said nothing.

"But first I'll have to inform all your personalities."

Barbara felt humiliated, but she didn't know what to say. She wanted to get better—to be whole—but she was scared. It was as if she didn't own herself anymore.

Dr. Walters studied her face. "First, I'd like to call on Enid. May I do that?"

Barbara nodded, but nothing happened.

"May I please speak to Enid?" he asked forcefully.

Barbara sighed. Then her eyes shut, and her head rocked forward. There was a tremor in her torso that made her head shake like she had palsy. He waited.

"Yeah?" she said.

"Enid?" he asked hopefully.

"Yeah?"

"I'd like to, if I may, go back into your early life. Is that all right?"

"No, it isn't all right, okay? Do it to her. When I get a chance to come out, I don't want to remember the sordid details. Don't put me through that shit. I want to have fun."

Again Dr. Walters was dazzled by her personality change. He would challenge anyone who said this was a put-on. It was impossible. Once you got to know Barbara, you knew she could never put on this kind of act.

He experienced a sensation that was not unlike being drunk. If he could summon one, he could probably do it again and again. It was obvious to him that he was wasting his time with Enid.

"May I please speak to Dana?"

Barbara began to feel dizzy and slightly nauseous. In the distance she thought she heard a teakettle whistling.

She picked up her bag and rummaged through for her tortoiseshell glasses. "Yes, Dr. Walters," she said, businesslike, putting them on.

He was mesmerized. At first it was difficult to tell Barbara from Dana. "I've asked the other selves if I could go back into the past. Barbara was compliant."

Dana's smile was conspiratorial. "Barbara is always compliant. What did you expect?"

Looking at Dana reminded him of his colleague, Beth Belmont. She should be in here witnessing this—someone should. It wasn't that she was too busy, which she was, he realized. He hadn't called her in because he didn't want to share it with anyone. He didn't want anyone to steal his thunder.

"Enid wasn't as helpful," he said.

"Enid is restless. She hasn't been out enough. By the way,

Thornton is Barbara's mother's maiden name. The Thorntons were quite prim and proper."

"Would you be able to go back into the past?"

She shook her head. "I can't. I wasn't there. I only came out when Barbara's father died and she began to act out her Enid personality. I take care of them. Like that first visit in your office. It was I who came out. Barbara had a dizzy spell and tried to cover for it. I came out to help you. I gave you Enid's card."

"Interesting. Dana, may I please speak to Barbara?"

Her face flushed a deep rouge and contorted with the effort. But in seconds the features of Barbara settled back on her face, and the eyeglasses had been folded back into the bag.

"Barbara?"

"Yes," she said. It sounded weak.

"I want you to tell me about your mother now. We've talked about your father, but every time we begin to talk about your mother you change personalities."

"Where do I start?" she asked dully.

"I'm going to take you into the past. When you were a very little girl. As far back as you can remember . . ."

About fifteen minutes later Dr. Beth Belmont, sitting with a patient, her chair opposite the wall Barbara sat near, was startled to hear screams. When the screaming subsided, she heard sobbing that sounded harsh and hoarse like a dog barking.

She tried to figure out, without losing her concentration on what her patient was saying or openly acknowledging the noise, which patient Alvin had in there. Then she remembered the multiple personality case. He had said something about seeing her for a double session early in the morning. Fascinating case. She imagined the screaming was an expansion of the problematic nature of the case. She had never treated a patient for dissociative personality disorders.

At ten forty Barbara, her hair hanging in her eyes, her complexion looking sallow, stumbled out of the office.

"Have a nice day," Dr. Walters said warmly. When Barbara reached the door, he put his hand on it and looked into her eyes. He said, "This is why I want you here in New York. Where you can be treated."

Her face was expressionless. Going out of the waiting room, she noticed a man with a face tick sitting in one of the wicker chairs, reading a magazine.

It was in the cab that Barbara tried to sort it all out. She could never trust herself on public transportation coming out of there. She was trembling. Everyone would stare at her. The worst part was that she was sure she was beginning to get better. She could account for three whole days, but in approximately the last hour and a half she could remember only about ten minutes.

Tears began to spurt from her eyes. She had sat there in that chair and—she was like a trained seal—he did something to her or *them.* She turned her face to the window so the cabdriver wouldn't see how upset she was. What did she do to deserve this? It was a living hell.

Almost choking, she felt the anger rise up like bile. The dizziness. The headache. She smiled, wiped away the tears, and felt around in her bag. The wallet, her business cards, a lipstick . . . but not what she wanted. There were those silly glasses. That wasn't what she needed. Nothing sharp and shiny. She'd have to stop at the apartment.

She hadn't been allowed to come out at the psychiatrist's office. He didn't summon her. Though, how could he? He didn't know about sweet, little Priscilla. The one who had a collection of nice, shiny sharp knives.

# CHAPTER 17

Dawn Snow sat in an Eighty-second Street coffee shop on Broadway, eating a cheese danish and sipping some tea. She had nine dollars left in her pocket. A dollar and a half would go to pay the bill, and then she would have seven fifty. That was enough to take that tap class on Columbus Avenue. It would make her third class of the day.

Might as well blow her last couple of bucks. All the rest of the week she would have to work office temps to make up the rent and pay for classes. That small check she was expecting wouldn't go too far. But the thought of taking the tap class made it all worthwhile.

She slung her lime green dance bag over her shoulder, paid her bill, and smiled at the waiter, who smiled back. It was fun to take three classes a day. Everything was fun since she moved to New York.

The waiter noticed her. He took in her sparkling smile, the full dance bag. He saw them come and go, the happy hopefuls, especially in this neighborhood. But this one had something special, he thought to himself. Maybe one day she would make it, and he'd see her name in lights somewhere.

Dawn didn't know which way to go. It was dark out now.

Eighty-second Street was pretty dark and empty. On the other hand, walking up Eighty-third might make her a few minutes late.

Aw, the hell with it. She'd take the dark street and walk fast. People got paranoid about New York anyway. What difference did it make which street she took as long as she got there in less than five minutes? Maybe if she changed into her leotard fast, there would be time to practice her double pullbacks.

Priscilla had walked the city now for miles, but no street seemed right, no person ignited the bubbling rage inside her. Her purse was open slightly, and she fingered the sharp knife safe inside it. Then she approached Eighty-second Street, and she saw the young woman swinging her bag. She watched the way it bounced against her hip. Mum had had a bag like that. Priscilla turned the corner, walking softly. She was wearing sneakers. The only sound on the street were Dawn Snow's midheeled sandals, which slipped off her heels slightly when she walked and made clickety-clackety noises on the sidewalk.

Dawn was lost in thought. Her class was five dollars, which would leave her two fifty, but her office temp check from the week before would be waiting in her mailbox when she got home.

She was humming a tune she was learning to sing when Priscilla came close behind. She never heard her. When the knife tore down her back from the base of her neck, under the clump of taffy-colored hair, and screeched silently down to the base of her spine, she was so shocked she couldn't say anything, had she been able to. Priscilla watched her fall, crumbling into a pool of her own blood.

She wanted something from this one. Some souvenir. In the big bag she might find something. She looked around. The street was empty, but she thought she heard the sound of voices somewhere, maybe coming from an open window.

She didn't have time. But it wouldn't do to run. She stooped down and wiped the blood off her knife onto a part of Dawn's lightweight jacket that was still clean and dry. Then she put it into her purse. Walking energetically but not noticeably fast, she went toward Amsterdam Avenue and hailed a cab. In the cab she fell against the seat, her head throbbing. Within minutes she was Barbara again. When she got out of the cab, she looked at her watch, which said eight thirty. She wondered what she had done for about the last seven and a half hours.

When the buzzer sounded, Barbara pressed the button and told the doorman to let Jonathan up. She was still buttoning her blouse. Quickly she tied a wraparound cotton skirt around her waist. She was moving slowly. He had called to get together, that he was in the city. She had just come out of the shower. No particular reason. It was just that she had felt strangely unclean.

It hadn't helped. She still felt unnerved and unusually jumpy. It bothered her very much that after feeling so well she couldn't account for a whole afternoon again. She was sure it had something to do with that session at Dr. Walters'. She felt humiliated —used. What she really wanted to do was stop seeing him. It was nothing more than a business transaction, she thought angrily. She paid him every week. And yet she knew it was too late to leave him. She would be afraid without him. He knew what her problem was. He could cure her. Even though she detested the sessions, she had to trust him. She wanted to be well so badly.

When she opened the door, she was still fidgeting with the top button on her blouse. Jonathan wanted to kiss her hello, but she looked so distracted that it didn't seem natural to do so. Maybe he was being too demanding wanting to spend so much time with her when she was in New York, but he couldn't help himself. Barbara filled a need in him he was just beginning to realize he had.

"You look well, Barbara," he began.

"Sit down, Jonathan," she replied somewhat stiffly. "I'll get you a drink, and then we can decide where to eat."

He was just beginning to think that something might be troubling her, but before he had a chance to ask she had left the room. He thought of following her for a second, but it was as if he didn't want to give voice to anything that might spoil their evening. His dates with Barbara were always so perfect.

In the kitchen, Barbara poured two glasses of white wine from the big half-gallon jug. Halfway through the second glass she realized there was more wine on the counter than in the glass. She stopped pouring and gripped the counter. She shut her eyes and shuddered. But she knew there was no way to stop it.

When she came into the living room, the first three buttons on her blouse were unbuttoned and her hair, which was usually parted serenely in the middle, fell to one side, hanging in her eyes. Her shoes were off, and she sauntered into the living room like a native Hawaiian girl manipulating a grass skirt.

It was a few seconds before Jonathan would admit to himself that something unusual was happening to Barbara.

"Why don't you ever take me dancing?" she said, pouting.

He choked on his wine. "I didn't know you liked to dance . . ." Then he added, "I don't know how."

"Well, I do and you never take me anywhere. Just those long, boring dinners. I despise Indian food, by the way."

Jonathan stared bleakly into his glass of wine. He felt like he was sinking into the quicksand of depression. What had he done to deserve this? She had never acted like this before. Why was she picking on him?

He wanted to ask her, but instead his ears and nose pinked with anger and he retorted peevishly, "Well, we certainly don't have to go to any more Indian restaurants. But I wish you would have told me before I wasted your time."

Was this their first fight—or what? He didn't understand. It was almost as if she weren't herself anymore, which was impossible.

"Bet your ass we don't have to go anymore," Barbara chirped. Then she laughed and moved closer to him on the couch. She chucked him under the chin. "Say, you're cute, after all. How come such a cutie like you is such a stick-in-the-mud?"

Jonathan stood up as if the couch had hot coals on it. "Maybe I'd better leave," he said indignantly. He was trying very hard not to cry. Women had always disappointed him, belittled him, rejected him. And then he had found Barbara. She was sweet and understanding. He was thinking as he walked from the subway to her house that evening that he was going to ask her to marry him soon.

"Aw, stick around. We'll have some laughs," she said, slapping him on the thigh.

Then he watched in horror as she tried to stand, then slipped, falling back onto the couch. Mesmerized, he saw her head turn around in circles, to his horror reminding him instantly of *The Exorcist*. He reached out to help her in some way, but she recoiled, blinking her eyes rapidly and fighting not to slip off the couch.

So he just stood there watching her, not knowing whether to sit or stand. His stomach was churning.

Moments later, she spoke. "I'm sorry, Jonathan, that you had to see that."

He was relieved that she sounded like Barbara again, but he was confused. Her voice had a stern edge to it—a voice almost like that of his second-grade teacher, whom he had been afraid of. He watched as she crossed the room and looked through her bag. She took out a pair of glasses with tortoiseshell frames and put them on. "I didn't know you wore glasses?"

"Only when I'm writing," she said. "I was writing just now. That's why I acted so brash and brazen." She swallowed hard. "Did you believe my act?"

He stared at her, the sad, sickening feeling still with him. "You know how I feel about women who act like that," he replied. Then he sat down. "But if it was part of your work . . . Which character is that in your book?"

"Oh, one of the women on the soap."

He shook his head. It had been too much.

"Oh, Jonathan," she pleaded, "I'm sorry if I shocked or surprised you, but maybe it's better this way." She took a deep breath. "Maybe it's better for you to see just what kind of pressure I'm under."

Dana waited for his answer. Maybe that would save Barbara. Then again, maybe it wouldn't. But it was a valiant try. She knew how important Barbara's relationship with Jonathan was —how it kept her stable. Wasn't it just like that devil Enid to come along and ruin things for her?

"I think I'd better go, Barbara," Jonathan announced dully. "I'll call you."

She saw him to the door, and they looked at each other.

He made no move to kiss her, Dana thought sadly as she shut the door. She adjusted her glasses, which were slipping down her nose. It was better he left. Poor man. What could he get out of this?

# CHAPTER 18

The meeting was at Stephen Knight's mother-in-law's house. Had Johanna lived, she truly would have been his mother-in-law. So while she really wasn't, she had become a surrogate mum and her house had become his house ever since the night he had lost Johanna. He stayed there because he was afraid to stay alone.

Annie, her pale blue eyes roaming around the cluttered, dirty apartment, took in her surroundings. So different from her spacious clean flat with everything in order. The baby, Rachael, was with a sitter, and Kenneth had been cheered to find she was lunching with some lady friends. He would be very angry if he knew she was with these two men.

Brian Harrington, the third member of their group, had some real conflicts about being there. It seemed awfully radical to him. But then he thought of his Jane being knifed just after rush hour on the Underground. And the coroner's sad message. She had been almost three months pregnant. And she hadn't told him yet.

Stephen sat on the couch, unshaven, with a notebook resting in his lap. "I propose we call ourselves Three against Victimization," he said.

"That's fine," said Brian, his beautifully articulated British accent a contrast to Stephen's cockney, "but it doesn't abbreviate well. Three against Victimization. That's TAV. Not very catchy. Nothing you can do with that."

"Well," said Annie, hesitant and shy at first to speak, "we don't have to abbreviate it. Actually it's more dramatic sounding and important this way."

"Another thing that bothers me," said Brian, wringing his hands nervously, "is if"—he began to tremble slightly—"if there's another murder. Then do we shift the name to Four against Victimization? Or maybe Five? God, I wish they would stop that monster."

"I wish he had never started," Stephen added bitterly. "But it would be the name even if we had to change it to Four against or Five against . . ." A flickering smile lighted up his face for a moment and then vanished. He had thought about this endlessly. It was his main preoccupation. He hadn't worked since Johanna's funeral, and he didn't care if he ever did again. All he wanted was to see Johanna's murderer captured. "One of the things we have to do relentlessly," continued Stephen, the self-appointed leader and organizer of the group, "is keep after the press for more coverage. There clearly isn't enough."

"Clearly," echoed Brian.

"Clearly," said Annie in her soft voice.

"There was that other case, that ax murder in Soho, that stole the headlines," Brian Harrington said.

"The public must be outraged," Annie declared adamantly, balling her fists.

"Yes, they must," agreed Brian, thinking he was almost getting used to Annie's American accent.

"Then there's Scotland Yard," Stephen said provocatively.

"The great Scotland Yard," Annie added sarcastically.

"They haven't solved the case yet," Stephen said.

The pitch was building up in momentum to that of a revival meeting.

"No, they haven't," Brian seconded, nodding.

"Maybe they need a little help," Stephen ventured. "Maybe a bomb scare threatening them would make them try harder."

There was an uncomfortable pause. Annie stared at the ceiling. Brian bit his fingernails. And Stephen waited.

"I wouldn't get into that," Brian said at last. "I don't think we should do anything militant."

"At least not yet," Annie agreed.

"What do you suggest we do, then?" Stephen asked equitably.

It was Annie who spoke up. Her eyes seemed darker to Brian at that moment. "Let's follow them."

The two men stared at her.

"Follow those two detectives, the ones who get their names in the paper. Let's get some sort of disguise and see what it is they do or they don't do. Maybe they're hiding something. Maybe they know something they don't want the public to know." She brushed back a clump of flaxen blond hair from her face and smiled at them sweetly. "Let's kick a little ass."

London is the busiest international air center, they say, in the whole world. Its main airport is Heathrow, and the number-two spot belongs to Gatwick. The men from Scotland Yard almost wished the murder had occurred in Gatwick. It would have been slightly less difficult than trying to find out who stabbed Julia Davidson in a ladies' room in the busiest international air center and got away. And now after ten days and a monumental effort on behalf of Scotland Yard the murder was no closer to being solved than when the body was first found.

The same was true for the other two cases, the unfortunate woman who was stabbed in the Underground and the tour guide, knifed in almost broad daylight in one of London's poshest districts. The pressure from a city that derived much of its income from tourists was enormous. Only a few days after Julia Davidson's murder in Heathrow Airport, all the airlines had called the Yard to register formal complaints. Air travel to London had fallen off.

Out of the millions of people who passed through Heathrow Airport daily, Scotland Yard had to find the murderer. After stabbing Julia Davidson, he could have gotten on a plane to India, South Africa, the Soviet Union, the United States, anywhere. Or he could have slinked out of an exit and disappeared eventually into the London streets.

After five days and an army of computers working overtime, they had evidence that a J. Davidson, a J. L. Davidson, and a Julia Davidson had flown out of Heathrow Airport on the night she had been killed. J. Davidson had flown Air India, and J. L. Davidson had been on BA. Julia Davidson had flown TWA to New York City, and that was whom they were interested in, although the other names had to be investigated as well. Julia Davidson had been going to fly TWA to New York City on Wednesday evening, the twenty-second of May, before she had been cruelly mutilated and murdered. They needed to find out how it was that she reportedly made the trip anyway.

Detective Inspector Cavendish and Detective Sergeant Hollings were at Heathrow Airport early that morning to further investigate the death of Julia Davidson. Other men from Scotland Yard were investigating the clues in the other two murders. Trailing Cavendish and Hollings were a heavily disguised vigilante group calling themselves Three against Victimization. They were there that morning because Stephen Knight, under cover, had followed Hollings into a restaurant and listened very closely on the other side of a potted plant.

He was standing now behind a passenger with three pieces of beautifully matched luggage. His abundant strawberry-colored hair was slicked under a rubber dome, with hair sprouting out on the sides. His jacket was padded and very thin rimmed wire spectacles slipped annoyingly down his nose, tickling him. He looked at least twenty years older and thirty pounds heavier. Not far away, slightly to the left, was Brian Harrington, feeling self-conscious in a policeman's costume and twirling his club nervously. Right behind Cavendish was Annie, her pale yellow hair buried under a wig of bright red curls. Her limpid blue eyes sparkled behind dark blue–rimmed window glasses. Her middle was covered with padding, which she wore underneath a pale lavender maternity dress.

They ignored each other.

When Cavendish and Hollings disappeared, she would eavesdrop on their conversation.

Inside the small room, Cavendish and Hollings met with two airline executives and a stewardess from Pan Am.

"You asked us to check the computers and our personnel for a discrepancy of any sort. I don't know if this is what you're looking for, but we don't want to leave a stone unturned, do we?"

Cavendish nodded.

The stewardess spoke next. "There was a woman. She wanted to return a ticket. She said she suddenly didn't feel like flying that night. I put the credit card through and it took. But then it showed up on the computer printout. It was a mistake. Computers make them. It lapsed, you see."

"But it went through that night?" Hollings asked, his notepad out.

"Yes, at that time, it went through and she got her credit. Now we're stuck. She no longer has a Pan Am credit card. Another thing that bothers me is that the ticket was put in the name of Barbara Hargrove. And yet the credit card was in the name of Dana Hargrove."

Hollings and Cavendish stared at the woman hungrily. It was meager stuff compared with what they were up against.

"Tell the detectives what you told us, Eunice," prompted one of the executives.

"I remember seeing *Barbara Hargrove* on the ticket. Then I noticed *Dana* on the credit card. I asked her what her real name was. She replied, 'Dana Hargrove.' "

"What was the billing address on that account when it was active?" Cavendish asked.

"A post office box number, Inspector Cavendish."

Hollings' pen was poised.

"In New York City."

Cavendish nodded wearily. The day had just begun, and already they were faced with the kind of impossible obstacles that made this case more unsolvable by the day. It was aging him, and he didn't like that.

One of the executives handed him a computer printout. "There's one hundred and eighty-six more names that canceled flights on that night."

Cavendish and Hollings would receive the same reports from all the other airlines.

"If there's any way we can help you," one of the executives said, "don't hesitate . . ."

Hollings asked the stewardess, Eunice, if she had a description of the woman named Barbara and Dana Hargrove.

Cavendish wondered seriously about the best use of his time here. Other men could have covered this. So there was a discrepancy in someone's name and a credit card with a New York box number. All that had to be checked. But he was convinced they couldn't possibly be looking for a woman. The logistics of a woman having the sheer animal strength and daring to be a mass murderer seemed to him to be impossible. And unprecedented, for the most part. Time was wasting. He watched Hollings taking notes.

"Her hair was brunette, shoulder length," Eunice recited. "She was fairly attractive, no great beauty but better-than-average looking. A pleasant-looking woman, if you know what I mean. But not someone you would pick out in a crowded room."

"Could you be more specific?" Hollings asked politely.

"Well, she was wearing glasses. Tortoiseshell frames."

"Any visible scars or blemishes?" Cavendish pressed, wanting to move on.

"No, none that I recall."

"What was she wearing?" Hollings asked.

"Let's see." The stewardess looked up at the ceiling. "A gray dress, I think. She was carrying a trench coat."

"Her teeth?"

"Well, she didn't smile really, I don't think."

"Earrings?"

"I don't remember," Eunice replied forlornly. She had a formidable collection of pierced earrings.

"That's all?" asked Hollings.

"That's about it," the stewardess answered.

Hollings closed his notebook. They took the computer printouts, shook hands all around, and left the office to blend in with the crowd in bustling Heathrow Airport.

"We'll have to connect with the New York City Police Department on that post office box number," Hollings said.

Cavendish grunted. They would have to check everything. "I just have this feeling, though, that we're going off on a bit of a tangent, if you know what I mean."

"Sir?"

"All this stuff about these women. It keeps us from finding the killer."

"But you don't think," Hollings said cautiously, "that the killer might have been a woman? It seems to point that way a tad, doesn't it—at least for now, that is? And the witness in the Underground saw a woman running away."

"Yes, but, Hollings, do you really think a woman murdered three women in cold blood? It doesn't make common sense!"

"I would have to think about that, Inspector, sir," Hollings replied softly.

They proceeded through the jostling crowds in the airport, being careful not to step on any small children, completely unaware that they were being followed by a pregnant woman with red curly hair. Annie stayed as close to them as possible. She heard every word of their quiet conversation. As they neared the TWA counter she smiled. There was no shut door this time.

Annie added a pair of sunglasses to her disguise as she kept doggedly close to the two detectives. She couldn't remember when anything had fascinated her so much. The baby was boring compared with this. And the baby didn't do anything about the burning hatred she felt against the person who had stuck a knife in her mother's back. She would never give up until they found him.

Nearby, pretending to walk nonchalantly, was the inwardly shaking Brian Harrington. He had moved cautiously after the two detectives, following Annie's lead. If trouble broke out in the airport, if anyone even yelled for a bobby, if he even saw another bobby, he would run, all right. Far away. It was an idiotic costume, and he wished they were through so he could take off.

Stephen Harrington, a *London Times* folded under his arm, was making his way closer with shuffling, mincing steps. It would be easy to get into earshot of the two detectives. It might be easier to plant a bomb scare in Heathrow Airport to threaten them to move faster.

Annie positioned herself in line in front of the TWA counter, standing to the side of the counter, blending in. The two detectives and the man had stepped aside to talk. As she strained to hear she realized, with a jolt, that even if she weren't so elaborately disguised, they still wouldn't recognize her. Even when she was growing up in Boston, she had respected the police department. They would take care of things. After the conversation she had just heard, she wondered about the world-famous Scotland Yard. Something seemed wrong to her.

"It's just that I have this photographic memory," the man was saying. "I read about it in the papers—that her name was Julia Davidson. And then I remembered writing out a boarding pass for her just before she went on the plane. Hard to believe, isn't it?"

Annie could feel her stomach juices begin to burn. For a moment it really felt as though she were pregnant again.

"What's hard to believe?" Cavendish asked. "That you remembered the name or that the same Julia Davidson flew on the plane?"

"Oh, that she was murdered. That's what I meant. I don't think *she* flew on the plane. I just issued her a boarding pass."

"It was a woman," Hollings asked.

"Oh, definitely," the man said, looking at him somewhat oddly.

"Can you describe her?" Cavendish asked.

Hollings opened his notebook. Annie all but stopped breathing so she could hear.

The man looked up at the ceiling as if he were trying to form a mind picture. He wanted, above all, to be correct. But even though he had such a perfect memory, the woman had not stood out as memorable. "Well, she had dark hair, parted in the middle, I believe."

"A brunette?" Hollings added.

"Yes. Not bad looking, mind you, but she wasn't that good-looking either."

"Did she wear glasses?" Hollings asked quickly.

"No, not that I remember. No, can't say that she did."

"Anything outstanding. Her teeth?"

"Oh, no smile on that one," he replied. "I do remember that.
All business and a bit of a scowl."

"What was she wearing?"

"A coat of some sort. Raincoat. I suggest you track down the
stewardesses on that flight. I don't know whether they'll be able
to help you or not. I mean, those planes are like little flying
cities. But they may come up with something helpful. You never
know."

You never know, thought Cavendish. In the end Scotland
Yard represented the worst kind of plodding detail work. He
was sure that all his men must have been bookkeepers in another life.

Annie saw Stephen Knight, altered, lumbering closer. She
gave him a subtle signal, her eyes going to the ceiling and then
to the floor. She had information. A woman had flown to New
York in her mother's place. She had the boarding pass. So she
must have had her mother's good navy bag. The leather bag she
had picked up in Rome and given her mother just this last
Christmas. She had remembered a pair of beautiful navy shoes
her mother had had that she never wore because she just
couldn't find the right bag to match. Julia always wore matching bags and shoes. Then she had the right bag. And then she
had been killed, and it had been taken from her. For what? So
someone could fly free on TWA under her mother's name? The
thought made her feel nauseated.

Stephen Knight interpreted the signal from Annie, promptly
sat down, and pretended to read his *Times.* His eye caught a
sandy-haired woman rounding up a crew of tourists, and he felt
a lump in his throat. She reminded him of Johanna. She had
done that. Gotten up early, rounded up a troup of bleary-eyed
tourists, and then put them up in their hotels. And she loved
her job.

"Don't they all look alike?" he had asked Johanna after a
while, listening to her talk about her day.

"No two tourists are alike," she had told him. "Even the
Americans."

Brian Harrington wished he could fade and dissolve into the
nearest wall. He had called in sick today. What if someone from

his firm decided to fly? Here he was, wandering around Heathrow all dressed up like a trained monkey. Well, the costume would be back to the rental shop by evening. And it did look almost like Annie and Stephen were on to something. Heathrow was so crowded. Just like the Underground. If he had known she was pregnant, he would have never let her take the tubes. Did she keep it from him because of her other miscarriages? Because she didn't want to disappoint him? He felt the tears well up in his eyes, and he sniffled loudly. Then he looked down. A little boy was staring up at him with wide eyes.

Cavendish and Hollings thanked the man and began walking away.

"You know," said Hollings, "it might have been a woman who murdered her, then took the bag and the boarding pass and flew back to New York. In that case, maybe she'll come back." There was no answer from Cavendish. "Or maybe we should send a few men to America?" There was still no answer. "For a while I thought the descriptions of the two women were the same except for the glasses."

Finally Cavendish spoke. "It's a common description. A lot of women have brunette hair and are average looking."

"But a woman did have the boarding pass and flew under her name," Hollings said.

"Don't suppose anything. Men can dress very skillfully as women. It's the fashion," Cavendish said. "Or maybe someone found the bag with the boarding pass in it."

They were silent then, each man absorbed in his own thoughts.

Annie, who was walking close behind, began to lose herself in the crowd. Her padding had begun to slip. It was time to stop and compare notes with the others. She had heard enough. And her ivory complexion had turned a noticeable shade of pink. She had heard too much. They were right. Scotland Yard didn't know what it was doing.

The two detectives drove back to the Yard, not saying much to each other, mulling over the details and the possibilities in the murder of Julia Davidson, trying to link it to the other murders.

Back in the office, Cavendish's phone was ringing immediately. All calls had been screened as to their importance. He half expected at this hour to hear from his wife.

Hollings was sitting in the chair opposite his desk.

"I see," said Cavendish in a low reply.

For a second, Hollings thought, with dread, that another murder had occurred.

"I see," Cavendish repeated, his anger showing clearly. "No," he said to the caller, "I didn't see you in the airport." He was motioning for Hollings to have the call traced. "I didn't know I was being followed." Then he was holding a receiver. "Hung up," he said.

"I couldn't trace it, sir. What was it?"

"They call themselves 'Three against Victimization.' "

"Not another terrorist group?"

"No, nothing like that. But they did threaten a bomb if we don't solve this case."

Hollings looked up sharply. "Stephen Knight behind this?"

"Clever reasoning," Cavendish complimented him. "I didn't recognize the voice." He began to pace around his office. "The oddest thing is, Hollings, that they followed us all afternoon. And what's even more curious is their foolish belief that the only one who could have committed these murders is a woman."

# CHAPTER 19

Jonathan Segal lived alone in an apartment in Brooklyn near Atlantic Avenue. He had a first-floor apartment, and he couldn't see out through the window gates to see if the sun was shining.

Jonathan was sitting at a table balanced by a book under one leg. He was staring dismally at a half-eaten bagel. He had neglected to put butter or jelly on it. His instant coffee looked and tasted like cold mud.

When he had walked out Friday night, she hadn't persuaded him to stay. Yesterday he had wanted to call her, but he couldn't. He had just walked around the streets of Brooklyn, feeling sorry for himself. How could she have acted like that? Why did she turn on him? He felt that everything nice he had liked about her had been twisted and thrown back at him as a mockery. It was like a bad joke. And then the way she had covered it up. That she had been acting out a character in her book. That was the part he disliked the most.

Let's face it, he thought, he had been tricked. He would never call her again. Ripping off a piece of the dry bagel, he crammed it into his mouth but choked trying to swallow it. And when he

choked, he realized that the tears rolling down his cheeks were
tears of grief and frustration. He was crying.

He kicked aside his chair and went over to the couch that
doubled as a pull-out bed. He had thought he had been lucky to
find this one-room apartment five years ago. Now it seemed like
a tiny prison.

What was his life *really?* Also a prison. He was just a librarian. It was just a job. Most people, he knew, thought he had no
personality at all. Except Barbara. She had thought he was special. She had made him feel important.

In an un-Jonathan-like gesture, he picked up an ashtray that
he kept for guests—though none ever came—and flung it
against the wall. He watched it split and shatter to the floor and
made no move to sweep it up.

To think that for weeks—no, months . . . actually since the
first time she had come around to the other branch of the library—he had been happy. That's how he knew the difference.
He wasn't even alive. For if he had never known how happy he
was, how would he know how miserable he was now? Why did
people have to get close to each other if this happened? He had
purposely avoided heavy intimacy. It was too risky. Now he
knew he had been right.

His hand reached for the phone and then dropped it like he
had touched hot bacon grease. Did he expect her to call him,
though? He grunted silently. Sure she would.

He looked around the apartment and saw some sunlight
streaking through the window. He had a right to feel hurt,
didn't he? She had disappointed him. Why should he pick up
the phone and give her a second chance. Why? Because he felt
like he was dying, that's why.

He dialed her number. The phone rang once, twice. He
waited while it rang ten times more before he hung up. His
imagination soared. If she could act like such a flirt with him,
could she do that with other fellows? Did she date other men?
Was she with someone now, not even thinking about him?

Barbara frosted her bagel generously with cream cheese, then
set it down, having no intention of eating it. Eva was slicing into
a steaming ham omelet. They were having brunch in a coffee

shop on the corner of Third Avenue and Eighty-sixth Street. Barbara's face was still shiny from the tears that had fallen.

"You don't remember anything? You blacked out, and the next morning you remembered he had left?"

Barbara nodded. "It's like being robbed. I don't even remember going out to dinner with him—unless one of the others did. But I just *know* something happened. I can feel it."

"Well, what did you do yesterday? Did you call him? Did he call you?"

"No. He didn't call me. I picked up the phone and then I put it down again at least a hundred times. What was I supposed to say? Did you notice anything different about me last night? Did I say something wrong? Could you tell me which one I was?"

"I see the problem," Eva said matter-of-factly.

"Dr. Walters doesn't want me to go to London and write my book," Barbara put in suddenly.

"Then you shouldn't," Eva said. "Do what he tells you to do. You could bring up this problem with Jonathan. Does he know about your relationship?"

Barbara looked unhappy. "He didn't say much. Only that it wasn't the best time for me to become involved."

Eva shrugged, not really knowing what to say.

"How many times do I get the opportunity?" Barbara asked mournfully.

"Well, maybe you're making a mountain out of a molehill," Eva comforted her in her usual let's-fix-it manner. "Why don't you just call him and say hello and then take it from there?"

"I can't do that," Barbara insisted, stirring the tea she wasn't even drinking.

"But you could wait for him to say something. Like whether you had a fight. Or why he left. Or what time he left. Or if you went to dinner. Or even which one you were." Eva put down her fork as her ham omelet had lost some of its appeal. "I'm sorry, Barbara," she said, looking into the eyes of her miserable friend. "This *is* weird."

When Barbara came home, she resolutely picked up the phone, determined to reach Jonathan and say something to open it up between them. The phone rang once, twice. When she realized he wasn't in, she hung up, not knowing if she was relieved or not.

She paced around her spacious apartment restlessly. She picked up a cut-glass paperweight and turned it over and over in her hand, then put it down. She stood in the middle of the room, stuck in time, not knowing what she wanted to do next.

Do what *Dr. Walters* says. That was the message she was getting loud and clear. But it made her angry. All her life she had done what people said. And now she wanted to do what she wanted to do. She thought of Dr. Walters, his hands on the arms of his recliner, staring at her, and she felt very angry. She didn't know exactly why. But she was free of him anytime she wanted to be, wasn't she? It was a business transaction. She could leave anytime she wanted.

But even as the first dizziness began, she knew she was lying to herself. She couldn't leave him. Even though all her instincts said he was making her worse.

There was no real earth-shaking reason why Alvin Walters had become a psychiatrist. He just had. Like one of his friends had become a gynecologist without too much soul-searching.

But now he could see why he had chosen psychiatry. Barbara/Enid/Dana Hargrove was the reason. He felt so stimulated by the case that even now he was writing a paper to present sometime next spring. The case had become an obsession, and he freely admitted it.

From all his readings, there could be other personalities lurking or waiting to be born. The new personality could be a male. Or a little child. It was like popping corn, he was afraid. The more work they did, the more personalities might spin off. He wanted to prevent that. Three personalities were enough to cure. He planned to kill Enid first, and then Dana would go naturally. That would leave Barbara the dominant personality, and he could treat her.

He gazed at, without really seeing, the fluttering gauzelike white curtains in his apartment. The author he had approached to do the book on Barbara had declined, wanting the patient to be fully experienced. He thought the book could be started now. The hell with it. He'd find someone else to work with.

Maybe it would be a movie, he mused. Why not? It had been thirty years since *The Three Faces of Eve* and over ten years since *Sybil*. Well, he had one, and she was an ex-soap actress. He would want to be a consultant when the movie was made, of course.

He recalled what Barbara had said in one of her nonhysterical moments under hypnosis. That the most vivid memory of her mother was when she used to sit in Barbara's dressing room and stare into the lighted mirror, studying her face, as if she were the star and not Barbara.

The mother. He pictured the actress who played her, looking a little like Joan Crawford. Yes, the mother. It was almost hard to believe. At first he thought it might have been the father. But the father was a superparent compared with some of the chilling tales he had heard about the mother while Barbara was under.

Beth Belmont had suggested somewhat subtly that he turn the case over to a specialist. That had pissed him off, but he didn't tell her. He didn't invite her to any more sessions either. He felt he could handle it as well or even better than a so-called specialist.

It was nearly dusk when Tammy and Carolyn pulled out of the precinct driveway.

"Think about it, Tammy."

"How can I back out with that drunk weaving in and out? Don't tell me he's going into the precinct! They'll only throw him out."

"But really, let's say you weren't a detective," Carolyn persisted, although it was clear Tammy wasn't paying much attention to her. "Let's say you were my best girlfriend, and we were having lunch at a real swank place, and . . ."

"I would never lunch at a real swank place. Try Wendy's. It's cheaper."

"Oh, you know what I mean, Tammy," Carolyn said, eager to make her point. "Look, how would I know if you had a knife in your bag or not? You could be my best friend, yet I wouldn't know that you had lost your marbles and were a killer."

"I don't think she does it that way. Kills her best friend."

"No," Carolyn agreed, happy that Tammy was at least on her wavelength. "But picture this. You're walking down that street. You're alone. You sense someone is following you. You even walk down the middle of the street. There's a little grocery store on the corner—you can see the lights. It's a little neighborhood affair, all warm and lighted up. You know you'll be safe on the corner. You walk faster. This other person walks faster. But this is what changes everything. Before this mass murderer, you thought it was naturally a man that would overpower you. Now you realize it might be a woman following you. And you don't dare turn—she might be the killer and somewhere in her bag or deep down in the pocket of her raincoat is a nice sharp knife waiting to slice through your back. Get my point? Isn't that more than a little creepy for the female population in New York to live with?"

"I like your little drama," Tammy agreed. "There's only one problem with Enid Thornton. She doesn't exist."

"Not so far she doesn't exist. But she did exist. Long enough to kill Polly Manklin, at least. Her bag didn't just roller skate over."

Tammy turned the corner and parked the car about a half a block away from the restaurant. The two of them walked, their shoulders touching, both hoping Mike Holler would show as he had promised over the phone earlier.

"There he is," Tammy said to Carolyn as they walked through the swinging imitation-saloon gates to the restaurant/bar. Mike Holler was sitting alone at the bar, sifting a handful of peanuts through his fingers, and sipping his third vodka martini.

He was thinking about Enid. They had told him that she was no longer suspected of being the victim . . . She was the suspect. Enid. That crazy broad. She could have killed him, for God's sake. Good thing he didn't get into her room. And yet to help them stalk her? The lady was off her noodle—anyone could see that. It went against his protective instincts. He sighed. He supposed he didn't have a choice, though. He signaled for another drink when he saw the two female detectives approaching his spot.

"Do you want to reenact the scene of the crime?" he inquired sarcastically, as ruddy-faced as before.

"I've heard that that sometimes helps," Tammy replied matter-of-factly.

"If you were reconstructing your evening with Enid Thornton, where would you start?" Carolyn asked.

"Oh," replied Holler, "that's easy. From the minute she walked in the door. I was sitting like I am now, much in the same place, and I noticed her. I have eyes in the back of my head at the bar. She sat opposite me, and then I went over and bought her a drink. Everything was great at the bar. She gave me the come-hither look, then I offered to buy her dinner on my expense account. Then something strange happened."

Tammy and Carolyn were waiting.

"She went to the ladies' room. And after she came back, she acted differently. It was like she was too good to have dinner with me. That made me angry. We were supposed to have dinner, and she stands me up like right in front of my face. I swear, no broad ever did that to me."

"What do you think happened to her in the ladies' room?" Tammy asked.

"Damned if I know."

"Maybe she made a phone call? Is there a phone in the back?"

"Nah, it's in the front." The bartender set another martini in front of him, and he scooped up the olive with his thumb and forefinger and sucked on it thoughtfully.

"Where is the ladies' room?" Tammy asked.

"Back there," Mike replied, like a man with the experience of waiting for many ladies to freshen up.

"I have to powder my nose," Carolyn announced.

"Me, too," Tammy echoed. "You'll excuse us for a minute?" She glanced at Mike with a smart-ass smile on her face.

As they made their way, weaving between chairs and tables and dodging waiters with big platters, Tammy said to Carolyn, snickering, "Tell me a woman detective can't do things a male detective can't!"

No one was in the ladies' room except for the matron, who was filing her nails in front of the counter. On the counter were

a little dish with two quarters in it and a whole array of ladies'
room freebies that most women hardly used. Tammy and Carolyn flashed their shields and I.D.'s immediately.

The matron was heavyset, her eyes watery. "No kidding,
huh? Lady cops," she said.

Carolyn tagged her for an over-the-hill prostitute.

Tammy reached inside her big bag and pulled out the new
artist's sketch they had on Enid Thornton based on Mike Holler's description. She was depicted as having shoulder-length
brunette hair, pushed behind one ear. An earring fell from the
other ear. She had a lively, animated look about her. Her mouth
turned upward at the corners.

"Ever seen her in here?" Carolyn asked.

"Honey, I seen a lot of gals that look like her. Dark hair,
earring. Everyone wears one earring these days. I mean, I really
don't look too hard at any of them. They do their stuff and
plunk a quarter down and then they leave. What's she wanted
for?" She blew a strand of waxen blond hair out of her eyes.

"Murder," Tammy informed her without emotion.

"Jesus," said the matron.

Carolyn couldn't help but think back to just a few days ago
when they were looking for her as the victim.

"So you never saw her?" Tammy asked, feeling a stab of
disappointment, although she had not hoped for more.

The woman shrugged. "Can't say that I have. But, hey, I'm
not the only matron on duty. There's another girl. Black
woman, Lurlean. She'll be here tomorrow."

"Is she on duty Saturday nights?" Carolyn asked quickly.
"That's when the murder happened, and she was seen in this
restaurant."

"Yeah, that's her night. Like I says, she'll be here tomorrow."

"Thanks," the two detectives called over their shoulders as
they left the ladies' room.

When they came back to the bar, they were hoping to question Mike further, but he had disappeared.

"Men's room?" Tammy asked.

"Left," the bartender replied. "He had a date."

"We'll be in touch," Carolyn said as they turned to leave.

Carolyn and Tammy made their way toward the front door.

"Sounds more like he picked someone up," Tammy muttered dryly. "Well, we've got all his numbers. Do you think we scared him into thinking he might be a suspect?"

"No, I don't think we really did that well enough. Okay, let's go back to the House of Horrors. When we come back tomorrow night to talk to the other matron, we might see him."

They drove back to the Nineteenth Precinct in silence, each woman trying to solve a different angle of the case in her head.

It was when they parked their car in front of the precinct that Tammy remarked, "You know, we never did that before."

"What?"

"Work separately in silence. I didn't come up with anything . . . Did you?"

Carolyn shook her head. They passed the small lobby and Tammy waved to the officer standing in front of the American flag hanging on the wall. As they walked the steps up to the third floor, Tammy kept her hand on the creaky banister and realized there was a piece of peeled paint under a fingernail. "There is one thing," she said. "If I were naming the killer in this case, I would call her . . . Jane the Ripper."

"Clever," agreed Carolyn. "I was thinking of about the same thing."

At the top of the stairs, red-faced, bulbous-nosed, unsmiling Captain Fulani was waiting for them. For one short moment it reminded Carolyn of a father welcoming two daughters who had stayed out past their curfew.

Coming up the stairs and closer, they saw he was holding the late edition of the *New York Post*. The headline was in big bold letters: JANE THE RIPPER.

"Son of a bitch," Carolyn said, "sir."

Captain Fulani's voice was low and tremulous. "The mayor called, the governor called, and I wouldn't be surprised if the President called. Do you two have anything new on this Enid Thornton?"

Tammy started to tell him about the matron they were going to visit tomorrow night, but judging from the mood he was in, it would be like setting a trap for themselves. The reality was they had nothing yet.

They all walked into the noisy task force room just in time to hear the shout. "Another stabbing just reported. It's the Twentieth Precinct, Captain Fulani."

That *wasn't* the news he had wanted to hear. He picked up the phone. "Yeah . . . Yeah . . . Slashed . . . Two days ago? You just figured it out . . . Yeah . . . Dinner . . . Soon . . . Yeah, that place in Little Italy . . . good spaghetti, fantastic tomato sauce . . ." In a moment, he hung up. He took out his handkerchief and wiped his forehead. "Okay, Zuckerman and Kealing. Check this out. This time we have an I.D. A dancer by the name of Dawn Snow. She's lying in the morgue with a tag on her toe."

# CHAPTER 20

It was past eleven o'clock when they walked down the stairway into the morgue in the basement of the building. A close, sweet smell lingered in the chilly air. In the corner was a freezer. Somewhere Dawn Snow was in a stainless-steel box, which the harsh fluorescent lighting would soon reveal. Tammy gulped. Only nineteen years old.

It was hard for her to look at the body under the white sheet when it was rolled out. She noticed the beautifully shaped dancer's legs; her protruding feet were turned out in a permanent ballet position. All Tammy could think of was her little Donny home sick with a temperature of a hundred and one. Had it gone up in the last hour? Did he hate her and think she was all kinds of a lousy mother for not being with him? Was her husband becoming a surrogate mother because she was a cop?

She looked down at the sweetly chiseled face of the dead girl. What the hell were her parents doing now? Sleeping? Watching television? They would send the usual telegram informing them of their daughter's death. Tammy already knew this kid wasn't from New York. Where would the telegram go? To a nice white shingled block on a quiet tree-lined street, with a church next door in . . . where? Kansas? Ohio? Arizona? She turned away. Okay, maybe she was an absentee mother sometimes, but if she could protect young girls from being cut up randomly like this one, was it really so unforgivable?

One of the pathologists handed them the contents of the dead girl's purse in a paper bag. Tammy ruffled through it. A wallet with seven dollars and fifty cents. The usual comb and lipstick. Then she fingered an envelope. A letter. And in the upper-left-hand corner a tiny sticker: Mr. and Mrs. Stuart Snow. She gulped. Flint, Michigan, natch.

She knew that it had to be run through for fingerprints but she carefully opened the envelope. Something fluttered to the floor. She bent over. A tiny square of wax paper with ten stamps inside. So she would be sure and write back.

Just then the pathologist said eagerly, "She's a little smaller. But we sewed her up."

"You did a great job," Carolyn remarked casually, a wave of nausea rolling over her. She hated visiting this vaultlike place.

"Maybe I'll go home now," Tammy said quietly.

"We'll take the car back to the precinct. I think you should. You know what they say about tired detectives—they make mistakes."

"No, it's not that. Donny's got the flu. I was just thinking how much I would enjoy smearing Vicks Vapor Rub on his chest. I mean, it isn't right, you know? A boy should know he has a mother when he's sick."

Then she thought of Mrs. Snow, who was going to find out very soon that there would be no letter from her daughter, Dawn.


It was barely ten o'clock Monday morning. Barbara and Jonathan sat on a park bench in Central Park.

"Think we can find a hot dog vendor?" he asked.

"Oh, Jonathan," she said, "it's too early. How could you think of a hot dog at this time of the morning?"

Her hand was resting in his, and he held on to it tightly. Jonathan was wearing jeans rolled up at the bottom. Barbara had never seen him in anything but a suit and a tie.

"What if my boss could see me now?" he quipped. "Just sitting on a bench in the park with you, contemplating a hot dog." He hadn't gone in to work this morning. He had phoned in sick. And it wasn't a lie. He had felt like he was very ill. And then a miracle. Barbara had called. And now they were together, holding hands on this beautiful June morning. And it felt like death had left his body.

"I'm leaving tomorrow night for London," she said.

Jonathan nodded. He could live with that.

They had, in reality, discussed nothing. She had only said that she had tried to reach him Sunday. He had admitted that he had tried to call her, too, but she wasn't in. He didn't say that Sunday he had wandered about the city aimlessly, had ended up on the Bowery, looking at all the lonely old men lying against buildings. That he had crossed over into the twinkling lights of Chinatown and wished she were there to share his dinner with him. The dinner he hadn't had.

She had not told him the agony she had been through—not knowing what she had said, who she had been, if he would ever want to see her again. She didn't say that at one point Sunday evening she had dialed his number over and over and over.

Barbara leaned a bit into his shoulder. "Jonathan," she said firmly, "I think we should talk."

Jonathan held his breath. He didn't like to talk. Whatever it was she wanted to talk about, he didn't want to hear. But he knew he had to.

Barbara swallowed and sighed. She had thought this over very carefully. In fact, she had hardly slept on Sunday night. If he were to know the truth about her, he couldn't know it all at once. And maybe she would never have to tell him that she was three separate people. Maybe she wouldn't have to. She would just get better. She had been doing fine until she got back to Dr. Walters.

"The thing is, Jonathan, I'm seeing a psychiatrist."

Jonathan let his breath out slowly. That was all?

"I have some emotional problems I have to work out. Do you mind?" Some people had strange notions about psychiatrists. Her mother had hated them. "What do you think?" Barbara asked bravely, wondering what he would really think if she told him the stark truth. "I wanted you to know . . . because sometimes I might get a little carried away, um, like I did Friday night, and . . . I think we can work it out."

She waited for some clue as to how she might have acted Friday night, but Jonathan didn't say anything. He was staring at a woman pushing a baby carriage and a dog jumping and yipping, following the turning wheels.

"What are you thinking?" Barbara pressed softly.

He was thinking that he had learned long ago that you couldn't have everything you wanted. That something was better than nothing. He coughed, although he didn't need to. "I think people should do what they have to do to get by. If you need to see a—uh—physician, then you should see one." He watched the woman pushing the carriage come closer as she passed them by. He wished he were the tiny little baby safe and cozy in that carriage, just for a second. The truth was that he didn't believe in psychiatrists.

They were silent. There was no more activity to watch in the park. Finally he ventured, "Are you sure he's a good one? There are a lot of charlatans about, and it's very hard to tell. Especially, God knows, in New York City. You should have a good one, Barbara."

Barbara thought of Dr. Walters. She didn't know if he was a good one or not. She was afraid to think about it.

Just then a little girl materialized before them. Keeping her eyes fixed on them, she swung a tiny hula hoop around her slim hips. They laughed at her together. Her mother caught sight of her, ran over, and brought her back to the next park bench.

"I wonder what it would have been like to have been a child?" Barbara said wistfully. "I was always working."

"I know what you mean. I never felt like I was a child either." He held her hand even more tightly. It was right. They did belong together.

A couple of the men were sitting around Patrick's Bar, off Columbus Avenue, bullshitting. It had become a favorite hangout where men from all the precincts could meet, discuss cases, get some feedback. Hank Patuto came there to unwind. He didn't believe in choosing your watering hole too close to your precinct. And Patrick's was far west and way uptown.

"You still banging that broad?" one detective asked another.

"Which one?" a short, chubby detective asked. His belly was hanging out over his pants. He was drinking beer and chewing gum at the same time.

"Coil."

"Oh, yeah, her. The one who had trouble with the IUD. No, the wife found out. She was waiting for me outside a motel one afternoon. That was the end of that."

"Anyone else?" someone asked.

"Like I said, my wife put an end to that. Threatened to divorce me if she caught me playing around again. There's the mortgage, there's the kids, one's ready for college, there's the car payments . . . And there would be alimony, *heavy* alimony. No, just me and the wife now." He raised his glass in a halfhearted salute, and there were a few laughs as predictable as a soundtrack.

"I hear what's-her-name, the rookie from the Fifth Precinct, used to pose in the nude for *Playboy* magazine," a detective said.

"Yeah?" Everyone leaned in. There was a lot of interest.

Hank Patuto was impatient. He cut right in. "What do you think of this case they're calling Jane the Ripper?"

"Oh, yeah," someone said, "that task force thing. The papers never let go of it. Biggest case to hit the city in a long time. I think about it a lot when I'm not thinking about my own less mundane cases, if you know what I mean? That's a case. Nice tits, Kealing. Don't mess around with Zuckerman, though. Married. Tough mama. Cut you right down to size."

"Something bothers me about that case," Hank Patuto announced flatly.

A lot bothered him about the case. Mostly that he wasn't on it. That he considered himself cheated out of his chance by two conniving female detectives, two broads. He would be on that coveted task force now if they hadn't tricked him.

"Yeah, whatsat?" asked Squirrelly Smith.

"It doesn't hang together, if you get my drift. The case is made up of hunches. It's been created by the media."

There was a low whistle.

Squirrelly said, "So what exactly are you getting at?"

"Just this," Hank continued as he raised his eyebrows, "do you really think a woman—c'mon now, with this Jane the Ripper thing—do you guys really think a woman is capable of a mass murder like these knifings? And if so, why never before? Suddenly we got a two-ton amazon going around the city, ripping a woman in half with a paring knife or whatever? Shit."

They were leaning in, hanging on his words, because he had lowered his voice almost to a menacing whisper. It was a dramatic effect of his. The man who was chewing gum cracked it loudly, then stopped when he saw the other men glaring at him.

"Good point," said a detective lieutenant from the Sixth Precinct in the Village where one of the murders had been committed.

"I mean," said Hank, warming up to it now, "it's e–mo–tion–al. Just like two broads to cook up something like this. So they found a pocketbook in a hotel and it had a woman's name in it that was murdered. Does that mean that the woman who had the hotel room for a day or two is a mass murderer?"

"Yeah, it makes a lot of sense what you're saying," said the gum-chewing detective.

"Most cases are based on hunches, at least at first," Squirrelly pointed out. "They're doing the best they can."

"But it's slow," Hank insisted, drumming his fingertips on the table. "And I just don't believe as far as a cow can piss that a woman is behind all this. I mean, it looks good in the papers . . ."

The men were silent. Each was trying to bring up another case of a woman slasher beyond Lizzie Borden, but no one could. He did have a point.

"Fulani's a good man," came a voice.

"The best," said another.

"Did they check the angle of the thrust of the knife?" Hank demanded angrily. "Did you find *that* anywhere in the papers?"

Hank Patuto raised his hands, aware that he might be giving himself away. "Okay. I'm just saying there should be a more scientific way of knowing whether a man or woman is doing the killings."

Sooner than Hank wanted the subject changed, the men be-

gan to trickle out to go on duty, home, or to see their girlfriends.

Hank Patuto sat alone, frustrated and angry. Damn it. It was
his case. He had let those women trick him out of it. Women
were always tricking him.

He stood up abruptly, almost knocking his chair over. In his
pocket was some change. He lifted out a handful and then
picked out a quarter. He dialed a number quickly.

Placing his hand over the receiver, he said hoarsely, "Patuto
here. I got another lead for you. There's a lot of talk in the
department that the killer on that case is not a woman. That's
right. There are no real facts yet. Not Jane the Ripper. More
like Jack the Ripper. Maybe you can fit it into the late edition of
the *Post*."


The noise level in the cramped task force room on the third
floor of the precinct sounded to Tammy like a long-playing
record scratching to a close at the wrong speed. The task force's
special call-in number was ringing faster than they could process the calls. One officer sat answering the phones, wearing an
ice bag on his head.

Carolyn tripped over three people trying to get to their desks.
"How's little Donny?" she asked Tammy.

"He'll be okay. Fever's gone down." She brightened up. "I
made him some chicken soup last night."

"Good. How are you?"

"Me? I never get sick—you know that."

"Good, I'm glad you're feeling hale and hearty . . . because
we have visitors waiting outside. The average middle-class parents of that baby hooker who got ripped in two. They drove in
from Connecticut."

"Oh, God," Tammy said. "Now we have to face this?"

"Yes, Fulani says we have to do it because we're women and
we're more understanding and sympathetic."

"Biologically or historically?" Tammy asked, not waiting for
an answer. "How did they track them down?"

"Put out feelers on Eighth Avenue. Checked the streets.
Talked to a few pimps. And then they contacted the parents,

who are sitting out there in a high degree of shock. She was a runaway, Tam."

"She was about . . ."

". . . in her senior year in high school."

"Shit. I *hate* this," Tammy said vehemently, smashing her fist down on the desk.

"Exactly my sentiments," was the reply from a detective trying to inch past their desks.

Carolyn brushed her hair with her fingers. She buttoned her navy linen blazer and brushed some imaginary lint off her gray pants. Tammy smoothed out the folds of her denim skirt as she got up.

They went down the steps slowly, silently, until they reached a small office on the second floor where the hooker's parents were waiting. Taking a deep breath and exchanging glances, they went in. The woman was wearing a hat. The man had on a suit and a tie.

Tammy said it first. "I can't tell you how sorry we are, Mr. and Mrs. . . ."

"Hardy. I'm Arthur and this is my wife Deborah."

The Hardys from Connecticut, thought Carolyn.

She was their only child, thought Tammy. Had to be. That was always the scenario for these things.

Carolyn started. "Did your daughter . . ."

"Anna-Marie." Mr. Hardy supplied her name softly.

"Did she have any . . ." She stopped. Out of habit, she was going to ask if she had any boyfriends. Carolyn looked at Tammy for some mute support, but Tammy wasn't even mentally in the room. Parents whose kids got killed wasn't her strong suit.

She couldn't ask if Anna-Marie had any girlfriends stalking her. Unless the killer was a hooker and there was jealousy or revenge involved. Was Enid Thornton a high-class hooker as well as a murderer? The thing was, she had to ask these people something. They had driven all the way from Connecticut for answers.

Carolyn took a deep breath. "Is there anything you can tell us about your daughter?"

Deborah Hardy took a ragged tissue from her bag. "Not

much. You see, she ran away from home. I guess we didn't know her too well. I guess we failed her somehow."

Mr. Hardy put his hand on his wife's arm.

His wife went on through her tears. "We sent her to the best private schools. We gave her piano lessons, ballet lessons. I never had those opportunities. She has—had a wardrobe, the best that could be bought in Hartford, Connecticut. Sometimes we would take her shopping in New York City, at Saks, Bloomingdale's. She was our only child."

Tammy and Carolyn exchanged glances. They weren't going to get any closer to solving the case by crying with the Hardys.

"Can we take our daughter home now and give her a decent burial?" Mrs. Hardy pleaded. "They said we couldn't have her."

"I'll see that all the arrangements are made and she's released to you as soon as possible," Carolyn replied soothingly as she rose from her chair.

Mrs. Hardy impulsively hugged and kissed Carolyn. Mr. Hardy pumped Carolyn's hand gratefully.

On the way back up the steps Carolyn asked Tammy, "How come they thanked us so profusely?"

Tammy shrugged. "People do strange things in grief. Tomorrow they'll hate us because their daughter was killed."

They went back into the task force room. The huge blackboard stood to the right of the center of the room. On it was written Polly Manklin, Hooker, Woman in the Village, Dawn Snow. Carolyn walked over and erased the word *Hooker* with her wrist. Then she printed carefully: *Anna-Marie Hardy.* Tammy nodded her approval. It seemed more respectful.

Carolyn brushed the chalk dust off her hands by smacking them together. "Ready?" she asked Tammy.

"For another set of parents? *No,*" Tammy replied emphatically.

"We have to go back to that restaurant and interview the other attendant," Carolyn reminded her.

Tammy grunted.

"Cheer up! Maybe we'll find something."

"In this case, I doubt it," Tammy said gloomily. "We've got a woman in a white outfit, very, very chic, murdered on Park

Avenue—a rich divorcée, we find out; a seventeen-year-old screwed-up kid who comes to New York for kicks and doesn't even get kicked in the ass before she's sliced in two; a beautiful young dancer who's greatest crime was walking down the wrong street in the dark; an anonymous lady in the Village who walked down a small street in the light and was so careful she kept her money in her shoe. And then you have Enid Thornton, who would have given Houdini some competition."

"Did you make that chicken soup with the skinny noodles or the fat ones?"

"Skinny," Tammy replied, her voice harsh, not willing to part with her cynicism.

"Yeah, I like that kind better," Carolyn said.

They walked down the precinct steps. "Who . . . is . . . killing . . . these . . . women?" Tammy muttered softly, each word staccato.

"Well, we think it's Enid Thornton," Carolyn reminded her somewhat facetiously.

"They put the sketch on the air, didn't they? I never have time to watch television."

"I saw it last night on Channel Four. It's just such an ordinary sort of sketch. In the newspapers, too."

"Even with the earring in one ear?"

"Doesn't stand out. I see a lot of women and girls with all kinds of earring arrangements in their ears."

"What kind of a woman would murder a young girl like Anna-Marie Hardy?" Tammy shook her head.

"Would you carry on like that if the murderer were a man? It's someone who definitely doesn't like hookers or women who wear white or dancers with dance bags."

"And what about the woman in the Village on Waverly Place?"

"Well, maybe," Carolyn conjectured, "maybe she doesn't like women."

"That's what I'm finding hard to swallow," Tammy admitted as they reached their car. "A woman killing women."

"I told you, but you wouldn't listen."

Except for small talk, which they used to cover up their tension, they rode down to Thirty-sixth Street in relative silence.

"Let's hope this woman is there," Carolyn said, the tension creeping back into her voice.

"You know, I'm getting tired of this restaurant and we've only eaten there once," Tammy commented dryly.

They walked in, said a few words to the manager, got a nod from the bartender, noticed Mike Holler wasn't there, and then went directly to the ladies' room.

Lurlean was sitting in her chair. She looked up, two paper towels ready.

They identified themselves.

"Cops?" she asked, almost fearfully. It was apparent no one had told her they were looking for someone.

"I'm Detective Zuckerman, and this is my partner, Detective Kealing," Tammy said. "We're looking for a woman whom we believe was in this rest room on the night of Saturday, the twenty-second of May."

Lurlean just stared at them. Then she shook her head and laughed, although there was no smile on her face. "Now how am I supposed to remember that? So many ladies come and go."

"If we showed you an artist's sketch of her, would that help?" Carolyn asked, already pulling out the piece of paper.

"Might," Lurlean replied, shrugging. "But probably not. I just do my job. I don't study *nobody.*"

As Carolyn handed her the sketch, she reached into her apron pocket and pulled out a pair of glasses. She scrutinized the drawing.

"The woman was wearing a white outfit," Tammy began hopefully. "And the earring in one ear. That was rhinestone."

Lurlean nodded. She sat down in her chair, not taking her eyes away from the artist's rendering. "And you say this would have been about two weeks ago?" Her hand was under her chin, which she was stroking with her forefinger and thumb while she was thinking.

Tammy and Carolyn stared at her. She was nodding.

"And the hair, it was brunette," Tammy said.

Lurlean nodded. "It's the earring I think I remember—if I'm right. You say it was a lady in a white outfit? Kind of a pants suit, one-piece, a little low in the front?"

Carolyn nodded enthusiastically, almost afraid to interrupt her.

"Yes, well, come to think of it, now that you bring it up, I do recall a lady like that. And I don't notice too many of them. I remember because this is a quiet job. Nobody gives you no trouble, if you know what I mean. That's why I like it. But this lady, she got sick in here. A kind of spell passed over her, dizziness, you know. And then she was okay again."

"So you saw her!" Carolyn declared triumphantly.

"Yes, I did . . . But I don't want to get involved. I didn't want to get involved that night, and I don't want to now."

"If you *don't* help us and get involved," Tammy stated matter-of-factly, "more innocent women might get killed."

Lurlean looked at her, not comprehending.

"She kills women. Killed four so far."

"Lord have mercy," Lurlean declared. "Jane the Ripper. I read about it in the *Post*. And *she* came in here?"

"Yes, that's why we need your help," Tammy said, not caring if she was pleading. "We might need to talk to you again. We need more description—anything you remember. And we might need you to identify her in a lineup."

Lurlean nodded, sighing deeply. "Well, I guess I ain't got a choice. Like I said, she got sick. Said she was okay. Then left. There's not a whole lot to tell here. But she didn't look like someone capable of killing. That's for sure."

Tammy and Carolyn waited quietly for Lurlean to say more, but her face was blank.

Just when Tammy was beginning to think they should go and come back when they had more evidence, Lurlean said, "What I remember most about her are those little candies."

" 'Candies'?" Carolyn asked.

"That's right. She emptied her bag looking for something, and then when she found it she put it all back, piece by piece— lipstick, comb, powder, whatever . . . But when she left I found two little candies on the counter. I know they weren't there before, so I figured she had overlooked putting them back in her purse. I put them in my apron pocket."

"Do you have them now?" Carolyn asked, hungry for anything.

"I ate them," the woman replied sheepishly.

"I see," Tammy said, disappointment obvious in her voice.

"Is there anything *else* you can tell us about the woman?" Carolyn asked, hoping for something more substantial.

"That thing she was looking for in her bag. It was eye makeup. She sat down in front of the mirror, and she found her makeup and she put it on. And then she sort of took sick."

"Anything else?" Tammy pressed, unwilling to leave a good lead, thinking that there was an explanation as to why she had stood up Mike. Maybe. Depending on how sick she really was.

"That was about it," Lurlean said. "Never used the facilities, mind you. Just put on her makeup and left. I was happy she didn't get real sick and cause trouble."

Tammy and Carolyn exchanged well-practiced glances.

"Well, thank you *very* much, Lurlean," Tammy said sincerely. "If we have any other questions, you'll be here?"

Lurlean chuckled. "I'm not going anywhere. You know, those little candies was real good. But those were the only two I'll get. You can't get them in the United States."

"What's that?" Carolyn asked.

"Well, they were so delicious—kind of rum-flavored on the inside with chocolate toffee on the outside. So I saved the wrapper and went to Woolworth's to get a pound. But I couldn't find them. Woman behind the candy counter said it was because they were British candies. She recognized them. Couldn't get them in the dimestore. She said maybe at some gourmet store somewhere, but she didn't know where. Never found them. Real good."

"British candies," Carolyn said, barely breathing, staring right into Tammy's eyes.

"No wonder," Tammy mumbled.

# CHAPTER 21

Jonathan kissed her, a lovely kiss on the lips, and they stood there just embracing. It was eleven o'clock at night. They had spent the day exploring Central Park, eating hot dogs from wagons, and taking in a movie. They had even squeezed in the Circle Line Cruise around Manhattan and held hands. Then they had gone out to dinner in Chinatown, which had been Jonathan's suggestion.

Jonathan broke the embrace. "I *do* have to go to work tomorrow."

"I know," she said as he left, giving her one last backward glance before he pulled the door shut behind him. But when the door closed, and he had gone, Barbara felt a longing. She had wanted more from Jonathan—thought this time there was going to be more. But there hadn't been.

Jonathan walked down the long hall until he reached the elevator. He was happy. But he'd have to wipe the smile off his face before the uniformed elevator man saw it. He didn't want to do anything to make Barbara look bad in her own apartment. He didn't want to do anything hurtful to Barbara. That's why he hadn't made love to her. Not after what she had told him about her emotional problems and seeing a psychiatrist.

Besides, he was nervous. He had always found that having sex complicated the relationship. And he wanted this one to be as smooth as possible. For as long as possible.

When the elevator came, Jonathan got in, thinking that it was good for them to wait. As the elevator sank he also realized that he was afraid she wouldn't think he was any good.

Barbara went into the kitchen to rinse out their wine glasses. She was lonely, and it felt like an empty ache. If only Jonathan had stayed over night. But why hadn't she asked him? She was too shy, that's why. Too afraid of being rejected. It didn't occur to her to ask Dr. Walters to help her. She thought of talking to Eva just as the floor became suddenly like the waves of an ocean, and she began to be afraid she would drown. She clutched onto the counter so that she wouldn't fall, her head heavy under the weight of the painful headache.

There was a giggle, and for a second, she wondered who else was in the room with her, then realized no one. She went into the living room and clicked on the radio as she passed it. She turned the dial to some nice jazz music and, clicking her fingers in time to the beat, walked, hips swaying, into her bedroom.

Funny, she hadn't hung up all her new dresses. She wasn't allowed to do anything. She dumped the boutique bag on the bed and lifted out the gold jumpsuit with the wide belt. That would do perfectly. In the back of her dresser was a small jewelry box with her earrings. She picked out crystal drop earrings that hung almost to her shoulders. Tonight she would push her hair behind her ears and wear both earrings.

She liked the jumpsuit. It was cut low. Real low. Slipping it on, she jiggled her torso in time to the loud music. The front of the outfit shifted and moved with her body, revealing even more of what she was forced to keep hidden when she was Barbara. Oh, it was so good to come out. That creep Jonathan hadn't even wanted to touch them. Hé didn't even desire her.

She rummaged in her closet for the perfect pair of shoes to go with the gold jumpsuit. Way, way in the back was a box of red suede ankle-strap heels with a bow. Just perfect for dancing the night away.

Touching her face, she realized she had done everything backward. She had forgotten her makeup, which she would have to put on. And no wonder. Barbara only wore light eyeshadow and a touch of blush. Sometimes she didn't even wear lipstick.

Well, she wasn't Barbara. And she didn't run around looking like the head mistress at a girls' school.

Enid took out her makeup case at the bottom of the dresser in the back of the drawer and went into the bathroom. She darkened her eyebrows, rubbed in shiny brown eyeshadow, and swept on some brown mascara, which lengthened her lashes and made her brown eyes look even darker. Too bad she didn't have any gold makeup. After applying dark berry blush, she put on her contour line, her lipstick, and slicked on some shiny orange gloss. Tonight was going to be super. She had been cooped up long enough.

In the back of the closet on a shelf, she found a gold evening bag. It was Barbara's, but it would do. God knows it never saw much action. Dancing into the living room, she turned off the radio in the stereo unit. That had been there when she moved in with Dad. Dear old Dad. He hadn't been around much because he was always out boozing, but she had inherited his ability to charm people.

The elevator operator opened the door and practically gaped at Barbara. For a second, he wasn't sure if that was the same woman he had just brought up with the gentleman or not. Going down, his back to her, he decided he had made a mistake. It just couldn't be.

Downstairs, she walked past the doorman, who didn't recognize her either, and decided to hail her own cab. She couldn't take just any old cab. On the corner of Ninety-fifth and Park, one slowed down. She looked inside. He was a young driver with a ready smile and friendly eyes. Perfect.

As she got in she noticed he was looking not only at her gold jumpsuit but also at the way the top separated when she sat down.

"Tell me, cutie," she said, "where's the best place to go to dance? I'm from out of town."

The cabdriver smiled. She looked fairly classy, but he knew what she was after. "The Pineapple," he replied. "It's in the

East Fifties, off Second. That's the 'in' place to go. Better than Studio 54 ever was."

"Well, terrific. I'm kind of an 'in' person," she said, her voice low and very intimate sounding.

The cabdriver felt for one frivolous moment he would like to take back his cab and go with her. She looked like fun. When he saw the generous tip, he took off his cap to her. "Have fun now," he said, smiling, thinking she couldn't miss.

The minute Enid entered the Pineapple, she spotted him. He was tall, dark, and handsome, standing at the bar, casually eyeing the door. Swinging her hips more than a little, knowing that the shiny gold material moved with her body, she walked up to the bar. She ordered a Scotch and soda. He caught her eye and smiled. She looked away first, then looked him squarely in the eye and smiled broadly.

Grabbing his drink, he walked over to the other side of the bar and joined her. He signaled the bartender, asked her what she was drinking, and bought her a fresh one.

They sipped their drinks in silence until he asked, "Want to dance?"

"Sure," she answered gayly, and they entered into the undulating sea of bobbing and dipping couples. Enid smiled up at him, her earrings thrashing about in circles.

"Come here often?" he asked, his smile showing perfectly even teeth.

He was an attractive man—black hair with flecks of gray and large light brown eyes. And he had picked her because he found her sexy and pretty. She liked that. "First time," Enid replied, laughing as her hip bumped headlong into a strange man's rear end. "I love to dance," she said blithely. And as she danced, the front flap of her outfit separated a little more.

"Then that's why we are," he bantered, chuckling, not taking his eyes off the flapping gold material and her revealing cleavage. "By the way, what's your name?"

"Enid. What's yours?"

"Alan."

Alan. Who had a name like that? Oh, yes, Dr. Walters. Well, she wouldn't tell him about going dancing. He was a jerk, anyway. Nothing but a square, trying to hold her back from having fun. Everyone was always trying to keep her from having a good time.

"I know a quieter bar, an out-of-the-way place," Alan practically shouted.

She looked at him, meeting his eyes, and with a teasing half smile said, "Later. If you're a good boy. I love to dance, remember?"

He nodded and laughed, fascinated with her and her light-hearted way. Enid was absorbed in the music, clicking her fingers, swinging her hips, alternatingly rolling her eyes and closing them. He watched her very carefully, especially the way that top gold flap clung to her neck and then fell away. She was stacked.

He thought as he smiled back at her and moved his body to the music along with hers that she was going to be fun. For a night. While his wife was away.

Wiping her forehead with the back of her hand, Enid said, "I need a drink, honey."

They returned to the packed bar, and he bought her another Scotch and soda, which she drank as if it were a soft drink. He suggested they move to an empty table in the back and talk a bit.

"You're a real good dancer," he complimented her when they sat down, his eyes focused below her neck.

"You're not so bad yourself."

"What do you do, Enid?"

"Oh, I'm a model. You know, lingerie."

He looked impressed. "I'm with J. Walter Thompson," he said quickly.

"Who's he?"

"That's an advertising agency. I work there." He didn't. He was unemployed at the moment, but if he told her the truth, he didn't think she'd go to bed with him.

"Oh, *that* J. Walter Thompson." She giggled. "Listen, sweetie, I didn't come here to gab all night. Let's dance some more!"

Alan threw back his head and laughed. "You're somethin' else, Enid." Enid. He wondered what her last name was. But if she gave him hers, he would have to give her his. And he didn't want anything that heavy.

He followed Enid to the crowded floor, his eyes on the way the gold material clung snugly to her ass. It was a nice, round ass. And if the top of that gold jumpsuit fell away one more time, he was going to carry her out of there.

They danced another dance, and as it drifted into the next one Alan said, "This is like a mammoth traffic jam in here." When she didn't answer him, he suggested, "Let's split."

Enid just laughed at him and kept gyrating her body.

Alan decided to ask her again, just in case she hadn't heard him. "I said, let's leave and go to the other bar."

She darted her tongue across her teeth petulantly and puckered her mouth. "Let's not and say we did."

The way she had said that pissed him off. It sounded kind of singsong and smug. He hated that kind of behavior in a grown woman. Taking her arm, he all but pulled her off the dance floor. "I *said* we're leaving."

"And I'm *saying* I don't want to go!"

"Wait a second," he said, his face twisted with anger, "I bought you two drinks and you've been flirting your tits and ass off, and *now* you decide to give me the cold shoulder? What gives?"

She looked him directly in the eyes and smirked. "Well, maybe it's that I don't think you're man enough for me," she answered evenly. Then she laughed at him.

His right arm flew back, and before anyone could restrain him his fist landed on her jaw and she fell to the floor. People stopped dancing. A man said, "Hey, buddy," but it was too late.

Enid was lying on the floor, looking like she was trying to swim ashore. It seemed as if a hundred faces were staring down at her. More than one hand was offered to assist her. Her jaw hurt and she tasted her own blood. Then someone turned the volume down, and all she saw when she looked up were mouths moving.

Tears came to her eyes as the blinding headache washed over her. She heard the voices say something that sounded like, "Hey, miss, are you all right?" But she couldn't answer. She shut her eyes tightly and shook her head. When she opened them she found herself lying on the floor. She didn't know where she was or who the people were standing above her. With a panicky feeling, she realized it had happened again. She had lost her memory.

Waving away the hands that were trying to help her up, she scrambled up on her knees, trying to stand. She faltered on the high heels when she looked down and saw the red suede shoes with the bows at the ankle. Oh, God, she thought, how disgustingly gaudy. And there was a gash in her hose. She clutched the flap of that silly gold outfit to her neck. Otherwise it would fall down and she would be naked. With a thousand eyes looking at her like she was a freak show, she stumbled toward the door.

Tears of humiliation fell down her face, splashing on the shiny material. She wanted to scream: *This is not me. Don't stare like that. I'm not crazy.*

She stood on the sidewalk, praying a cab would come by quickly. She knew that long after, when she was alone, she would feel all those eyes staring at her, scrutinizing her, as if she were a fish in a see-through bowl.


It was a record-breaking sellout for the first and second editions of the *New York Post.* On Tuesday, the eighth of June, the story finally broke, and the *Post* was the first to cover it. On their way to work, millions of people were reading about yet another woman stabbed and slashed to death.

The catchy *Post* headline was the grabber: SNOW WHITE DROWNS IN BLOOD.

Had the cops on the task force been riding the subways that morning, they would have heard what the public thought. Everyone was talking about the case. Mostly women.

"I don't know if I want to take the subway to work, anymore," said one young secretary who worked for an importing firm.

"How would you come to work?" her friend asked.

The subway lurched around a corner, and a woman holding onto a strap almost fell across their laps.

"Bus," replied the young secretary.

"Oh, c'mon, these murders weren't committed on the subways. You just have to be careful. Don't take them after dark."

"But the underpass, the one I change over to, coming home at night, to get the uptown IRT, that's dark. It's always scared me. Now I'm more scared."

"I don't blame you," chimed in the woman grasping the strap.

The two young women looked up and then ignored her. "You don't understand," continued the secretary. "I used to be afraid of strange men. Now no one's safe. Not only is a woman going around murdering women, but I'm still afraid of strange-looking men."

"But there've been murders before in New York," her friend said.

The secretary spoke in hushed tones. "It's all different, now that it's a woman. I hate to say this, but how do I know it's not you?"

But the cops on the task force weren't riding the trains, and they left the man-on-the-street interviews to the media. Most of them had found the *Post* headline disgusting. But Tammy and Carolyn were in shock over a subheadline, also in bold letters, on the second page of the paper: COPS DISAGREE AMONG SELVES. And then in a caption: "Murderer might be a man."

They read the article together. How clumsily some of the department—persons not named—felt the case had been handled. How even the mayor wasn't so sure the city was putting pressure on the task force to consider a man as well. How officer after officer, including women, did not believe a woman was capable of committing four murders. Not even women detectives boasted a better physical strength than men.

Tammy and Carolyn looked at each other. They saw that in a corner of the room a group of detectives were talking about the same subject.

Tammy and Carolyn could easily overhear the conversation.

"I never thought it was a woman either, to tell you the truth."

"I do think it's a man. I agree with everyone else. No witnesses, no real proof . . ."

One voice stood out from the rest. They both recognized it at the same time. Carolyn turned to look first, then looked back. They both knew the task force had been expanded.

"I don't think the killer's a woman, and I never have," boomed the voice. Then they saw his raised hand of acknowledgment and the mocking smile. Hank Patuto was now on the task force.

When the call came, Captain Fulani was in the task force room, in the middle of a meeting, writing on the big blackboard. He had just printed: *Man vs. Woman Killer.* Both Tammy and Carolyn realized that the tide was going against them. Now they were the only detectives on the task force who still believed it was a woman. And all because of a newspaper article.

And let's face it, their leads didn't amount to much—a handbag and a sketch of a woman with one earring.

For about fifteen minutes Tammy had been trying to get the captain's attention. They hadn't yet had a chance to tell him about the ladies' room attendant's recognizing the woman in the sketch and the two pieces of candy from Great Britain. But it was as if he were ignoring them.

"Captain, telephone call," someone shouted from the door.

The captain raised his hand. "Take a message."

"Can't take a message, Captain," said the man, then turned to talk to someone else.

Captain Fulani sighed, put the chalk down, wiped his forehead, although he wasn't perspiring, and walked out of the room. He went into his small office and picked up the phone. In front of him was a map of New York City with four pushpins, each a different color, sticking out of the areas where the murdered women had been found. There was no pattern, he thought. They would just stick more pins in the map, most likely. "Captain Fulani here," he said.

"Detective Inspector Douglas Cavendish from Scotland Yard." The line crackled with static.

"What can I do for you?" Fulani asked politely, wondering what he could do for anybody at that moment.

"I had a piece of business—a favor—I was hoping you could see to for me," Cavendish said, "something I can't do from here."

*Figures,* thought Fulani. Why me? The call must be a mistake. The man probably thought he was still with Manhattan South, unaware he was now the head of this task force. That was it.

"I was looking to track down the name on a post office box number," Cavendish went on. "Do you have access to computers? Or can you send someone to do this? I'd appreciate it. It's hard to do it from overseas."

Fulani grunted. What the hell was this man getting at? They needed more shitwork like they needed a hole in the head. The syrupy, meticulous British accent was beginning to unnerve him.

And then came the kicker. "Someone called my attention to the New York papers, so I called you. Your name is in the paper."

"You mean the killing of that young dancer?" Fulani asked.

"What young dancer? No, we didn't get that."

"Just happened."

"That's why. Interesting . . . No, I mean the others and the odd fact that our murders coincide with yours."

"I beg your pardon?"

"With our *killings.* Don't you read the London papers, man? We have had the same rash of stabbings. Three. Same M.O. Jane the Ripper, I believe you call it."

The men who hung about the room were surprised to see Fulani's mouth drop open and stay there.

"Well, to tell the truth, we overlooked the case here, too. Someone brought the similarity to my attention. I say, Captain, do you really think it's a woman?"

Captain Fulani recovered slightly. "What do you think?"

Cavendish was silent for a moment, then said, "What do *you* think?"

Captain Fulani didn't want to say, "I asked you first," but it was interesting that obviously neither would commit himself. "I thought it was a woman, but now I'm not so sure," he finally admitted. "There's just no real evidence here."

"I'm under a lot of pressure here, too, to search for a woman suspect, but I personally don't believe a woman *could* be responsible for all these killings."

"And how do you account for the similarity in all these cases?" Fulani asked.

Cavendish cleared his throat. "There might be some connection between the killings here and yours. We were trying to locate a woman who had a box in the post office. To make a long story short her name didn't match her credit card, and that was under a post office box number in New York."

"Why were you tracking it down?"

"She canceled a flight the night of a murder, and her name stood out from the rest. Just a routine check. We had a woman who was knifed in the ladies' room of Heathrow Airport."

"Holy shit!" Fulani sputtered. "And the murderer got away?"

"Straight away," replied Cavendish.

"Well, this woman you were looking for, what was her name?" asked Fulani, his pencil poised over a note pad. If the names matched, he might be able to get excited.

"Dana Hargrove was the woman we were trying to trace in New York."

"Enid Thornton was the woman we thought it was when we thought it was a woman," Fulani explained, then realized what he had just said.

"The woman who was murdered flew to New York."

"You mean someone flew *for* her. Anyone can steal a boarding pass. That does point to a woman."

"London has gotten rather androgynous lately," Inspector Cavendish commented dryly. "I don't think it takes too much of a twist of the imagination to think it might have been a man dressed adroitly as a woman."

"That's what I've been thinking for a long time," Fulani admitted. "This is a serial murderer."

"What is that you're calling it?" Cavendish asked.

"Well, a mass murderer is someone who fires at random from, say, a machine gun. But a serial murder means that there are killings at random, one after the other. We've got another Son of Sam here. Only I wouldn't go so far as to say it's Daughter of Sam."

Cavendish was relieved to talk to someone who thought like he did. "Sure, it could have been a man dressed as a woman.

The bag could have been tossed aside. If it wasn't the murderer, *any* woman could have flown to New York on that boarding pass."

"Sounds like you've got a headache like we do," Fulani admitted.

"I'm wondering, Captain Fulani, if it's the *same* headache?"

"You mean a murderer who's flying back and forth to throw everyone off track? Perhaps I could send some men from the Yard over there?"

Fulani began to feel pressured. It was *his* task force, and he wanted *his* men to make the collar. The city was building up to a feverish pitch with the help of the media. He'd have to think about accepting help from Scotland Yard. "It could be a coincidence, you know. Ever hear of a jealousy killer? Someone who knows about our killings and is copying—got the idea from us, so to speak?"

Cavendish stroked the ends of his long, curly mustache. It was obvious that the New York City Police Department didn't want any help from the Yard. Maybe they were close to something. "Let's keep in touch, shall we?" Cavendish suggested slyly. He gave Fulani his numbers and that of Sergeant Hollings and decided, if need be they could send some men over to follow Fulani's men without their knowing about it.

Captain Fulani sat quietly for a few seconds, then lighted a cigar with a shaking hand. "I want to see Zuckerman and Kealing in here on the double," he directed crisply to one of the men standing at the door. "Oh, yes, and send in Hank Patuto." Funny, even before the *Post* printed that piece about the doubts surrounding the probability of the murderer's being a woman, Patuto had said the same thing. He had seen him just last night over at Patrick's. It was good to have a few with the men, find out what they thought. A lot of them couldn't stuff that it was a woman either. He had outright offered Patuto a place on the task force. And Patuto had accepted with the understanding that he leave his regular caseload.

Tammy and Carolyn walked in just behind Hank Patuto. There was one chair in the small office. He sat down and they stood.

Captain Fulani pointed to the phone as if it could talk. "An inspector from Scotland Yard called. A Detective Inspector Cavendish." His voice started to rise. "We *should* have known this. There's a rash of stabbings in London just like ours. They've had three. Same M.O."

Tammy and Carolyn exchanged glances.

Then his voice became even louder, and his face got redder. "From now on, I *don't* want to be *embarrassed* this way!" he screamed to everyone in his office. They listened intently but didn't know what he was talking about. He turned and went back to his desk, sat down, and lowered his voice. "From now on, we should get the overseas papers, Goddammit. Especially the *London Times*—or whatever they have there. That's at least in English. Send someone to pick up a couple of papers or watch the goddamn TV!" he barked. A man disappeared.

It was Carolyn who spoke up first. "Captain Fulani, sir, we talked to a ladies' room attendant at the restaurant where Mike Holler said he was with Enid Thornton. And she recognized the sketch. Said she left some candies behind. They were British."

It was Hank Patuto who leaned forward and asked, "Do you have them?"

"She ate them," Tammy replied simply. It was unfortunate but true.

Patuto snickered.

"So there's nothing, no evidence again," Fulani stated flatly.

Tammy didn't necessarily like the word *again*. "Only that it reaffirms the possibility that she could be from Great Britain, or that she'd been there recently, sir."

"Or she could have gotten them in a special store here," Patuto chimed in, smiling angelically at them.

Carolyn remembered the phrase, When you're hot, you're hot, and when you're not, you're not. She had a funny feeling they weren't hot anymore. In fact, she wasn't even sure that what they said mattered.

"Where was I?" Fulani asked, feeling his blood pressure rising.

Before you were so *rudely* interrupted, thought Tammy. She heard her voice, and it was small and thin and unlike her. "Is his murderer a woman?" she asked.

"He said he's under some pressure to think so, but he thinks the murderer purposely planned his M.O. to make them think that. He personally doesn't think it's feasible. A view shared by many of us here."

*Clunk,* thought Carolyn.

"Crap. Jerking off. That's the stuff we're doing," Fulani snapped. He was clearly agitated. The mayor was calling daily, the governor was on the mayor's back, and the media was depicting New York's Finest as an army of mindless robots. "I think we should begin to consider the possibility that it might be a man impersonating a woman."

Patuto nodded in agreement. Tammy and Carolyn made no move; they saw that panic was setting in. And as far as Patuto, he was on the task force and they had to be careful. Sooner or later he would screw them. He was a very vindictive man. Most cops were.

"I wonder," said Carolyn, noticing that she felt awkward about speaking up, "if the murders are being committed by the same person?" She was careful not to say *woman.*

Tammy wasn't so careful, and she felt angry and rebellious. "The same woman could be traveling back and forth. Businesswomen do that."

Hank Patuto laughed. "Do you really think a woman like that with responsibility is flying back and forth with a knife unnoticed?"

"She could be crazy," Tammy retorted. "Anything's possible."

Hank Patuto knew now that whenever he spoke, he had the attention of Captain Fulani. He spoke calmly as if he were addressing hysterical women. His was the voice of reason. "And what if it's one killer in London and another one here? I don't think we should concentrate on a woman. Personally, I think we're being duped, and it makes me angry. I think the person we're looking for is a man. At least consider that it might not be a woman. Admit we made a mistake."

Captain Fulani sighed. "We'll have to go to the streets, round up the parolees, check out the releases from mental hospitals, lean on our informers. I'll have to get some more men on this case. Without a lot of fanfare, we're going to have to start over."

Tammy looked over at Carolyn for some support. But Carolyn was frowning, studying the floor.

# CHAPTER 22

Barbara was sitting in the tiny waiting room thumbing through a magazine that was, she noticed, almost two years old. She couldn't help but envy the glowing woman she saw walking out. If only she could be her.

In a matter of minutes he would come out and greet her in his usual fashion, and she would go into that office and lose herself, becoming other people—women she didn't even know. Then she would walk out, not feeling like that fortunate woman but feeling thoroughly wretched. Her life was a living hell. And each time she went into that office, she felt like she was facing an operation.

At exactly nine o'clock he stood in the archway that separated the waiting room from the little hall and said, "Hi!"

"I didn't know you had another patient before me," she said, walking ahead of him into his office. "You know, that other woman."

"Oh, yes, her appointment's at ten after eight. She works. She's a secretary."

"Oh," Barbara replied flatly, studying the knobby bumps in the beige carpeting. Did he mean she should work?

"I was a secretary, too. Well, a typist. Before I got all this money."

"I didn't know that," he answered as if it were a part of the jigsaw puzzle that was her.

"Yes."

"So, what's been happening in your life?" he said, smiling.

She didn't lift her eyes off the carpeting. "Something awful happened to me last night. It seems like it's getting worse. I woke up and I was lying on the floor in this discotheque, and all these people were looking down at me, pitying me." Her voice cracked. "At first I thought it was a nightmare. But it was real, all right. I couldn't get up."

He noticed she was wringing her hands as if she were washing them.

"And I was wearing this tight gold outfit and very high red shoes. Finally I stumbled up and ran out of there, feeling humiliated, like everyone was watching me. I don't remember coming there in the first place." She was blinking and trying not to cry, her eyes still fixed on the carpet.

Dr. Walters nodded. This was progress. She was aware she was a multiple personality.

"So, I came home and ripped off that gaudy gold outfit and cried myself to sleep. I was *her*, wasn't I?"

Dr. Walters' voice was soft and soothing. "Yes, you were most likely Enid. She likes to go dancing and would have felt at home there."

"And that's where the dresses come from? When I have memory lapses, I might be shopping . . . Right?"

He nodded sympathetically, wondering what this woman would do without all that money she had. She wouldn't be flying to London twice a week, that was for sure. Maybe it wouldn't be a bad idea if she became a secretary again. It would stabilize her. "I would like to keep taking you back to your past," he said firmly.

She looked away, seeming to examine the oil painting over the couch.

"I know, I know, it's distasteful to you. But that's the only way we're going to get you well and merge your personalities.

We don't want you waking up on any more strange floors, do we?"

It never ceased to fascinate him, when he put her under, how her face twisted into a tortured expression. Her mouth slid up on the side as if it had been shoved by a hand. Her eyes became slanty, and the right eyelid drooped. A fairly attractive woman, she looked almost ugly when she talked about her past, and he was beginning to understand why.

She had a nervous habit of putting her hand over her mouth as if she had spoken out of turn. She was doing that at the moment. "Where did I leave off?"

"You were fired from your job on the soap opera. Your mother and father got a divorce. Your mother was angry with you and beat you several times for getting fired."

"For growing up," Barbara corrected him. "That's why my character was killed. I got too old to be 'Cookie.' They got another girl. I think it was also because I wasn't very good. Only when I was little. I really wasn't a good actress. That's why I didn't go on."

"Okay, Barbara, you were twelve years old when this happened. I want you to fall into a deep sleep, and when you wake up you'll be twelve again."

As he was hypnotizing her, he watched the play of emotions across her face.

"Mum moved us to Hammersmith. She was born in London. Though none of her family were left when we moved. But she said she wanted to go back. That America was too crude. Besides, she wanted to move far away from Daddy."

He had reached for a yellow pad and was taking notes. He never took notes. Didn't believe in it. He thought it was better for the patient's trust if he just remembered every detail of his or her life as if it were the only life he was holding in his head. Every once in awhile he made a note after the patient left. He had been trained to do that, and he rarely made a mistake he couldn't cover for. But with this case, he couldn't afford any slipups. Besides, he didn't think she was really aware of him.

As they sat there he jotted on his pad:
Hammersmith. Relation to why she's in Hammersmith now.

To write book or recapture years with mother. Get her out
of Hammersmith. ASAP.

Barbara's voice, which hadn't really been confident even
when she first came in, at twelve was higher and less sure of
herself.

"Does your mother—I mean, mum—treat you better now
that you're not working? She did some pretty wicked things to
you, Barbara. Things mothers don't usually do to their children."

Barbara didn't answer. She started to cry.

He clearly remembered their last session. He had taken her
way back, and she had screamed so loudly he had become
alarmed.

Now Barbara's face was streaming with tears.

"We used to play a game called 'Catch Me If You Can.' I
would hide in the broom closet or under the bed or behind the
piano—anywhere. But she would always catch me."

"And then what did she do to you?"

Barbara half sobbed, half choked. She began to stutter. "She
—she—she used to tie me onto the piano stool and spin me. My
feet dragged on the floor. She would spin me and spin me until I
threw up, and then she'd leave me there, smelling it with my
eyes shut tight."

He was beginning to notice that her voice was taking on a
slight British accent. Interesting . . . "Now, Barbara," he
said, "can't you tell anyone—a friend, your teacher, a counselor
—about how mean your mother treats you?"

Barbara got angry. "She's not mean. She takes care of me.
She's my best friend. We do lovely things. It's just when she gets
in one of her moods."

"I see. Well, tell me what's happening in your life? Who are
your little friends?"

She stiffened. "I have no little friends. I'm not popular. Just
the American girl. I hate being me."

"So you go to school in Hammersmith. And after school,
what kinds of games do you play?"

Barbara snickered. "I don't have time to play games. Mum is

a nurse. When I come home, I have chores to do—clean the house, get the dinner, sometimes polish the silverware."

"And what about doing your homework? Do you get any?"

"Oh, I hardly have time for that. I'm not good in school anyway. I'm not very smart."

"You don't mean to say that a little girl who could memorize a script . . ." But she wasn't listening to him. He had lost her. He had to be careful. "Boyfriends," he suggested. "Do you have a boyfriend or a crush on a boy like girls usually do at your age? Hammersmith can't be too different from the United States."

"I'm afraid of boys."

She began to look around the office, and he felt she was seeing the furnishings in his office rather than something in that flat, long ago, in Hammersmith. Quickly he made a decision. He pulled her out of the hypnosis and waited until, as Barbara, she woke up. Then he held his breath and followed that with, "May I talk to Enid, please?"

Barbara's teeth were chattering, and her eyelids were half shut, the whites of her eyes showing. He heard the familiar laugh first.

"Enid?" He felt relieved that he had gotten her and that it was so very easy.

"Yeah, that's me. Hey, I was having a lot of fun last night until she horned in on me."

"Tell me what happened?"

"Oh, I was dancing with this guy, and he got fresh, and—"

"Wait a second. Were you flirting or teasing? Leading him on?"

"Yeah, well, he didn't have to smack me one."

Dr. Walters nodded knowingly. "So Barbara didn't horn in on you. You got caught." He smiled at her.

Enid threw back her head and laughed. "Oh, you're on to me. I play my little games with them. How come you didn't play your radio?" she asked.

He laughed with her for a moment, then said seriously, "I don't listen to radio or watch television. I'm too busy. I want to do a little work now. I want to know more about what it was like in Hammersmith when you were all twelve. Were you there?"

"Was I *there?* Listen, that woman was a witch. Who would want to come out, you know? I overheard her once talking to some lawyer on the phone. She was trying to cheat that poor little creep out of the money she had made on that soap. It was supposed to be in a trust fund waiting for Barbara, but the witch wanted it. So the father, the drunk, put it way away. Couldn't touch it until Barbara was thirty. Guess he figured his liver would go kerplunk one day, and he didn't trust himself not to borrow from her to drink. But I'm glad she's got dough now. I've got swell clothes. Not that I get enough time to wear them, you know?"

He laughed again. "Do you go to Hammersmith now?"

"Not very often. I tell you, it's getting harder and harder to come out."

"Are you aware of the work she's doing there?"

Enid waved away the question with her hand. "Oh, c'mon, she couldn't write her way out of a paper bag."

"I thought she was writing a book?"

"A couple of pages, that's all."

Suddenly he said, "Could I please speak to Dana?"

The head rolled back slowly as if she were reluctant to stop being Enid. Sagging in the middle, she bent over and he saw that she was reaching for her bag. He was continually amazed at the ease with which he could bring on her personality transformations. It was like controlling the strings to a puppet. He watched as Dana put on her glasses.

"And what do you think, Dana?" he asked, almost conspiratorially, as he would address a colleague.

"She does write," Dana said. "She's just not used to expressing herself."

"But you didn't know the early Barbara or the treatment she suffered under her mother," he said, knowing he had the upper edge.

"And *you* don't know how closely attached she is to Jonathan," Dana countered. "She doesn't speak about it enough."

"That attachment is too difficult to control."

"She loves him."

"She only thinks she loves him. She's experiencing certain needs that have been repressed."

"She's falling in love," Dana insisted.

"Let me talk to Barbara," he demanded. Then he thought better of his approach and added, "May I speak to Barbara, please?"

She looked at him wearily.

"May I please speak to Barbara?" he repeated as if she hadn't heard him.

Dana carefully took off her glasses and put them into the bag. Then she sat there. Dr. Walters watched her. For a few moments it looked as if it wouldn't work this time. But then he was relieved to see her start to shake uncontrollably, shutting her eyes and gripping the arms of the chair. When he felt sure she was Barbara, he said brightly, "So let's talk about Jonathan."

Barbara's voice cracked a bit as she spoke. "I like him a lot," she said shyly. It seemed as if she were afraid he was going to argue with her.

Dr. Walters smiled like an indulgent parent. It was okay.

She kept talking, a little more buoyed up. "Men usually have hurt me. But not Jonathan. He's different."

"Did your father hurt you?" Dr. Walters asked quickly.

"No, I mean boyfriends. But Jonathan's so nice and sweet and gentle."

"Jonathan might hurt you," he said. "That's what I'm afraid of."

Barbara stared at him.

"When he finds out."

"But he doesn't have to find out."

"Barbara, when two people become intimate, they get closer. I suggest you bring him in, and the two of you can share a session."

Barbara was horrified. "Will you make me change into those other people in front of him?"

"If I don't, he won't believe it. And that way he'll be prepared for what you might do," he explained. He looked at her searchingly, his voice entreating. "Isn't it better that he know? That everything be out in the open?"

"I'm not sure. He might leave me."

Dr. Walters shrugged. "He might. But then, he may not be

right for you later on, too. You may not even *want* him when
you're cured."

"You mean one personality?"

He nodded and smiled at her. "Yes, and it will happen. I'm
trying to go as fast as I can."

"Who will I be?" Barbara asked. "Will I still be me?"

"You'll be *better* than you," he assured her, letting himself
get excited.

They sat for a moment, each thinking about what had been
said.

Barbara broke the silence. "I've been having some strange
dreams lately."

He stared at her. He didn't usually believe in analyzing
dreams. It was all right for him to know about them, but he
didn't want his patients to get into dreams too deeply.

"They're not just sleeping dreams," Barbara added. "When I
wake I still have the feelings, like longings."

He was sure her dreams centered around sex. Someone as
bottled up and repressed as she was. He had been waiting for
something like this. "So what do you dream of?" he asked,
folding his hands in his lap.

"Killing people . . ."

"Killing whom?" he asked, unclasping his hands.

"I don't know. Women. Anyone who reminds me of my
mother in any way, even the littlest way."

"In what way would a woman remind you of your mother
that you would harbor feelings of murdering her? What would
she say to you?"

Barbara shook her head. "Oh, I wouldn't even have to know
her that well. Sometimes I dream about killing women who
wear white."

"White? Why white?"

"Mum was a nurse in Hammersmith. She *had* to work. She
spent a lot of time in a white uniform. Then when she came
home she wouldn't change. I hated her white uniform."

"I think you just hated your mother," he said softly, knowingly.

"No, you don't understand. Sometimes if I see a woman
whose hair falls toward her face like my mother's, that will

trigger it. Or a woman who walks with the same brisk, no-nonsense walk as Mum. Or even one who carries a big bag like she did. It could be anything. It happens a lot. Anything that reminds me of her or some woman who resembles what I remember she looked like . . . I want to kill."

"And what happens in those dreams of yours?"

"I do kill."

"What is your weapon?"

"My weapon—my weapon is a knife," she said slowly. She had never been so open with anyone in her life.

"A knife," he repeated.

"I stab them," she said, bowing her head.

"That's when you're dreaming?"

"Yes."

"And when you're awake?"

"I'm just aware of it. This feeling that I want to kill. But only someone who reminds me of my mother. It's an anger."

"Describe that anger. What does that feel like?"

"It feels like I want to kill," Barbara answered simply. She sat there then for several moments before going on. "When I was a little girl, I used to rip things. Tear them in half. Destroy them. Like dolls, coloring books, any toys I had."

"I see. You ripped your own toys. Were you angry with your mother?"

"Yes." She was wringing her hands as if she were washing them.

"So you killed your toys." He was getting to something. "How?"

"With a knife"—she was thoughtful—"but they didn't bleed."

He was smiling again. "Barbara, can't you see the progress you've made? You're talking about your feelings of anger toward your mother. When you first came in here, you didn't even know where those feelings were. And those feelings make you a multiple personality. But all that anger against your mother, and the terrible way she treated you, is very repressed."

Barbara stared at him, not looking down or at the plants but directly into his eyes.

"You're not a killer, Barbara, believe me." He smiled at her approvingly. "Your repressed feelings are seeping into your dreams, and that's a very healthy way to handle them. I know you well enough to say you would have a hard time killing a cockroach."

She looked down at the floor and said softly, "I don't have cockroaches in my apartment."

He noticed the time. "Well, our time is up. Don't be ashamed of your feelings of wanting to kill your mother. You do want to kill her in your mind, but we will kill your mother for you one day so that you can be well. Don't punish yourself for those feelings. They are nothing to be ashamed of. I'd like to see even more anger. Use it." Then he added, "You're doing *very* well."

She nodded, happy that she seemed to be doing something right.

"I'll see you Friday." As she was walking to the door he asked, "Going to Hammersmith?"

"Yes, tonight." He had never asked her that in quite that way.

He frowned. "I'd like you to come every day eventually. The work needs to be done." He left it at that.

She opened the door to his office and walked down the small corridor very slowly, feeling heavy and awkward, the terrible pounding of a headache beginning, the anger a sour taste in her mouth.

It was the stewardess who first noticed the woman. The trouble was that she was just too busy to tell anyone and they were, as usual, shorthanded. Not that it was anything earth-shaking, mind you, but the lady sitting between the two elderly gentlemen was acting a bit peculiar.

Her face had changed. Every time the stewardess passed by, she scowled very noticeably. But at nothing. The two old men were both snoozing and nodding in their seats. The woman, seemingly very angry and perturbed, was sitting in the middle with a magazine on her lap. But she wasn't reading it. She was ripping it to bits.

# CHAPTER 23

It was early Wednesday morning. The shopkeepers were just starting to open up. Some children were running after a dog in the street. The dog turned briefly. They threw a stick at it, and the dog, its tail wagging frantically, jumped for it and missed. Yipping, it lunged at the stick, which was lying in the middle of the street. The children skipped along, leaving the dog behind.

She laughed, enjoying it, throwing her head back. The dog was running in circles now, chasing its tail, biting the stick. The children had turned the corner and were disappearing. It was fun to notice little scenes like that. Life wasn't all glamour and glitter—or hard knocks, for that matter.

The sun had just come up. Time to go to sleep. And dream marvelous, wonderful dreams. He had had to go to work this morning, but she could sleep. The sound of her heels clicking on the sidewalk made her think of castanets. Her caftanlike dress moved with the lovely morning breeze. They had loved her last night at the club. And so had he.

She tossed her head, shaking about her curls. Her dangling earrings, which just teased her shoulders, jingled like silent bells. She was carrying a silver evening bag with thin straps. It hung about her shoulder, but in a moment of being utterly impossible, which of course she was, she took it off and swung it in little circles. No one was on the street. It didn't matter what she did.

No one was on the street that she could hear.

About a hundred paces back, walking noiselessly, stealthily, was another woman. Her nylon-stockinged feet were encased in white thick rubber-soled sneakers. She was carrying a bag, too, and she had something in it.

The woman twirling the silver bag accidentally dropped it. Stooping delicately, she picked it up, tossed her hair, and continued on, swinging her bag and whistling merrily. When he was finished working, they would have a drink and then they'd go dancing again. Maybe she'd move in with him. Maybe he'd take care of her.

From a distance the dog barked. The children were gone. The street was empty. It felt so right. Priscilla could feel the anger within her climbing to a deafening crescendo. She had to satisfy it.

She walked faster, fingering the clasp on her bag. Inside was the sharp knife she had found in the apartment. Light-footed, barely breathing, she caught up to the gaudily dressed woman, who was lost in thought.

It was the swinging bag that set her off. Mum had had an evening bag, and she often swung it in circles just that way. She was going to have to kill the woman less than a foot in front of her. Before she ruined someone's life like Mum had ruined hers.

Priscilla released her shiny knife from its cushioned compartment. This was the part she lived for. It was like sliding down a zipper. The knife cut through the skin, slashing the material, the blood gushed out, soon the person crumpled in a heap, and then she was gone, quickly, almost painlessly.

Precision. That's what she loved. Raising her arm, she saw the knife dig into the flesh and she smiled. There was a half-hearted scream, which sounded more like a whimper, before the shiny, gaudy dress fell in a bloody puddle around the woman on the pavement.

Almost momentarily she was running quietly down the street like any morning jogger. She turned once and watched the red pool spreading wider. Satisfied, she bounded around a corner and then began to walk more casually. No one had seen her. Her anger was sated.

When she turned the key in her front door, she thought she heard someone shouting from somewhere, but she ignored it and went in. Once inside the flat, she took out the bloody knife wrapped in a towel and ran it under the water. Then she put it back in the drawer.

Lockey, miffed, came away from her perch by the upstairs window. "Doesn't even bother to talk to me," she complained to her husband. "I was going to invite her to have a cuppa."

"Aw, mind your business. You can't be waiting and watching for her to come in all the time. She has her own life to lead." His eyes, during this discourse, never left the television screen.

Lockey sighed. She didn't care what he said. The girl was a bit strange. She needed looking after.

Only a few blocks away, the children, who were chasing the dog back down the street, stopped silently when they stumbled across the blood-drenched body. The dog sniffed around, barking, getting the tips of his paws crimson red. One of the little boys started to cry. Another girl said, "We mustn't stand here. Let's get someone." Her eyes were wide. "I bet this is a case for Scotland Yard."

They ran down the street, screaming. The dog remained, guarding the dead body.

Priscilla flopped down on one of the giant pillows she had bought to place along the floor. And when the headache began to spiral around her, she curled like a fetus into the softness of it. She burrowed deeper and deeper as the dizziness felt as if it were tumbling her around. Then it stopped and Barbara sat up and rubbed one eye with her knuckle. She looked at her hand. There was mascara on it.

She wasn't sure for a moment whether she had come in and fallen asleep in the cozy pillows or had another memory lapse. Not that there was that much difference. She couldn't remember how she had gotten back from the airport. Lately everything seemed to blur. She couldn't remember even the smallest segments of time.

She needed to work. More than ever she needed to justify her time spent in Hammersmith. Downstairs by the typewriter, she recalled then, were the first two chapters of her book. Eagerly she went down the stairs to read the memoirs of an ex-soap star.

There they were. Stacked neatly on the little table. She read the first two chapters without stopping. When she was finished, she threw them on the floor, shocked. She hadn't written that. Maybe one of the others had, but not she.

Who was that wonderful person described here, the one who took her on that interview when she was just four and got her on that soap opera? That enchanting, marvelous person had also dressed her up so nice. Especially that red velvet coat with the fur collar. *Cookie* she had named her. Again the work of that all-knowing, all-doing perfect mother. Mum had done it all for her.

She saw it like a picture, then. She was very little. Her mother was a big, giant woman standing at the top of the steps. In her hand was a jumprope. She was waiting for her. To punish her for not knowing her lines and making a mistake. But she would do it in such a way that no one would see. Barbara started to cry and plead. If only her fan club could see her now.

Barbara put the pages down, depressed. It was that nice way, sure. But it was also the other way. People wouldn't want to read either. If she made it nice, it wasn't honest. But she couldn't tell the truth. The pages she had just read were about as stupid as the soppy character she had played on that soap. And yet she had loved it. Loved the attention.

She'd have to start over. Her mother was right. She was a failure. She'd never make a comeback. No one would ever know who she was or what she could contribute to the world.

Not far away, Metropolitan Police cars were speeding to the scene of the latest slashing in the residential area of Hammersmith. The press was not far behind now, hot on keeping it a sensational piece of news.

A man was bending over the body. "The work of that Jane the Ripper, they're calling it now. Well, that's four women so far. A bloomin' epidemic."

"Cavendish will be right here," another man said.

"Got away with it in broad daylight. Cold blood."

"Couple of children playing near here. They didn't see anything," another man offered.

"Wait a minute, wait a minute," the man who was bending over the body said. He had a thick cockney accent. Everyone was quiet. "This here woman needs a shave then, don't she?"

They all moved closer.

"I see what you mean," someone said solemnly.

The little group was clustered as close as they could to the bloody pulp that was the body. They studied the pink paint on the lips and the long, tapered fingernails painted a bright silvery blue.

"Like Boy George," someone uttered softly, respectfully.

"I'll be damned. It's a he-she!" another exclaimed more loudly.

The man stood up, took off his cap, and scratched his head. "Cavendish is going to find this very interesting. They now have three unsolved murders of women, and the fourth turns out to be a man. Didn't think a woman would have the force to kill a woman, let alone a man that looks like a woman. Still a man, though, wasn't he? Even if he was all decked out. Wonder if the press is right—all this *Jane* the Ripper stuff."

# CHAPTER 24

By afternoon, everyone on the streets of Hammersmith and people all over London were talking about the latest murder. One woman announced in a shoe store not far away from the slashing that she was going home and not coming out until they had found the killer.

Another woman reminded her that the victim had been a man this time. "Propaganda, that's all it is," the woman said, rushing out. "No one knows for sure if the killer knew what or who he or she was killing. Someone's killing women. Make no mistake. And I don't want to give them a reason to be tempted."

Just seconds after Stephen Knight heard the news on the radio he contacted the other two. He spent his days and nights listening to the news or watching the telly, ready for another nasty killing. In between broadcasts he thought up new ways to follow up on the case or antagonize the Yard. He had had a photograph of Johanna blown up into a poster, and it sat over his mother-in-law's fireplace mantel. Though Mum didn't like it all that well. She said it made her feel sad all the time.

In an ancient pub called The Swan on the corner of the Hammersmith shopping center strip sat Detective Inspector Cavendish and Sergeant Hollings downing a couple of good, strong ales for lunch.

Cavendish was unusually gloomy.

"I don't think that's her real name," Hollings said.

"His," corrected Cavendish.

The body had been removed from the street, but the blood remained as a chilling reminder. There was still a big blood stain in the Underground commemorating the spot where Jane Harrington had been stabbed. Passengers stepped around it when they could.

"Crystal Ball. What kind of name is that?" Hollings asked as if that were what was really bothering him. He took a swig of frothy ale. What was bothering him was that the victim, this time, wasn't a woman. The point was: Did the murderer somehow know?

It was almost as if Cavendish had read his thoughts. "There's something fishy about this case. Maybe the killer knew what he had. Maybe the killer was also a man dressed as a woman. Because if that's the case . . ."

". . . you don't think a woman is doing it," Hollings finished for him. "No Jane the Ripper."

Cavendish declined to answer. Instead he said, "Captain Fulani in New York should know about this."

"Pity," said Hollings. "The papers will bury him, that's all. No one else will know. Imagine writing on a wallet I.D.: 'In case of emergency, notify: Nobody.' And the name. Crystal Ball. Another blind alley for us on this case."

"Well, it's a subculture, you know," Cavendish replied. "We'll check the spots, ask around." He knew he sounded optimistic, but that was just to keep up appearances. He had no illusions about this case. It could very well go unsolved.

Not very far from them, Barbara sat staring out the window and trying to write the third chapter of her book. She had been out marketing and heard the talk throughout the neighborhood. That a woman had been murdered in cold blood, not six blocks away. That was the reason she couldn't concentrate. She didn't feel safe. How could she write? Restlessly she walked around the small, as yet unfurnished, bedroom where her typewriter

and table were kept. She had a strange feeling that she should
go back to New York. That she was needed there.

It was Lockey who saw Barbara leave, a carry-on bag slung
over her shoulder, a smallish suitcase in her hand. "That's
odd," she said to the Mister, who had fallen asleep across the
room in his chair in front of the television, "now she's going.
Without even a word. Yahoo," she yelled, "Miss Barbara."

But Barbara couldn't hear the voice coming from the upstairs
window. She was looking for the taxi she had called. Perhaps if
she would have just acknowledged her, Lockey wouldn't have
felt so insulted, because she was sure Barbara was ignoring her.

A big black taxi that always reminded Barbara of one of the
cars in a thirties American gangster movie pulled up, and she
got in. She didn't see Lockey move away from the open window, didn't know she had made note of every detail.

At just about that time, Cavendish placed a phone call to the
task force in New York and told them a man had been killed
this time. The cab drove away. The Mister was still snoozing
peacefully in his chair, and the telly was blasting. He could
snore until suppertime as far as Lockey was concerned. Something was odd, and she was determined to find out what it was.
It was her flat to let. She had a right to know who she had let it
to. She went to the pegboard.

Tiptoeing down the stairs, she looked to both sides when she
reached the door. Then she turned the key slowly, as if she half
expected someone to be in the flat.

It was still. And bare. It wasn't furnished properly. A
wealthy girl like that? Didn't seem right to her. Everything in
the apartment, except for the oversized pillows, Lockey had
helped provide. She was good for carrying things but not good
enough to talk to . . . Was that it?

Lockey walked around the upstairs of the maisonette flat,
trying to put the pieces of the puzzle together in her mind. She
went into the kitchen and looked around. There was the little
stove Barbara had liked so much when she had let the flat.
Lockey patted it. Didn't look like the girl got much use out of
it.

It was too clean. Like the rest of the kitchen. The whole

apartment gave off the same aura. Like a ghost lived there. She looked around the kitchen, out the window at the parked cars. At the stove, then the small table. And then she screamed, frightening herself by her own sound, and clamped her hand over her mouth. The Mister might come running, and then she'd be on the spot.

But in the middle of the table was a glove. One beige fabric gardener's glove. And the glove was clutching a knife while blood stained the table. Lockey dipped her finger in. It wasn't paint or nailpolish. It was blood.

Maybe she had cut herself when she was doing the gardening. Where was she now? Who had attended to her hand?

She looked around as if someone were behind her. Her heart beating fast, feeling the panic begin to grip her, aware of the tomblike silence of the flat, she started to run, tripping once.

Her hands shaking, she opened the door quickly and breathed, then locked it and looked around. Smoothing out her housedress, she walked calmly upstairs, a little tear trickling out of her eye. She could never tell the Mister.

Before she had been afraid for Miss Barbara, she seemed so fragile. Now suddenly she knew she was afraid of her.

As Barbara moved through the grueling procedure of the line for customs she wondered a little why she had made such a reckless move. It would be about nine o'clock in the morning in her flat in Hammersmith. But it was four o'clock in the morning at Kennedy Airport. She could have written some more, fixed it.

When the taxi from Kennedy stopped in front of her Park Avenue apartment, it wasn't quite dawn. Driving into Manhattan watching the brand-new morning's pink sheen on the buildings and bridges, she had felt she was the only person in New York. It was the only time of the day when she didn't see the doorman.

She had tried to sleep on the plane, but she never could. It was an impossibly cramped situation, and she could never doze off with her legs tucked under her. She wondered idly if when she had her memory lapses and became someone else she slept. Oddly enough as bone tired as she was, her head was clear. Her body was in a temporary stupor, but she felt purposeful, almost buoyant.

Going around the apartment, she closed the venetian blinds, noticing the dust that was accumulating on them. She wanted the apartment darkened when she slept. But before that, she needed to eat. Airplane food never satisfied her. It never looked as good as it did in the commercials.

Absentmindedly she snapped on the television for company as she went into the kitchen. Taking out two eggs and a dish and fork to scramble them, she thought of Jonathan and smiled. He would be surprised that they would have more time together.

There was an early morning newsbreak on the television that she could just barely hear. Something about a murderer they wanted to catch. They were showing a sketch. She walked into the living room, but when she got to the television set they had taken it off. She shivered and felt, at that moment, very alone. It was as if she couldn't get away from danger.

She looked in the refrigerator and found some cheese. Slicing tiny chunks of cheese, she tossed them into the egg mixture, half listening to the television. There was some number to call. They had a task force. Killing. All these murders. She felt a wave of dizziness pass over her, but it was light. Hunger, that's what it was. She was starving and tired, although she knew she enjoyed her life, traveling back and forth. It made her feel important. Yes, things had never been so good. She had her work and Jonathan and money, which enabled her to afford the therapy, and soon her problems would be behind her. She gripped the counter when she thought of Dr. Walters, and her knees buckled slightly. Reaching up into a cupboard, she took out a box of Ritz crackers.

As she was slipping her cheese-fried eggs onto a plate, she noticed an open drawer. On top of the silverware tray was a big knife. A really substantial knife. Fascinated, she took it out. And as she stood and ate her eggs and crackers she wondered where it belonged and why she had forgotten where to put it. Well, she was getting sleepy. She had been up about, what, almost thirty-six hours. No wonder her mind was a little rusty.

At that moment a headache rippled through her brain like

the crackling of thunder. She sank lower and lower as if an invisible hammer were pounding the top of her head. She had fallen to her knees, and her hands were palms down on the floor. She jerked a hand up as she noticed the bits of sharp broken china and realized she had dropped the dish. For a moment she couldn't figure out where she was. Was she in the flat at Hammersmith? No, she was back in New York.

And then she noticed the knife, and she knew why she was back in New York—and just what it was she had to do. Yes, there was no putting it off. Her bag was on the couch in the living room. She turned off the television and took out her airline tickets, a small notebook, her compact, and the case for her sunglasses. Perfect. There was enough room for the knife.

Voices swirled around. She looked again at the television set and saw a blank screen. So the voices were inside her head. They were telling her what she had to do. Before, they had been just a buzz, something she could ignore. Now they were playing like a full orchestra. Her mother's voice was the loudest, urging her on, but her father was there, too, and he agreed. For once in her life her parents agreed. Even the doorman downstairs spoke to her. They all told her it was time.

When she left the apartment it was not yet rush hour. People were walking their dogs. Joggers ran by. She couldn't look at the doorman. That would be too revealing. She was holding his voice inside her head. She couldn't embarrass him by talking to him.

The air was exceptionally clear that morning. She could almost smell the buds on the Park Avenue bushes. It would be a warm early summer day. The knife was resting inside her beige cowhide bag, and she noticed she was walking alone now. Her voices had left, and the crescendo inside her head had quieted down. She walked east on Ninety-sixth Street. There was time. She was in no hurry. The side streets were empty. In an hour the picture would change as people started running for buses and disappearing into the subway. She ran her tongue across her teeth, feeling the excitement mount.

A man looked at her closely. But all he saw was a fairly attractive woman wearing a pantsuit and carrying a beige bag. Priscilla wondered if he wasn't looking through her. The body wasn't that beautiful. Not that she cared. Determined, she just kept walking.

It was a long walk, but it was worth it. Finally she pushed the revolving doors and smiled at the man behind the desk. He looked up in recognition and nodded back.

At the elevator bank, she pressed the button and waited. She was alone. When she rode up, she was also alone. Getting off, she saw another bank of elevators adjacent to the hallway. It was a good place to stand and wait and watch.

Downstairs Dr. Alvin Walters was thinking about the woman he had spent the night with. He would have to end that relationship. She was getting too dependent on him. That was the trouble with being a psychiatrist. He was so compassionate— women just naturally wanted to lean on him. In the elevator he thought of his nine o'clock patient. She wanted to terminate. He didn't think she was ready.

The elevator doors opened, and he took his keys from his pocket. As he was opening his office door he experienced the oddest sensation that there was somebody or something behind him.

He turned quickly and saw her. She smiled at him, as if she had a sheepish secret, and was holding something behind her back like a bouquet of flowers. Why did she look so different? he thought. There were lines under her eyes and her hair was combed, teased, so that it seemed to be sticking out. And the smile. It was triumphant.

"Barbara," he said patiently, "you made a mistake. Your appointment is tomorrow. While I'm always happy to see you, I just can't see you now. I have a patient coming at nine." He turned to open the door.

Smiling gleefully, she brought her arm up and let the knife sink into the base of his neck. Now he would never find out about her and stop what she had to do. Shocked, he made a move to turn while the knife sliced through his back, cutting his suit jacket in half. "I'm Priscilla," she said, "not Barbara. I'm the one who kills."

Pitifully he sought out her wild eyes as he crumpled to the floor. "Mistake," he uttered in a painful whisper, then stilled. Blood was trickling from his mouth, and Priscilla stepped back, enjoying it, loving his last word. Yes, he had made a mistake. But he wouldn't make any more.

She turned. He had been quiet like all the others because she had taken him by surprise. The hall was empty. Elevators would be too risky, though. Moving swiftly to the door marked Stairs, she began to run down them. She felt exhilarated. He had reminded her a lot of Mum—telling her you can do this, you can't do that. And she had wanted to kill Mum so badly before she died.

Combing her hair in the elevator, which was approaching the seventeenth floor, was Vera Stevens, ready for her nine o'clock appointment. This appointment was so important to her that she had written out the main issues on index cards so she wouldn't forget anything. She hadn't slept a wink the night before. Everything had just kept rolling around and around in her head. Now she felt calm. Dr. Walters would figure it out for her. He would tell her what to do. He was very good about that.

She was still rehearsing in her mind everything she had to tell him when she turned the corner. Her eyes were level with the door, and it took a few seconds before her mind became aware that there was a pool of blood inching down the hall, threatening the tips of her shoes. Her eyes closed, her hands over her mouth, she screamed. It was loud and hideous and she couldn't stop it. Her psychiatrist was lying face down, body twisted, the blood seeping out of him.

A door down the hall flew open. A man in an undershirt and pants, holding a rolled-up newspaper, peered out. He just stood there gaping.

Another door popped open. A woman with two rollers on the top of her head, wearing a blue-flowered duster, peeked out over her chain. Her hand flew to her mouth. "Oh, my God!" she screamed. "Oh, my God! I knew when they let psychiatrists in the building there would be trouble!"

"Someone should call the police," the man said. "We shouldn't just stand here."

Vera Stevens's screams turned into frantic little whimpers, and her throat began to feel raw. She fingered her index cards sadly. Her problems would be harder to solve now.

"Who do I call?" asked the man.

"Call 911, for God's sake!" the woman across the hall barked. "I'll get the super, call downstairs, tell security. Security, ha ha, that's a laugh."

Both of them closed their doors, leaving the horrified woman alone in the hall. They had looked at the bleeding lump once, then very carefully avoided it.

The operator answering the 911 call felt a growing excitement as she jotted down the information. Hanging up, she announced to everyone else, "There's been a slashing."

"Call the task force at the Nineteenth," someone advised her.

She didn't make the move. "It's in a building, though. An apartment on the West Side. And it was a man who was stabbed."

There was a silence. "Where's the building?"

"On Seventy-first and Central Park West."

"That's the Seventeenth Precinct," someone said.

The woman was in a quandary. Should she call the Nineteenth's task force, like they had been instructed to? Or because it didn't exactly fit the M.O., should she call the Seventeenth Precinct? She had to do something. They had to send someone!

"Call the Seventeenth," someone instructed her. "It was just a man stabbed in an apartment house. Jane the Ripper only goes after women."

They knew they had fallen from grace, as it were. Tammy and Carolyn left unsaid what they didn't want to know. They could be kicked off the task force and put back on regular duty. There was an unspoken agreement between them, although neither had a chance to say anything, that they would continue with the case anyway.

When the phone call from 911 came into Captain Fulani's office, the operator spelled out her name, in case he wanted to say who had taken the call when it broke in the newspapers. Now it was Fulani's dilemma. Was it a jealousy case? Did it belong to the Seventeenth? It didn't fit the M.O. Or—and he reached into his jacket pocket and pulled out a Rolaid—the

M.O. was stretching amorphously to include men and apartment buildings.

He thought of Cavendish and the call he had received from London. Was that coincidence? A man had been killed over there. And now it was a man in New York. He belched and vowed to stick to cheese sandwiches instead of the lousy spicey crap they were ordering out. The point was, maybe women ran around killing women, but he'd bet his paycheck that women didn't go around stabbing men. He thought Patuto was right.

"Get me Hank Patuto!" he yelled.

"He went down to the Village on a couple of leads," a man said shortly, standing in the doorway.

Fulani tossed a dime on his desk. Heads it was. "Zuckerman and Kealing," he said. He got up and went into the task force room.

"Zuckerman and Kealing," he repeated. They both looked up. That's it, thought Tammy. We're off the case.

"Call came in. Apartment building on Seventy-first and Central Park West." He gave Carolyn a piece of paper with the address. "Man has been stabbed. Don't know if it fits the M.O. or not. If not, we'll turn it over to the Seventeenth. If it is, Patuto will take it."

It wasn't until they were out of the precinct that either of them spoke. "I feel like a God damned secretary," Carolyn said.

" 'Patuto will take it,' " Tammy mimicked.

They drove almost wordlessly downtown. As they parked near Columbus Avenue Carolyn said, "You know, I feel like a go-fer."

"The case ain't closed yet. Let's see what we got here."

In the lobby they flashed their shields and I.D.'s before two dark-skinned Arabic men, who seemed to be patrolling the front desk. They seemed very nervous. They thought they had seen a delivery man go up at about that time. They had said it was okay. But they couldn't remember seeing him come down. Outside of that, there was nothing out of the usual.

They walked toward the mirrored columns and waited for the elevator.

"Classy," Tammy said, then whistled softly.

Carolyn looked at the mirrors through the revolving doors. "Here come the Crime Scene Unit and, looks like, the medical examiner's people."

They didn't wait. The first thing they had to do when they got to the seventeenth floor was clear it. The weeping Vera Stevens was put in a car and sent home, just a little ahead of the press, who had just gotten the call.

The woman who had called the 911 number said sarcastically, upon seeing Tammy and Carolyn, "I thought they called the *cops!*" At the same moment, the crew that had been behind them came onto the floor.

"Now we're seeing some action," someone said.

An officer, a patrolman from the neighborhood who had been called, was standing in front of the elevators and having a hard time with a woman who refused to be sent back downstairs.

"My office is on this floor. What's the trouble?" she asked him.

"Like I said, there's been a murder on the floor. Can't let anyone up, careful of whom we let down. Sorry."

"Don't tell me *sorry,*" she replied angrily. "My office is 17F, and I have a patient coming in five minutes."

She walked past the officer and strode down the hall. Tammy and Carolyn looked up at about the same time she screamed. It was a short screech, followed by a long gasp. Then Beth Belmont went about composing herself professionally.

"What happened?" she asked.

"Someone stabbed him," Tammy answered. "Killed him."

"Oh, my God!" Her hands flew to her face.

"You're . . . ?"

"Dr. Beth Belmont. I'm a psychiatrist. I rent the other office from Alvin. We're—we're—colleagues. I don't believe this."

Carolyn had her notebook out. "Can you think of anyone who might have wanted to murder Dr. Walters?"

"No. No one."

"What about one of his patients?" Carolyn asked.

Beth shook her head and sighed. "Oh, God, do those things happen?"

"Are you familiar with his patients?"

She looked away from the body and the men who were working on it. "Can we go into my office? I'll give you his files." She had her keys out. "I can't stand here. It's very hard to look at someone whom you—you . . ." Her voice trailed off. She would have to take a Valium. Any minute now her patient would come up on the elevator, and she would be turned away.

In a green khaki-colored file cabinet beside his bookcase were all of Alvin Walters's patient case histories, active and inactive up to two years ago. It was a gold mine of a source if the killer had been a disgruntled, vengeful patient.

"The key," Beth said. "I wonder where he keeps the key?"

"Try it. Maybe it's just open. After all, it's his office," Tammy said.

Beth approached the file cabinet as if she were trespassing. Sure enough, it opened. Everything was in alphabetical order. Pendaflex files hung from the sides with all the pertinent information about his patients. She glanced through them, running her fingertips across them. It wasn't much. He didn't take notes —she knew that. But there was something about each patient. Most of his patients were female.

Occasionally he had discussed a case or two with her, so some of the names were vaguely familiar. She lifted them out, still in shock. Somehow she expected him to ask for them back.

Tammy and Carolyn left the office wondering if this belonged to the Seventeenth Precinct or not. The body was slashed the same way, but the body was a man and he was murdered in an apartment building. And it seemed premeditated.

After they had left, Beth Belmont wandered around the office. She had taken a Valium, but it hadn't taken effect yet. The plants, she should water the plants. Alvin would want her to do that. He wouldn't want his plants to die.

One thing bothered her. She had given those two detectives all his files. But nowhere in his case histories was the one that had fascinated him so. The lady with multiple personalities.

When they got back to the Nineteenth and walked past the desk and waved to the patrolman sitting there, Carolyn stopped in front of the stairs and said, "I *wish* they would put elevators in this relic."

"Now, now," said Tammy. "That's not what's really bothering you. Changing the decor of this museum isn't going to change the case."

"I have a funny feeling that things are going to get worse," Carolyn muttered.

"Me, too."

The floor was busy, and no one looked up except Hank Patuto. He smiled at them. "Guess what, ladies?" he taunted, his mouth curving into a smirk.

"Tell me . . . I can't *wait* to hear," Tammy replied in a tone that belied her nervousness. Had he taken over already?

"They're taking the picture of that woman off the air." They were still staring at him when he added, "And you didn't hear about Scotland Yard?"

Forgetting to think up a smart retort, Carolyn shook her head and Tammy said, "No."

"They had another murder," he announced smugly. Like one privy to privileged information, which he was, he went on. "It was a man. A man dressed like a woman. So how can a woman be slashing a man? In fact, no one believes anymore, least of all the city, that it's a lady killer. Now what do you ladies think of that?"

Tammy and Carolyn looked at each other and walked away. *They* still believed it was a woman. Who ate British candies. Maybe the same woman. But they knew that no one would believe them.

# CHAPTER 25

A copy of the *New York Post* sat on the coffee table. The headline was in big bold letters: SHRINK SLASHED. The paper was upside down. He turned it right side up and studied it again.

It wasn't a woman this time. It had been a man. And he hadn't been murdered on the street. It had been right outside his office in one of those glitzy high-rise apartment buildings. Go figure.

He flicked on the television set. Time for the news. It felt like all he had done lately was wait for the news and watch this story.

He picked up a stick of chewing gum, unwrapped it, and shoved it in his mouth. There was bound to be something about this new murder. The set started to snow. Agitated, he jumped up and adjusted the knob. There was an announcer with a microphone and he was on the street.

He was talking to Detective Hank Patuto, who was saying that they did believe this latest case, the killing of the man, was the work of the slasher. When he was asked if it was the work of a Jane the Ripper, he declined comment.

Then the announcer started interviewing people on the street, centering on folks in front of a bus stop.

"Excuse me, sir," he said, holding the microphone down a little. "How do you feel about the recent reign of terror, the slashings?"

The little bald-headed man stepped closer and replied loudly into the microphone. "It's a terrible thing for the city of New York."

"Do you think a woman is doing all this—a Jane the Ripper?"

"Nah, I never thought that. Women don't kill that way. When they do it, it's always with the wallet. Like the alimony I have to pay my two ex-wives."

There was a short ripple of laughter throughout the crowd.

He next interviewed a passerby, a woman in a suit, carrying a briefcase. "Do you think the slasher is a woman, ma'am?"

The man sitting in front of the television put his gum behind his tongue. He didn't want to make a noise or miss a word of this. This was key. This was what he had been looking for.

The woman stopped as if she were doing him a favor to get a second of her time. "Of course I don't think it's a woman. This is set up by the sexist media. It's good copy. But ultimately they're still trying to make a woman the victim."

The man got up impatiently and switched off the set. Pacing around the living room, he changed his mind and turned it on again. He saw the announcer interviewing a man in a yellow hard hat. "If Jane the Ripper were doing it, it would be an all-time first. No, these murders are being committed by a man. A very clever man. Women aren't capable of that. Maybe he wants everyone to think he's a woman, though."

Irwin Dinkle put his chin in his hands, his elbows resting on the coffee table, and thought about that. And the interviews before that. The body he had seen lying in a pool of blood on upper Park Avenue had had a bag attached to her. She was Enid Thornton. He had seen it. He had held his breath until they had identified the body as Polly Manklin. He had watched the tearful funeral on television and cried with the family. Then they decided the killer was Enid Thornton. Every time he turned on the television there was her face, or a drawing of her, and a number to call. This Enid was supposedly quite a lady. She had zipped open three more women.

"Shit!" he said out loud. Yes, he could go to the police. But that wouldn't make any difference now. Besides, they seemed to be so screwed up they didn't even care. He could tell them a lot of things to ease his conscience. About the picture in the small photo album, her I.D. in her bag. It was of a brunette, like the sketch they had on the air. But she had no earring in one ear and was less glamorous. Same woman, though. He was positive about that. But what was the sense? The cops were about to change their minds again. He could smell it coming. And if they were now going to look for a man, why should he lay his ass on the line and say that he had seen the body *and* the bag, and that they had the wrong sketch of Enid Thornton? Enid Thornton didn't do it anyway.

Jonathan always bought a *New York Post* to read on the subway, going home from work. Not that he was into sensationalism. But after a day of seeking out pedantic books, it was a way of relaxing. Tonight he bought a paper out of habit but didn't really look at it. He was due over at Barbara's. It was lovely of her to come back early. He wondered if it was because of him and hoped it might be.

It was so nice out that he decided to walk the forty-odd blocks up Park Avenue instead of taking the stuffy subway ride.

He straightened his tie. It was a perfect night for a light dinner. Perhaps they could go to a Japanese restaurant and then later . . . He smiled. It was time for them to make love. He felt good about that tonight. Everything was in the timing.

He thought about the nice evening they would have and the turning point in their relationship, and it seemed a short walk, rather than a long one.

When he reached her apartment on the corner of Ninety-sixth Street and Park, he announced himself to the doorman and waited to go up. The doorman rang once, twice, then turned to Jonathan.

"No answer. She's not home."

Jonathan thought a minute. Barbara was a very punctual person. She must have gotten caught in traffic. He looked down at his watch. It was one minute after seven. Okay, so she would be a few minutes late. He sat down on a tufted apple green love seat to the right of the elevators and folded his hands, watching the people come and go in the building. A few were walking dogs, mostly curly French poodles.

At seven thirty he got tired of studying people, but he didn't have the patience to pull out his newspaper from his briefcase. Instead he counted the minutes. All the way until eight o'clock. He was beginning to feel somewhere between worried and disappointed. He was also getting hungry.

At nine o'clock his hunger and immobility began to make him edgy. The doorman nodded at him and Jonathan took it as a suggestion to leave. From nine to nine thirty he waited outside the building, careful not to wait on the Park Avenue side where the doorman might see him. At ten o'clock he began waiting across the street because dog walkers were beginning to eye him suspiciously. A few minutes past ten, not understanding what had happened, his hunger having leveled off into a dull headache and nausea, he decided to take the subway and go home to Brooklyn.

For her appointment on that Friday, the eleventh of June, she dressed very carefully. A pale blue summer dress with a full skirt and white flat-heeled sandals. She wondered to herself as she poured a glass of orange juice, Did it really make a difference? She was facing an ordeal, not a fashion show. Lately she didn't even want to eat breakfast before she went. She was afraid she'd lose it.

If just once he would give her some real support for even showing up. Tell her she was brave. Tell her it took guts to subject yourself to that. She realized she was crying. Sometimes she thought she hated him. No wonder she dreamed of killing him. Come to think of it, she had had that nightmare last night. She brushed the tears from her face. No wonder she was crying senselessly.

She wished he could cut out a little block in her mind, adjust some knobs, and she'd be well. What she needed was a fairy godmother to wave a magic wand over her. Then she'd be well and she wouldn't have to remember anything that went before.

Sighing, she closed the door and ran down the hall to catch the elevator. There was too much she couldn't remember now. Lately she couldn't even remember when her memory lapses occurred.

When the cab pulled around the circle, the crystal chandeliers were glittering through the large windows, and Barbara saw that it was actually a few minutes after nine. She hated to be late for anything, especially him. As luck would have it, the elevator seemed to take years to reach the main floor. She was rushing so much she almost tripped over the painter's cloth that was lying on the floor. Someone must be painting their apartment. Still, it was dangerous to leave something like that out where people could trip over it. She put her hand on the doorknob, and it didn't give. It was only then that she slowed down and saw the note taped to the door.

She read it and shook her head, her hands over her mouth. Oh, *no!*

A woman was just coming out of her apartment and saw Barbara standing there. "Don't you read the papers or listen to the news, lady? He was stabbed. Killed," she said harshly.

Barbara stumbled blindly down the hall, tripping over the painter's canvas, seeing now the upturned corner with the blood stain. She had dreamed of stabbing him, and someone had actually done it. The note had said his colleague would call to help his patients. But who would really help her now?

There were police officers and plainclothesmen in the lobby. Walking quickly past them, she let the revolving doors push her out of the building. There was a phone booth on the corner. Digging into her bag for her wallet, she found a quarter. She dialed information first and wrote down the number. Cars and trucks and buses were passing up the avenue, and it was impossible to hear.

When she dialed again she stuck her finger in her free ear. "Jonathan? Listen, I have all day free. Can you tell them you're sick or something and meet me?"

Jonathan had not slept more than two hours the night before. He had waited for her to call and she hadn't. In reality she had just decided to stand him up. Anger was not something that came easily to Jonathan Segal. Today it did. "Where were you last night?" he demanded.

"Last night? I just got back from London. Where do you think I was?" She could barely hear above the street noise.

There was a silence. She was making a fool out of him. "Barbara, you got back from London the night before, and we made plans to meet last night. I wanted it to be a special evening. I waited for you." He caught himself. No use saying he waited for three long hours.

Barbara was sobbing loudly now. It was too much to handle. Her secret was too hard to keep, and now she didn't even have a psychiatrist to help her with it. Jonathan had never spoken that harshly to her. He hated her now, and she didn't blame him.

"Stop crying," he said patiently. There were people lined up for help in front of his desk.

She couldn't stop. A day, she had lost a day. And how could she tell him where she had been if she didn't remember? "Jonathan?" she begged. "Could you do me a big favor?" She was using all her control to speak evenly, to be heard above the roar of the traffic. "Could you ask no questions right now and just believe me when I say this is *very* important? Something terrible has happened. I need to be with you."

"Go home," he said firmly. Of course he had to do what she asked. He was needed. "I'll be over as soon as I can."

There was now a long line in front of his desk, and he saw that people were impatient. So there *was* a reason she had stood him up. But more important, she was in trouble. Jonathan remembered his mother. There were times that he was compelled to go rushing to her side. He mentally calculated his sick days, then proceeded to go through the motions of becoming suddenly ill. He ran his hand across his forehead as if he were checking for a temperature, he shook away feigned dizziness, and he prepared himself for a major coughing spasm.

She had canceled all her appointments for the day and was trying to reach his patients, to help them with referrals, to say something supportive. It was because of her that there was no police bar or guard at the door. She said it would be too jarring for patients who were still coming up to the door, who hadn't heard. The note was enough. It merely said that Dr. Walters had passed away and a colleague would contact them. It gave them a number in case of emergency. But she wasn't answering her calls.

She looked around her little office. It would be impossible to practice here anymore. She got up and moved into his office. Something was bothering her. Even with two more Valium and an emergency call to her old analyst in Chicago, she had been awake half the night. That patient wasn't in the files. The one that had meant so much to him. The one with several personalities. She couldn't remember her name. And she couldn't figure out where the files had gone.

What mystified her was why he hadn't consulted her more than he had. Alvin wasn't a specialist in multiple personalities. He was a psychotherapist. She couldn't remember whether he was into psychoanalysis or if he really even approved of it.

Finding the file was now almost as much of an obsession as the case must have been for him. She remembered the woman but not her name, if she ever knew it. She had only seen her for a minute or two, and she hadn't seen her change identities, although she had certainly heard her agonized screams through the connecting wall. Come to think of it, she couldn't say that she remembered exactly what she looked like. Except that her looks weren't too memorable.

She looked carefully around the office. There was the recliner he'd never use again. The couch, the chair to match, his textbooks. His ex-wife would sell everything—she was sure of that. Alvin wouldn't have approved. He would have liked less what she was planning to do to him. Have him cremated. Less bother.

She shuddered. Just a short while ago, it seemed, he had sat in this office. And now the building was charging the apartment for a new strip of carpeting to replace the bloody reminder.

She checked behind pictures, under pillows, under the couch, in every book of the bookshelves, and there was no case history. No mention of the multiple personality case he had prized. Without thinking she decided to open his desk to see if there were keys to some hidden cabinet somewhere. And that's when she saw it. Flat out in the desk drawer were two full file folders.

She pulled them out and saw the name typed on the label of each. Barbara Hargrove. She opened one up and saw written notes from his sessions. This was the dissociative personality disorder. Curious, she walked over to the couch and, her legs tucked under her, began to read the accounting of his sessions with her.

It was early afternoon of a dark gray, drizzly day in London. Although it was foggy, the BBC cameras were there anyway. As were several radio stations and reporters from many of the London papers. There were picket signs that said: "Clean Up the Yard" and "Blood for Blood." Considering there were only three marchers picketing and chanting on Victoria Street in front of Scotland Yard, there was a multitude of coverage.

There was also a crowd that had gathered to watch the spectacle. Close by was a big wooden sign that read: "Three against Victimization." A knife was stuck into the center and surrounded by huge red painted drops of blood.

A reporter shoved a microphone in front of Annie's mouth. Her throat was sore from shouting. She saw a television camera taking aim at her. She knew that her husband would know what she had been up to, and at that moment, she didn't give a damn.

"I'm here," she said in a loud but slightly quaking voice, "because my mother was murdered in cold blood in Heathrow Airport. She never had an enemy in her life. She wasn't even a British citizen. She had the rest of her life to live. She had a new little granddaughter to enjoy." Several women in the crowd began to cry. Annie's voice became bolder. "Why hasn't Scotland Yard solved these murders yet? I want to know who killed my mother so I can sleep at night."

A cheer rose from the crowd. "Stop these senseless killings!" someone screeched, and the mob was brought to a near-riot pitch. It was a newsworthy event in that no one had ever protested against Scotland Yard before. No one had ever complained, either.

"Where's the Fourth against Victimization?" asked one reporter who was clearly amused.

"We haven't found—uh—him yet, but he's welcome to join us," Brian Harrington said. The attitude of the reporter angered him. He was not risking his job anymore. He had taken so many days off they had fired him.

He began to chant and soon the watching crowd enthusiastically joined him. "Don't just sit there . . . Find the Ripper."

Detective Inspector Cavendish and Detective Sergeant Hollings stood by the windows that lined the side facing the street and watched the demonstration.

"We *could* go down and make an appearance," Hollings suggested.

"I don't want my mug on the telly tonight," Cavendish replied. "I'm sure I'd have to make a statement."

"And . . . ?"

"What can I say except that Scotland Yard agrees one hundred percent that it's an abominable situation and we're trying our best. Working round the clock. Trying as hard as we can to find the killer."

"Jane or Jack?" Hollings asked slyly.

Cavendish walked away from the window and started back for his office. "That's why I don't want to go down there."

Two detectives from the Yard were getting into a car parked close by. They had seen part of the protest but had to answer a call. It was quite near the sight of the last murder, but it was just a routine call. Someone who thought they had a suspect. There were a lot of folks accusing others of being suspicious. People were just plain scared. Phones were being answered day and night at Scotland Yard. Hardly enough detectives or cars to take all the calls.

They rode through the village of Hammersmith in silence. After this they had a few more stops. It seemed endless.

"Here's the address," said one detective as he slowed the car and parked. "Probably nothing will come of it," he grunted.

"Nothing's come of any of it," the other detective chimed in.

They buzzed the bell and almost immediately the door opened. "You must be Scotland Yard, then," the woman said. She was a short, stocky woman with steel gray hair pulled back into a tight bun.

"Right you have it. I'm Detective Rutherford, and this is Detective Sunshine."

She studied their identification briefly and then let them in.

"I'm Mrs. Lockwood. And I made the call." She lowered her voice. "If the Mister knew, he'd kill me." She opened the door to Barbara's flat and the three of them went in.

"Not too cozy, is it?" commented Detective Sunshine, referring to the bareness of the flat.

"I told you," she said, "it's the same downstairs, and she has *plenty* of money to buy furniture, believe me—the way she goes back and forth to the States."

"Is that why you called us?" asked Detective Rutherford in a monotone.

"I want you to look at this," Lockey said, then led them into the kitchen.

From the big kitchen windows they could see their car parked out front. Both looking down at once, they saw the solitary object lying in the middle of the table: a bloody butcher's knife. It gleamed under the kitchen light except for one spot that was dull. That was covered with a red substance.

Using a towel hanging nearby, Detective Rutherford picked up the knife and looked closer. "Dried blood," he said.

Lockey smiled smugly. "Course it's blood," she snapped, wanting them to know she didn't pull them down there for nothing. "I found it right after that murder a few streets down."

"You were in her apartment?"

Lockey was defensive. "Well, she was out, but I wanted to check on a leak, and there was this knife. She takes off. Doesn't even say good-bye. Not that she gives much of a hello, you understand."

One of the men touched the sharp tip of the blade. "We'd like to take this for fingerprints. When do you expect her back?"

Lockey shrugged. "She doesn't check in with me, that's for sure."

"How long has she had the flat?"

"Since the end of May. She paid her rent in advance."

"Paid by check, then?" asked Detective Sunshine.

"No. She paid the month in pounds. Said she didn't have a British bank yet."

"What else can you tell us about her? Any reason you can think of for a knife with blood on it?" He wasn't terribly excited about it, but they had to check out everything—and this *was* Hammersmith.

"Well, she's not a butcher, is she?" Lockey replied sarcastically. She squinted her eyes as if she were looking into the distance. "And there was one other time I was curious about her. There was, uh, something wrong with the pipes downstairs, so I used the key and looked around—I mean, to see if there was a leak or something in the plumbing. I found a knife then, too. It was just sticking into the wooden floor. Something odd about her."

Rutherford began to write in his notebook. "What's her name?"

"Her name is Barbara Hargrove," Lockey said.

The detectives exchanged looks but said nothing.

"Could you give us a description of her?"

"Well, she's not too tall, not too short. Not a great beauty but not homely, either. She has brunette hair, falls around her chin about shoulder length, I would say. Brown eyes—or are they black? A little of both, I guess."

"Does she wear glasses?" Sunshine asked.

"Not that I recall." Lockey thought about it some more. "I may have seen her once or twice from a distance in sunglasses."

Both detectives recognized her name—Barbara Hargrove—from working on the case. She was the woman the stewardess had seen at the airport. The woman with the discrepancy. Dana Hargrove was the post office box name they had tried to trace in New York City.

Sunshine was getting just a little excited by this information, but he didn't dare show it. Besides, it might be just routine. The name *Barbara Hargrove* might just be a coincidence and that's all. And she might not be able to lead them to Dana Hargrove. "Do you have her address in New York?"

Lockey stared blankly. "No, I don't. She didn't pay by check or anything."

"Did she ever say at any time where she lived?"

"Just New York City."

Rutherford realized then that the Yard had made a mistake. They had tried to trace the post office box of one Dana Hargrove as the holder of the credit card and had done nothing to trace one bearing Barbara Hargrove's name. It may have led to something. On the other hand, they were tracing one hundred and eighty-six names from that airline alone for, seemingly, no reason at all. "No address, then?" he repeated. That was about the jist of it. She might not *have* an address. Who's to say she was from New York City? Who's to say she didn't cut her finger on the knife? They'd have to run blood tests on it and see how it compared with the murdered man's blood.

"Wait a second! Wait just a pretty second here," Lockey said, determined. Under the loft bed was a small piece of luggage. Lockey pulled it out, looked at the I.D. tag on it, and spun around triumphantly. "Barbara Hargrove," she read, and then gave the detectives her Park Avenue address.

# CHAPTER 26

There was something wrong when a psychiatrist was talking to herself out loud. Dr. Beth Belmont was the first to realize that. There was also something wrong with what she had just read, so she was having an inner dialogue and her lips just happened to be moving with it. She wished she could discuss this with another colleague, but she really didn't feel she could.

She was having a problem with Alvin's diagnosis. Not with the fact that the woman had several personalities. She believed that there *was* a dissociative personality disorder. It was easy, reading about the monster mother and the shadowy father, to understand why. It was unbearably sad—but plausible. What she didn't believe was the sterile perfection of it all.

Three personalities, just like Eve: Barbara, the known personality, quiet and unassuming; Enid, the flirtatious, outrageous coquette; and Dana, the quiet, distant intellectual, the analyst's helper who kept track of the other selves. It was too pat. It would make a good movie, but she didn't believe it. Alvin tended to be a little superficial sometimes, and she thought his interpretation of this case was just that.

It was just that it was such a tricky illness to treat. Up to the time of the publication of the book on Eve, then the movie about her, there had only been two hundred known cases of multiple personality. Everyone in the profession knew now that that poor woman had been ripped off by her doctor, who wanted to gain control of the movie rights. It was eventually shown that she had—hard to believe as it was—twenty-two personalities and not the three her doctors stopped at. They had refused to consider more even though she said she wasn't cured. Beth shook her head in disbelief. Thank God that Alvin hadn't been the type to capitalize on a patient's illness.

She had heard of a lot of shams around this unique disease. Many criminals pleaded a multiple personality to win a plea of insanity. It was almost losing its credibility. She shook her head, her lips still moving as if in prayer. This one was real, poor soul. Such suffering contained in one body. Such a sick, pathetic mother who lived only vaguely in a shattered memory. Beth felt tears come to her eyes. It was so incredibly unfortunate.

But so was the fact that Alvin Walters had been murdered.

She took a bright mustard-colored Kleenex from the box that still rested on the floor and blew her nose. They were looking for a male deliveryman that might have slipped into the building. Plus they were interviewing all his bewildered patients. But there was one they didn't know about.

She believed he might have been murdered by a patient. It could happen. Although she hadn't ever read of a case like that. She mentally ran through some of the male patients Alvin had discussed with her, and then she looked down at the file folder.

Could this patient have been the one who killed him? But according to Alvin's case notes, none of the existing personalities could have killed him. That was the catch. None of them were really "killer" personalities.

Pacing around the floor, her hand to her chin, she supposed it was because that was all he could summon. But what if—just suppose what if—there were other personalities, others he hadn't tapped? She shook her head. No, it didn't make sense.

Wait a minute! She rushed back to the notes. There was a very clear section where he reported that she had had dreams of killing women who reminded her of her mother. He had attributed it to repressed anger. Yet the patient, in the notes, went back time and again to this insistence of killing, of being a killer. Beth was reminded again of Eve. It had been an erroneous diagnosis. There were, in time, twenty-two faces to Eve before she was cured.

Beth looked up at the ceiling as though it were a hot line to heaven. "Alvin," she whispered, "I think you made a little mistake."

She collected all the papers lying on the couch and put them back into the two folders. There was only one thing to do. She couldn't keep this information to herself. Barbara Hargrove could have had a killer personality Alvin didn't know about.

In five minutes she had locked up the office. She had canceled all her patients for a few days, farming out the emergencies to another colleague. She had talked to most of Walter's patients and given them advice. More were sure to call as they found out. She sighed. She had an enormous workload. There was little time to play sleuth.

But she couldn't live with herself unless she told the truth.

In less than fifteen minutes she arrived by cab at the Nineteenth Precinct. She ran up the stairs, the files in her briefcase, and entered the lobby of the decrepit precinct house. Going up to the front desk, she announced herself, informed the patrolman that she wanted to see the two woman detectives she had talked to before because she had pertinent information on the case, and then waited there. There was really nowhere to sit.

The patrolman looked at her wearily. She looked legit enough, holding a briefcase and wearing a classy pantsuit, but in this precinct, all kinds came rolling in. Especially now. Upstairs it was a three-ring circus. He didn't even know if anyone would pick up his call—they were so busy with the task force lines.

He was wrong. A man was passing by as that phone rang, and he picked up immediately.

"Lady here to see someone," the patrolman at the desk said. "Said she has information on the case."

"I'm a psychiatrist," Beth mouthed, but he didn't see her.

"Says she wants to speak to the two woman detectives—that would be Zuckerman and Kealing."

Patuto looked around the room. They weren't in it.

Beth Belmont was further explaining in a whisper that she was the murdered psychiatrist's colleague, but the patrolman became confused listening to too many voices. Patuto now had twenty-five men under him waiting for orders, and the phones were all ringing at the same time. He wondered why he had been such a good Joe and picked up this one. Someone else should have answered it. He was too busy.

"Can you send someone down?" the patrolman asked.

"Take her name and number, and I'll have someone get back to her immediately."

The patrolman asked her for her phone number, and that made her furious. She had come all the way down to help *them*. Now they were telling her to go home and wait? Beth Belmont didn't wait for people. They waited for her. If they didn't want her information, fine. She had more important work to do.

As she was walking down the steps, she was so angry she almost didn't see Tammy and Carolyn approaching. They almost didn't recognize *her*—they were so tired and depressed. Patuto had sent them to interview a man, a suspect, but it turned out to be a wild-goose chase. If the suspect was the one they were supposed to be interviewing, he was all of eight years old. Another trick of the vindictive Patuto.

They all practically bumped into each other before anyone had a chance to say, "Aren't you . . . ?"

It was Dr. Beth Belmont who spoke first, and she spoke quickly, "Say, can we talk? I have something I found. Another patient file that I think is of interest. I think she might have killed him. But no one upstairs wants to talk to me."

Upstairs the exhausted Captain Fulani was summoned once more from a meeting in the task force room.

"Yes, Inspector Cavendish," he blurted out, even before the caller had a chance to identify himself.

But he was right. And the British detective sounded just as tired. "We have a lead we'd like you to check out. It's a Park Avenue address in New York. Name's Barbara Hargrove. That's the woman whose name came up when we were tracing Dana Hargrove. Maybe they're related. The thing is, she also rents a flat in Hammersmith near where we had our latest murder. Now maybe she went out and killed a squirrel in the garden, I don't know, but we have to check out this woman who is not in her flat at Hammersmith but believed to be in New York." He sighed and stopped to light something, Fulani wasn't sure what. "We'd appreciate it if you could do us this favor. It just might have something to do with your murders as well, you know."

Fulani agreed and promised to let the inspector know. He had Hank Patuto called in. More and more he had come to rely on this Nineteenth Precinct detective. Patuto agreed how important it was and agreed personally to go with two squad cars.

But when he came out of Fulani's office and picked up the phone to get someone, he got another call. And another call. And another. In two minutes, he had his hat on and he was on his way. They had cornered the deliveryman spotted in the building. This could be his collar. He could crack the whole case open.

As he was going out the door, he remembered he had started to make a phone call. Well, he would. It could wait, though. Because it wasn't as if it were important. It was a favor. So while he wanted to follow an order, which he would, he needed to be on top of a lead. Now.

When Jonathan rang the doorbell, Barbara was still wearing the sky blue summer dress. He thought how lovely, though pale, she looked.

Barbara wanted to fling her arms about him, she was so glad to see him, but she didn't know how to be impulsive. She had called Eva, who had been too upset to talk because of Dr. Walters. Barbara had ended up comforting her. Now she had someone to talk to.

He sat down on the couch and loosened his tie. "Now what's all this about?" he asked. He had used that tone with Mother when she had become particularly upset.

"Do you want a cup of coffee, tea? A cold drink?"

He shook his head, privately amazed at his attitude of assertiveness. "I want you to tell me what's bothering you."

Barbara sat in the armchair opposite him, nervously twisting the folds of her dress with her fingers. "About last night," she began hesitantly, wondering if it was the best way to start.

He looked aside. He wasn't sure he wanted to hear this. That she had been out with another man. Is that why he had taken off from work—to be hurt?

She looked at him. He looked perturbed with her, and she didn't blame him. Maybe she shouldn't tell him. She swallowed and licked her lips, which felt dry. She looked down at the rug, up at the chandelier, away from his eyes at the blue drapes that were blowing in the breeze. She was reminded suddenly that this was what it had been like with Dr. Walters. She began to feel panicky again. "Should I turn on the air conditioner?" she asked.

He shook his head, which looked bowed. "No, just talk," he said, somewhat sadly.

She began to speak slowly and had to bite her lip to keep from crying. Her eyes were fixed on the wooden part of the floor not covered by carpeting. "The reason I wasn't with you last night is because . . . I don't know where I was or even whom I was with or what I did. I have memory lapses . . . I—I stop being me. I have other personalities. I become someone else and then I can't remember what I've done. Do you understand?"

She searched his face intently as if she half expected him to bolt and run. But then she smiled. Dear, sweet Jonathan. He had understood.

Jonathan thought she had never looked more attractive. She had never been so sweetly honest, as if she were dropping a barrier he had always sensed but never been able to pinpoint. Thank God she hadn't been out with another man. He wasn't sure he knew exactly what she was talking about, but he didn't know that it mattered. He loved her.

"That time you stopped calling. I was another personality for a little while. I blacked out, lost time. That must have been Enid. She gets me in a lot of trouble. She's supposed to be brash and vulgar. I hate her."

He nodded, remembering how she had acted. Remembering how he had stayed away.

"Don't you see, Jonathan?" she pleaded. "That's why I was

so afraid to get close to you. I was afraid I'd be another of my personalities and you wouldn't understand or like me."

"Why didn't you tell me before?"

Barbara looked down at her toes sticking out of her sandals. She didn't remember polishing her toenails bright red. "I was ashamed," she replied simply.

"I think I saw a movie once on television—"

*"The Three Faces of Eve,"* she said, interrupting him. "I'm like that woman. Only it's worse. I'm not cured yet and my psychiatrist is . . . dead."

"You'll get another one," he assured her, trying to be of some comfort.

She shook her head. "You don't understand. No, that's not fair. How could you . . . Oh, it's so difficult." She began to cry piteously, large tears splashing onto her lovely dress.

Jonathan got up and went over to her, pulling her up by her shoulders gently and placing her head on his shoulder. "I don't care what's wrong with you," he whispered. "I love you." They kissed and he held her tighter—not shyly but passionately.

"I've wanted you for so long," he confessed.

"But why didn't you . . . ? I thought I was doing something wrong."

"I was afraid you'd be disappointed in me."

"Oh, Jonathan," she said softly.

And without saying any more, they walked hand in hand toward her bedroom. There were no words. Barbara lifted her dress over her head and, with no embarrassment, watched him looking at her in her bra and slip. He took off all his clothes and pulled her into his arms. He helped her finish undressing. The sheets were cool and comfortable, and they lay wordlessly clinging to each other. Then they began to touch, tentatively at first.

Barbara could feel the breeze from the open window almost dance over her naked body. Outside she heard a bird singing. Time seemed to stand still, and for that moment, she felt as happy as the bird sounded.

Then she felt him inside her and it felt right and complete. As the feeling enveloped her, beautiful tears came spilling from her eyes.

They brushed against Jonathan's face, and he whispered, "Am I hurting you, dear Barbara?"

"Oh, no," she answered, laughing in little gasps as she ran her fingertips through the baby fine hair on the top of his head.

Then they were silent as their bodies moved quickly in unison until they both stopped, satisfied. Though neither had screamed out their joy or made any sound.

Finally he spoke, his voice a little choked. "It was beautiful. Was it like that for you?"

Her hair was fanned out over his hairless chest. "Lovely. Love in the afternoon. I want it to happen again and again."

He laughed.

"I'm hungry," she said. "Maybe there's something in the kitchen."

"I'd like to take a shower."

"Of course, first door on the left. Clean towels in the linen closet," she chirped.

She heard the sound of the shower running and smiled. Putting on her bra and slip, she strolled into the living room. It was cute the way he had left the bedroom, she thought, with his clothes bunched up into a flower around his middle.

His briefcase was on the couch. She ran her hand over the cowhide. On top was a newspaper, the *New York Post,* and she smirked when she saw the headline: WOMAN BURIES LOVER IN NEW JERSEY. So like the *Post.* She didn't read any of those papers. Only the *Times.* But lately, she had to admit, she'd been so confused she hadn't even read that. She wondered why an intellectual like Jonathan bothered with that paper.

She was sure there were eggs and cheese in the refrigerator. They could have omelets and some chilled white wine. Feeling relaxed, she opened the paper out of idle curiosity. It was on the second page. SHRINK'S MURDER STILL A MYSTERY. She closed the paper quickly, as if she didn't want someone reading over her shoulder. Then slowly she opened it again to the same place and scanned it, her heart beating wildly.

Her eyes picked out the key words. " 'Dr. Alvin Walters . . . stabbed outside office . . . cremated today . . . still searching for murderer . . . checking patient file . . . deliveryman suspected . . .' "

Her eyes blurred over the next part. It said that although male suspects were being considered, they were still continuing to search for a woman—a woman who might be connected to the other murders in New York. The name of the woman they were looking for:

ENID THORNTON

ENID. That was that vulgar tramp she was supposed to be. When she wasn't herself. And THORNTON. But that's impossible. That was her mother's maiden name. That meant . . . the police were looking for her . . . *She* was Enid Thornton. But there was some mistake! Barbara started to shake. She couldn't kill anyone. Tears splashed out of her eyes. If only Dr. Walters were here. She was certain she was going to lose herself. Because she couldn't face it. That Enid was going around . . . *Oh, God!*

Jonathan, humming peacefully, was just turning off the shower and stepping onto the bathmat. Leaning over, he took out a big yellow towel and wrapped it around himself. He was hungry and he felt good. Sex with Barbara was natural, better than he'd had with any other woman. But that was because they loved each other. He felt hungry, starved.

Barbara felt a blinding headache coming on. The paper slid to the floor, separating and sliding under the coffee table. Rage bubbled inside her. Skidding a little in her bare feet, she ran to the kitchen. She needed to feel it, to touch it. She found it in the spoon drawer. A thick, sharp knife. Turning quickly, she thought she heard footsteps. There was someone in her apartment. Someone had broken in. And yet how fortunate. She felt like seeing blood. Her eyes glittering, her hands firmly on the knife, she stood waiting, hiding behind the open kitchen door.

Jonathan sauntered in, the towel still tied around his middle. "Got any food?" he asked, thinking he had seen her moving about.

But he saw she wasn't in the kitchen. He turned to go out the door and into the living room. Priscilla raised her knife. What was that half-naked man doing in her apartment? Grinning excitedly, she raised her knife.

He turned. God, he was suddenly thirsty. A glass of ice water was what he needed.

In the instant he turned she lowered the knife, and it almost sank into his chest, but instinctively he grabbed her wrist and held it there tightly in midair. His towel fell to the floor. But she didn't stop struggling. She wanted to kill him.

"Barbara! My God, what's come over you?" he shouted.

"I'm Priscilla," she replied through clenched teeth.

"Stop! It's me, Jonathan!" he yelled in panic.

Her eyes were wide and the expression on her face was almost savage. Keeping a firm grip on her wrist, he gave a sigh of relief when the knife fell to the linoleum floor, just missing his foot. But he didn't know what to do or say, how to take care of her.

Priscilla broke free of his grasp and ran her hands through her hair, making it stick out in all directions, then combing it back with her fingers, taming it. Eyes shut, she fell back against the kitchen counter, steadying herself.

Jonathan wanted to help her but somehow sensed he should keep away. His stomach feeling like hot acid, he waited almost breathlessly to see what she was going to do next.

Tears sprinkled out of the corners of his eyes. So this is what the woman he loved had to go through. She had even tried to kill him. Almost from a distance, he saw the scene in the kitchen. A helpless naked man and a woman in a bra and slip going through mysterious gyrations. He thought, then, there was little to keep him from losing his mind.

Below, on the street, an unmarked car pulled up in front of Barbara's apartment building. Dr. Beth Belmont was in the backseat, hugging her briefcase.

"She might not even be home," Tammy said.

"Imagine looking for a person who doesn't even exist. Someone that's another personality. No wonder we could never find Enid Thornton. That's why we need you, Dr. Belmont—to figure out how to treat her when we get her," Carolyn pleaded.

"I have to warn you that it might not be as harmless as you think," Beth Belmont replied. "Enid was a real person when she existed. But it's the other personalities I'm worried about. If

I'm correct in my assumption, she's got a killer personality there. And it's so enraged she was able to kill on the streets of New York single-handedly."

"And maybe in London," Carolyn added softly. Then she stated simply, "I want the collar. And I don't want any more slashings."

"Look, Dr. Belmont, we're very grateful for the help you've given us so far. You can come with us or not . . . It's up to you," Tammy said matter-of-factly.

Beth Belmont climbed out of the car. "I always wanted to be a policewoman when I was a kid." She clutched her briefcase to her like a shield.

Tammy and Carolyn felt for their guns in their shoulder holsters.

Barbara sat on the couch, feeling slightly dazed, while Jonathan brought her a glass of water. He arranged his suit jacket over her bare shoulders because she was shivering.

"What did I do?" she asked in a childlike voice. "No one ever tells me what I do."

"You tried to kill me with a knife," Jonathan answered, his head almost buried in his chest, the towel secured once more around his middle.

"Then it could be true," she said slowly, speaking as if every word caused her great pain.

"What could be true?" he asked, feeling his body fill with sadness, the euphoria they had shared replaced by a heavy depression.

"That one of my personalities is a killer." She picked up the newspaper that had fallen under the table but couldn't manage to put it together; it kept falling apart. Finally she stopped and crumpled the paper, then watched it fall from her hands. "I *killed* Dr. Walters . . . Don't you see?"

Jonathan stared at her, his mouth open, his eyes wide.

"I killed all those women. I mean *I* didn't. Something, someone inside of me. Can you imagine what this is like? I'm me, but I'm not me. I could live with that. But how can I live knowing I'm a . . . Oh, God, I'm a *monster!*" She fell on the floor, sobbing.

Jonathan sat there, staring into the distance, not looking at the wretched figure on the floor.

"I'm Barbara now. Sometimes I'm Dana, a very sensible lady, I understand. And then I'm Enid, the flirty one, the killer. I *hate* her. I could kill her."

"Priscilla," Jonathan corrected her quietly.

She looked up at him. "What did you say?"

"The personality that tried to kill me was called Priscilla."

"How do you know?"

"You—she . . . told me."

"Oh, my God! You mean there's a fourth one?" Barbara asked, shaking her head in horror.

Jonathan covered his face with his hands and began to cry. What if there were more? What would they do?

In the lobby, the doorman studied the shields of the two detectives and looked at the attractive woman with the brief-case. He agreed not to buzz up and felt sure that Miss Hargrove had come in. In fact, he knew she was home.

"There's a gentleman up there with her," he told the police.

"Jonathan, why don't you leave me—get out—before it's too late?"

Jonathan rushed over to her and pulled her up. "No! We'll go to your flat in London. No one knows you're a killer there!"

Barbara began to cry.

"I didn't mean *killer* . . . I—I meant . . . Oh, Barbara, it will be all right . . . We'll do something."

Just then the doorbell rang. It was scary.

"Who's that?" he asked her.

"No one rings my doorbell."

"You should answer it."

"No, you. I'm afraid."

Then they heard the word, loud and forceful and collective. "Police!"

"I better get it," Jonathan said.

"No!"

"Open up! Police!"

"Hide in the bedroom," he instructed quickly. "I'll stall them. And we'll leave tonight."

He rushed past her and found his pants, hurriedly stepping into them and zipping them up.

"In the bedroom," he ordered softly. But Barbara was looking confused, her eyes darting about vaguely. Barefoot, he rushed to the door, his heart pounding almost as loudly as the insistent knocking. His knees shaking, his mind blank, he opened the door not to burly policemen but to three women. He looked down and was staring at two detective's shields. He looked up again.

"We're looking for Barbara Hargrove," Carolyn said.

Beth Belmont was standing behind her. That must be *the* Jonathan, the boyfriend in the notes. He would need help on this, too, she thought compassionately. And she would find a specialist to treat Barbara before the trial.

Barbara had closed her bedroom door. Should she hide under the bed? In the closet? Behind the door? They weren't in the apartment yet. No, she thought, the best place to hide would be in the kitchen. In the broom closet. Like a mouse, she scampered barefoot to the other room.

"She isn't here," Jonathan muttered dully. He was bad at lying. He thought he heard a noise in the kitchen. He hoped they hadn't.

Barbara had bumped into the sharp, shiny knife that was still lying on the floor. She picked it up, then she dropped it. Knives. That's how the monster killed. Stay away from the knife, she told herself. But she had to hide it, put it back in the drawer so the police wouldn't see it. She picked it up again, but as her fingers closed around the handle a tremor rushed through her body. Tears streamed down her face as the pain split her head.

Her name was Priscilla. And she was named after a favorite doll. Her mother had cut it to bits—just like she was going to do—with a sharp knife . . . Just like the one she was holding. Kill! Kill! The rage she felt when she thought of her mother bubbled inside her.

* * *

"I told you, Barbara's *not* at home," Jonathan repeated, more forcefully this time.

"Look!" Beth screamed as the figure leapt crazedly out of the kitchen.

As soon as the detectives saw the knife poised in midair, they pulled their guns. Beth stepped back a bit.

"No, Priscilla, no!" Jonathan screamed.

For a moment the wild-eyed woman tried to locate his voice, then just as quickly dismissed it.

It was the voice of Beth Belmont that was heard over the shouting. "May I please speak to Barbara now?" she asked, her voice cajoling, her tone as low as a man's voice. Yes, that had been in the notes. But she didn't think she could pull it off. And Barbara with this killer personality had more energy than the four of them—she just knew it.

Suddenly the woman lowered the knife, confused. Then in a triumph of effort, she raised it and as Barbara said, "I'll kill her, Jonathan. I promise I will . . ."

He rushed to stop her, ready to grab for the knife, when the quick-as-lightning change came over her. Again the distorted grimace and the hideous voice. "Kill who? You little . . ."

It took only seconds.

They watched wide-eyed as she looked like a person disjointed under strobe lighting—first the meek Barbara jerking the knife, then the stronger Priscilla plying it free, getting more furious.

It was Beth Belmont who, realizing what was happening, leaped forward first, almost knocking Jonathan over.

But it was too late. The blood spurted forth, and as they rushed together, the body crumbled.

Beth ran over to Barbara and tried to find a pulse. "I'm afraid she's dead."

Jonathan and the two detectives stood dumbfounded, staring at Beth and the bleeding body.

"She wanted to kill her other selves . . . and ended up killing herself, too," Beth explained shakily.

"Suicide," Tammy said.

"How the hell could that happen right before our eyes? Unbelievable," Carolyn whispered.

"So was her whole life," Beth said sadly. "She was the real victim."

There was an outraged cry of disbelief as Jonathan fell to his knees and covered Barbara's bloody body with his own.

"It's not fair," he moaned.

The detectives reached for him, but Beth motioned them away.

He began to sob. He looked like a man trying to resuscitate a drowning body. She was dead. Just like that. And yet somewhere in the back of his mind, he knew that had she lived, her life would have been a living hell.

"Life isn't fair," he said, looking up, from one face to the other, then back down at the woman he had just made love to only an hour or two ago. "Life just isn't fair."

# CHAPTER 27

A week after Barbara had killed herself and the New York sensational papers were just beginning to write about a new subject, Cavendish and Hollings said their farewell in the offices at Scotland Yard.

"I suppose it makes the Yard look rather clumsy," said Hollings.

"Oh, I don't know. The point of it is that the reign of terror is over." Cavendish shook his head. "I never saw a case like that."

"I'll miss you, sir," Hollings said awkwardly.

Cavendish nodded. "And I'll miss all this, I suppose. But this last case told me I wasn't getting any younger. The world is changing, and it's time for me to retire, do a little painting, play with my grandchildren."

"Quite," agreed Hollings.

"Years ago we wouldn't have considered a woman, you know," Cavendish said more expansively. "And the woman— not even a killer. Well, there's no accounting for adrenaline."

A long silence followed. It was obvious that Cavendish's nose was out of joint because New York solved the case, but he wasn't going to admit it. He stood at the window, looking down.

"What about you, Hollings? What did you really think? About the killer, I mean?"

Cavendish didn't turn as Hollings said softly, "I've always thought women were just as capable of killing as men."

They met for the last time at the Antelope on Eaton Terrace for a farewell drink. Three against Victimization was disbanding. Strangers who reached out to each other and became close.

"I think it helped me to deal with losing my mother," Annie said.

"Funny, I thought I would hate the killer, but it didn't turn out that way. All I dreamed of was his arrest so I could sneak up and kill him the way he slashed Johanna. That's how this started. Now look at the end of it," said Stephen Knight. "Best be looking for a job again. Moving back into my own place."

"Sick," Brian Harrington mumbled. "Each murder just an unlucky coincidence."

"Well, it's over now," said Stephen. "Let's drink a toast, shall we, to the real victims and let it be."

Misty-eyed they raised their glasses in a toast.

"I'm going to try to be the best mother I know how," Annie said earnestly.

They clicked glasses.

"Let's meet every year and compare notes and keep their memory alive," Stephen suggested.

"I'll drink to that," Brian seconded.

They clicked glasses.

Lockey lighted two candles and placed them in brass candlesticks on the table, which was set with a fresh white linen and lace tablecloth.

The Mister didn't want any part of it. He just wanted the flat filled with someone who paid the rent—and never-you-mind-who-lived-there-before.

But it needed something. A little memorial service. Her prayer book rested near the candlesticks. The Mister had the television turned louder because he was getting a little hard of hearing. Poor Barbara, Lockey thought, turning to a prayer. She had never even finished her book.

He had come for her things. Gaunt-faced, grief stricken. That was her young man, Jonathan. And her friend, Eva, had accompanied him. They had held hands and looked around the sparsely furnished flat. Well, something good had come of it, she thought. She could always tell. They would be getting together soon, those two.

As she bowed her head in silent prayer she heard the doorbell ring. She blew out the candles but left the incense still burning. Brushing a strand of steel gray hair that had slipped out from her bun, she left the flat and the telly and the Mister beginning to fall asleep in front of it. She felt a flutter of excitement.

Opening the door, she saw a young woman, a newspaper folded in the crook of her arm.

"I've come to see about the flat you've got to let," the young woman said.

"Oh, yes, *yes* . . . I was expecting you, miss. Oh, you're in luck, you are." She let her in the door and walked her toward the empty maisonette apartment. "This flat was once occupied by a very famous soap opera star."